IN THE 'NICK' OF TIME

*Policing in the Sixties –
From Probationer to Promotion*

By
Tony Ford

Copyright © Tony Ford 2017
This book is sold subject to the condition that it shall not, by way of trade or otherwise, be lent, resold, hired out, or otherwise circulated without the publisher's prior consent in any form of binding or cover other than that in which it is published and without a similar condition including this condition being imposed on the subsequent publisher.
The moral right of Tony Ford has been asserted.
ISBN-13: 978-1545139950
ISBN-10: 1545139954

Much love and appreciation to my wife Judith, whose enthusiasm and assistance played such a significant part in the writing of this book, not forgetting my two sons, Philip and Andrew, for their suggestions.

AUTHOR'S NOTE

This is the story of a young man who joined the police at the beginning of the 1960s and during a period of eight years follows his progress, firstly as a probationer constable, still under training and assessment, and then as a fully fledged uniform constable. It starts with gaining experience in what in those days was called the 'slums', which would now be designated an inner-city environment, moving to policing a suburban area and then working in an ethnically diverse area with its mainly West Indian community. The story moves on to include his period as a member of the Plain Clothes Department, which acted as a vice squad and into the CID for a short period of attachment before finishing with his promotion to uniform sergeant. Because many of the events refer to particular operational practices and procedures which are no longer a part of today's policing it would be useful to provide some initial background information before embarking on this particular journey.

All these incidents take place in a northern city police force in the 1960s. Up to the middle of that decade policing was still based on the Victorian system with its emphasis on a localised police service, where the beat constable was a significant member of the community. Local knowledge of the area was important and officers established their own contacts over time, which in many cases were maintained for long periods. Because police forces tended to recruit locally most officers were in tune with community issues and were soon able to identify problem areas and personalities within a short time of their arrival on a particular beat. Before the introduction of personalised communication and fast response vehicles, the individual beat constable was very much on his own and had to rely on a combination of his wits and if all else failed, imposing his physical presence, when keeping the peace, especially in communities where violence was not unknown. Recruiting big men as police officers was seen to be important to reassure to public and ensure that public disorder was kept to a minimum, and as a result all police forces imposed minimum height limits when recruiting into their particular force. In general most police forces did not recruit men below five feet eight inches in height; some in fact increased the limit upwards leading to one or two forces who would not recruit men below six feet, such as the City of London and Nottingham City Police.

Problems occurred during the sixties as a result of the economic boom and increases in employment prospects which led to large numbers of police officers leaving the Service for better paid jobs. As a result of this boom and consequent reduction in police numbers a change in policing methods took place during this period, with the Victorian policing method, which was firmly community based and manpower intensive, being replaced by a new system. This new system made use of technology and mobility with the introduction of personal radios and 'panda' cars, which had the result of gradually loosening the ties between policing and the community, creating what Sir Robert Mark,

London's Police Commissioner, later described as a form of 'fire brigade policing'.

Somerford City Police which forms the basis for these stories is a typical northern city police force, such as Manchester, Liverpool, or Leeds, where the city is divided into territorial divisions. In Somerford the A Division is the city centre division with three outer divisions, B, C and D located around it. Each division had between 250 to 300 uniformed officers, together with their own CID staff. There were three important departments located at Police Headquarters; a specialist CID element, which included a fraud squad, a special branch and a criminal record office; a specialised Traffic Department, including the police driving school, an information room, which handled 999 calls and finally an administration and training department. The total manpower to police a population of about half a million would be between 1,500 and 1,700 officers.

Up to the middle of this decade the political control of a city or borough police force was the responsibility of the Watch Committee, which comprised aldermen and councillors selected by the city or borough council. They appointed the chief constable and other chief officers and expected a weekly report from the chief constable; they approved promotions and exercised control over policing to a far greater extent than the police authorities which replaced them. To give an example of their influence in Somerford before the Second World War the Watch Committee decided that most of the tallest officers recruited into the Force would be posted to the A Division. The reason for this decision was that they felt the city centre benefited from having tall smart officers who could assist the public with directions, when asked, and also provide traffic duty at busy junctions, which was necessary before automatic traffic signals were introduced. The rest of the Force soon cottoned on to what was happening and promptly christened the members of that division 'the wooden tops' a nickname which demonstrated, the 'high' regard this 'elite' unit was held. Our storyteller found that the gods must have been looking after him because, although his height qualified him for such a posting, he initially managed to avoid joining that division, although as we shall see fate eventually decided otherwise.

The other policy which most Watch Committees insisted upon was that they expected the police to keep an eye on the working class to ensure that violence, which they believed was associated with this section of society, should be kept to a minimum. In middle-class areas the police were encouraged to limit crimes related to property, especially burglary and shop theft. These policies reflected the political makeup of most Committees, which was mainly Conservative Party in composition; the change to Labour Party dominated councils in the North did not take place until the late 1970s. Every Watch Committee exercised a very tight grip on finances and as a result the chief constable was left with very little room for manoeuvre in relation to resources. In Somerton when the chief suggested that the full-time police band be disbanded so that more resources be given to traffic enforcement, he was slapped down by the Committee who told him that the band was a public relations jewel which was loved by the citizens, who would take exception if such a move took place.

Whilst police pay was awarded on a national basis, various allowances were also paid; these included boot allowances, plain clothes allowance, but there were many more. The most important was Rent Allowance, which was the one allowance that was locally awarded. From Victorian times the Watch Committee were liable for providing housing accommodation for its officers and this was either given by allocating police married quarters, usually attached to a police station, or a paid allowance for non-police accommodation. During the twentieth century Watch Committees provided less police housing and instead allowed officers to purchase their own housing for which the rent allowance was paid. This allowance varied from town to town due to the local price of housing and since the Watch Committee could set the rate, this was seen as one means which could be used to retain police manpower during this period.

Although to the average constable the chief constable and the Watch Committee were the important local element in policing, it should not be forgotten that the Home Office also played a lesser role during this period. Finance for policing was raised from two sources; half came from local rates and other through central taxation. The only experience most officers had of Home Office influence was during the annual inspection of the force conducted by HM Inspector of Constabulary, who on behalf of the Home Office visited the force each year and decided if it was doing its job properly and whether central government money was being spent appropriately. Every year officers used to parade in a local park and HM Inspector would stride up and down along the lines of uniform constables and ask questions of the men on parade. Things started to change after 1966 when the new form of policing was introduced, with the introduction of new wireless communications and 'panda' cars, and with this increased public finance the Home Office started to take a greater interest in policing which was been maintained ever since.

Another point to bear in mind was that from Victorian times, the police were the only local organisation operating a 24-hour, 365-day service and thus became responsible for all sorts of services, which today have been given to specialist groups within local government and other public bodies. In the city the police originally ran the fire and the ambulance services and some of these other responsibilities still remained. For example when an officer was appointed as constable he also became a Shops Inspector and amongst other powers was technically able to examine weights and measures in shop premises. Fortunately for both the local shopkeepers and the police, most officers were never called on to administer these powers.

All polices forces operated a 24-hour shift system, but there were a lot of variations. The majority used 6am-2pm for the morning shift, 2pm-10pm for the afternoon shift, and 10pm-6am for nights. However, some forces used 7am-3pm, 3pm-11pm and 11pm-7am, and others 8am-4pm and so on. It was usual practice to have overlapping shifts to provide cover and for the purposes of these stories the divisional van crew provided such cover. When the volume of police work to the particular shift is compared, most police activity was found to occur during the late afternoon to the early part of the night shift. The morning shift was generally the easiest for work rates, since during the week a lot of police time was spent on school crossing patrol duties from 8.15am for the period of an hour. A similar requirement existed from 3.15pm for an hour in the afternoon. After school crossing duties in the morning had been completed, time is used for pursuing one's own enquiries or for enquiries on behalf of other police forces, or executing warrants for issues such as failing to attend court when required, or failing to pay a fine, which resulted in the individuals named on the warrant being arrested and brought before the court. These warrants were also executed for other police forces, who would then be required to send one of their officers to come and collect the person concerned from the police station to which they had been taken.

These stories show that many of the old police practices from Victorian days were still in use. One of the most common was parading for duty, as it was known. The pay for police officers together with terms and conditions of work were not noted for their generosity; for example there was a requirement to report for work a quarter of an hour before the start of an eight-hour shift. There was no extra pay given for this time, which the older officers used to say was for queen and country, and although not universally liked, was accepted as a fact of life. The parade consisted of constables, all male in those days, lining up when the section sergeant turned up and briefed the officers. Occasionally the inspector would appear, but invariably it was the sergeant. Police parades for various purposes were quite common in those days; for example officers were expected to parade every Thursday to receive their pay. This would require officers to line up, salute the inspector who was in charge of the proceedings, step forward, sign for and then received the pay packet. He would then step backwards, give another salute and march off. Eventually police pay was paid monthly into bank accounts, although for a long time after many older constables still preferred the old system, since it allowed some of them to keep the amount they were paid hidden from their wives.

During the parade when officers came on duty, truncheons, or staffs as the police preferred to call them, were produced and held up, together with the pocket book for the sergeant to see as part of the inspection process. On night duty some of the older sergeants would insist on torches being produced and then switched on to show they were working. When each officer returned his staff to the staff pocket the business of the day commenced with the sergeant giving out information on local crimes, the activities of suspected criminals, missing persons and stolen vehicles. This last item was laboriously written down into the back of the pocket book. Finally various jobs were allocated and refreshment times were given when officers returned to the station for food.

The policy over when to use the police staff was an important factor which was drummed into the recruit at an early stage. It was made quite clear that when the staff was drawn it should always be used. It was seen as a serious weapon of aggression and not to be waved around ineffectually. Once the staff had been drawn out of the staff pocket a report had to be written explaining why such an action had been taken, unless a command had been given by a senior officer in a public disorder situation. Its use was similar to the supposed requirement of the Gurkhas, who it was believed never drew their knives, except against the enemy. The result of all this effort by officialdom to restrict its use meant that it was little used for its intended purpose. In practice the staff was very useful in breaking windows to gain entry into premises, this was done not only for police purposes but also to help members of the public who had lost door keys. No written reports were ever produced to confirm such use, but a close examination of the staff would have revealed that most uniformed constables had used it in the past for this purpose.

Another part of the Victorian beat system which foot patrol officers were obliged to adhere to was to maintain the 'points' system whilst walking the beat. Every foot beat within the City Police boundary was given four geographical points, which were numbered one to four. Officers were expected to walk around their beat either clockwise from points one to four via two and three or anti-clockwise from one to four, three and two eventually arriving back at one. Each day the system changed and officers were given which point to start off from and whether to patrol clockwise or anti-clockwise. The time allocated between points was three quarters of hour and the officer was expected to rotate around his beat from point to point. These points acted as potential meeting places for the sergeant to see the beat officer, sign his pocket book and discuss any important issues of the day. The other justification for this system was that it had been created to confuse the residents of the beat who would be unable to keep track of the beat officer who might surprise them if they were up to no good. As our storyteller got to know the residents he quickly found out that most local people were familiar with this system so that its crime prevention purpose was virtually meaningless.

During this period the City Police were reluctant to pay for overtime worked, preferring instead to give 'time due' as compensation. The system was formalised so that everybody was aware of what to expect. For example if an officer was working the afternoon shift and had occasion to attend court the following morning he would receive four and a half hours' 'time due', which would be entered on his record. If he was on the night shift a court appearance would provide him with five and a quarter hours' time due. All these extra hours allowed the officer to take extra days off, if circumstances allowed. This time due system was controlled by one of the inspectors who was expected to keep a sharp eye on the activities of junior ranks to ensure that no excessive amounts of 'time due' were built up.

One factor which is no longer so important was the relationship within the Police Service with the Armed Services. Most of the older officers had served in one of the Services during the Second World War and memories of that experience were not forgotten. In addition National Service was only beginning to wind down during this period and thus the vast majority of the younger men had performed National Service before joining the police and this was another form of common bond within policing.

One of the practices the City Police supervisors used which was not to everybody's liking was the insistence by sergeants, inspector, and senior ranks of calling constables by their collar numbers rather than their names, which seemed to the author a lazy and demeaning approach to take. Originally constables and sergeants had worn high-neck uniforms and around the collar were to be found the divisional letter and the number of the individual officer. By the time our storyteller had joined the service the buttoned-up jackets had been replaced by collars and ties worn with an open-neck uniform jacket, with the divisional letter and number secured to both shoulder lapels of the jacket. Regardless of this change the supervisory ranks still insisted on addressing constables by their number and not by name. The young man who is the storyteller in this book was given the number 340 of the D Division and as such that became his identification for the first three years of his service. Although this practice was detested it became ingrained in the memory with everyone over time so that even today police pensioners still remember old comrades both by name and number.

Bureaucracy and police work went hand in hand and the paperwork together with the time spent on providing this written work was phenomenal. The one constant problem a young policeman had to wrestle with during his formative years in the Force was the insistence of form filling. There was a form to be filled for every incident and these ranged from the straight forward, such as the crime report or traffic report, of which for the latter there were three; injury, non-injury and animal, to the more esoteric, such as an unusual light report. If all else failed there was the major incident report and the minor incident report which would cover anything which wasn't already provided for by the hundred or more forms which were believed to exist within the Force. All the reports had to be checked by a sergeant, who was trained to spot a mistake at twenty paces, which would result in another form being completed to his satisfaction. This pressure to fill forms was offset against competing aims to work a beat and not lurk about a police station wasting time.

All the events described are based on the truth to a greater or lesser extent and initially they take place during the first two years of service, which is the probationary period, when the Force is assessing whether it has selected the right candidate 'for the job'. During this period of time regular assessment reports of progress are completed by the officer's sergeant and inspector and at the end of this period if the officer has performed satisfactorily he is confirmed in the rank of constable. However, if his progress is unsatisfactory the force dispenses with his service and he leaves the police. After successfully completing the first two years the story then follows the career of a constable who, with ambition is able to move through a path which might lead to promotion. As a career sergeants and constables could then remain in the police for a total twenty-five years and then retire on pension, which was normal practice. This meant that in many cases men were able to retire under fifty and thus able to start a second career, if their health remained good. Senior ranks which meant inspector and above could on the other hand, continue to serve for a total of thirty years or up to sixty years of age.

One word of warning; these stories give the impression that a beat bobby's life was a constant rush from one incident to another which was clearly false. In practice there were often times of boredom, but the author has tried to present a selection of stories which give a feeling for the life and times, together with the environment in which the uniformed beat officer worked. After all, the changes in society and policing portrayed in the stories are less than sixty years ago, but they do illustrate how far we have come as a society over that period.

CONTENTS

Chapter One *1*
Chapter Two *28*
Chapter Three *47*
Chapter Four *71*
Chapter Five *98*
Chapter Six *127*
Chapter Seven *144*
Chapter Eight *174*
Chapter Nine *202*
Chapter Ten *223*
About The Author *250*

This is a work of fiction. Names, characters, businesses, organizations, places, events and incidents either are the product of the author's imagination or are used fictitiously. Any resemblance to actual persons, living or dead, events, or locales is entirely coincidental.

CHAPTER ONE

After school I worked as a porter at our local hospital and then decided to join the Royal Marines before my call-up papers for National Service arrived. I signed up and after completing my time decided to leave the Marines not really knowing what to do, but not wanting to do a nine-to-five job. When I returned to civilian life I had a pint with an old school friend of mine, Charlie Brooks, who was also thinking about the future. He had been working in an insurance office and had also come to realise that it was not the job for him. We both wanted something different and our thoughts turned to the police or the fire brigade which might offer the change we were seeking. We applied to both and the Somerford City Police were the first to respond and that made the decision for us to join the police.

We went through the usual interview process, a medical examination and also had to complete a couple of examination papers dealing with maths, English and general knowledge, and then had a six-month spell at the local Police District Training Centre, which took all the recruits from the local police forces. I didn't know quite what to expect at the Centre and found the training consisted of a mix of drill conducted by a sergeant from the county police, who was an ex-Grenadier Guardsman, some physical training, together with a lot of time spent on the criminal law. The law syllabus was extensive, covering a variety of offences including crime, traffic, and what was termed general law. We were expected to know about one hundred legal definitions of offences, from larceny or theft as it is now known, together with a wide variety of other offences ranging from fraud to death by dangerous driving. Their importance lay in the fact that if you knew these definitions they gave you the various elements which were needed to prove the offence. Not content with that we also had to familiarise ourselves with firearms offences, control of animal orders and the various offences dealing with aliens. Initially I along with the rest of my class made fun of this term suggesting that it might relate to science fiction, but we soon learnt that the term 'alien' was used to include foreign migrants and visitors from countries overseas. All this information was tested by examination at regular intervals and became the basis for future promotion exams. Whilst going through this syllabus it seemed to me at the time that a great deal of this information would never be needed by the average police officer and eventually the powers that be must have also woken up to this fact and changed the syllabus at the end of the sixties, when the law section of the programme was cut down by nearly half. In addition we were also expected to learn the Laws of Evidence which I found most helpful when preparing cases for court, since it enabled me to recognise what would be accepted by the court and what was inadmissible.

One of the rather obscure traditions to which I was introduced related to how to wear the police whistle chain. Some police forces required officers to place the whistle in the right-hand pocket and position the chain straight across the chest and through the tunic button opening, securing it to the button below. Other forces insisted that the whistle be placed in the left-hand pocket with chain placed across to the same button and down to the button below. The City Police required their officers to place the whistle in the left pocket and then extend the chain down the outside of the tunic level with the button below and the up to the one above to be secured inside the tunic. Given that all police uniforms were very similar, other than helmets, it was one of the few ways of distinguishing one police force from another. There were two main types of helmet in use at the time; the Metropolitan or County helmet which is most closely associated with policing through its use by London's Metropolitan Police, and the comb type helmet with its raised ridge leading down from the top of the helmet to the rear, which was used by the City Police. Other types of helmets could be seen usually worn by the smaller borough police forces, one of which resembled the Royal Marine helmet I had worn as a member of the Corps.

I knew when I joined that policing had a disciplinary element to 'the job', some of which was similar to what I had experienced in the Services. There was the requirement to salute officers of inspector rank and above and call them 'sir'. In addition being found drunk on duty could result in an officer being dismissed. Other requirements were not so obvious and were revealed as we became familiar with the discipline code and found that policing was given the right to interfere in the life of the officer to a greater extent than other jobs in civilian life. For example the City Police were able to decide where an officer could reside and in the event of his marriage, and assess whether his wife was a suitable person to be the wife of a police officer. Because I was still living with my parents, when I joined, our home was visited by the divisional administration sergeant who decided whether it was a satisfactory residence for an officer. I knew my mother would not be happy to find out that our home was being assessed for this purpose so I made an excuse and told her he was visiting over a uniform problem.

After returning from the Centre we were given a short induction course at the City Police Training School and both Charlie and I found we were both to be posted to the D Division. I had a week with a senior constable who showed me round the various beats, together with explaining school crossing patrol duties. He also gave me an introduction to the local area, including introducing me to some of the personalities I would get to know over time. I then spent a further six months being sent to various beats on a temporary basis, covering for officers on leave or absent on sick leave, which enabled me to get used to shift work and the geographical area of the Division. In order to keep abreast with the daily postings it was necessary to keep an eye on a sheet called the Daily Variations which was issued from Divisional Headquarters each day. If you failed to keep up to date difficulties could emerge. A common problem which happened to me on more than one occasion was turning up for duty on my day off; when that occurred colleagues could be expected to show no mercy. There was no sympathy from anybody and the only way forward was for me to return home on my bike.

I settled down to the rotational shift system which comprised of nights, afternoons, mornings, evenings and days. The last two shifts were mainly used to fill gaps which occurred in the afternoon or morning shift through unexpected illness or extended duty for court appearance. The night shift offered the most extremes. Usually it was quiet after closing time, although on Fridays and Saturdays it could be busy until one or two o'clock with late night revellers. On nights we were expected to check the front and the back of shops and other commercial buildings, twice, once before and once after the refreshment break to see whether any premises had been broken into, since very few had burglar alarms. The rear of shops required some getting used to as there was no lighting and walking along a back entry with a dim torch allowed the imagination to create all sorts of situations in the mind. On my first tour of night duty I remember walking along the backs of the shops on Thompson Street and hearing a dustbin lid fall to the ground. With my heart beating ninety to the dozen I made my way towards the noise and crept into the yard. Seeing the fallen lid I shone the torch and caught the yellow eyes of a cat sat on the top of the wall looking down, leaving me to let out my breath in relief.

After six months being dictated to by the tyranny of Daily Variations a welcome change arrived with notification that I was moving to Belltown and

Harrison Street Police Station to become a regular beat constable. Belltown was an inner-city area comprising of row upon row of terraced housing, known to all as 'two up and two down', which described the limited amount of accommodation within each house. I knew the area well since my father's family came from the district, in fact his younger brother, my uncle Len, still lived there with his family. My father had moved out of the area before the Second World War when he became a cashier of a hardware store; he married my mother shortly afterwards. She came from farming stock in the north and I remember her telling me the problems she had adjusting to city life with large numbers of people living cheek by jowl. I used to visit my relatives in Belltown as a youngster and one of the first memories that remained was seeing women wearing old fashioned black dresses and carrying large white jugs filled with beer. I remember my father telling me that it was part of the preparation for the evening meal expected by husbands returning home from work. There was still one remnant from the past working in the area when I joined the City Police. The first time I worked 'nights' I came across a 'knocker up', using his long pole to tap on people's bedroom windows in the days before alarm clocks. He could be found working the area from 4am onwards, but after twelve months I no longer saw him and assumed he had retired. Looking back now it is sometimes forgotten just how many people were living in these areas; on the beat next to mine it was estimated that nearly 15,000 people were resident in this small area and given the extent of human activity, one could see such a figure seemed possible.

IN THE 'NICK' OF TIME

On my first visit as I cycled up to Harrison Street Police Station, the premises from the outside looked a bit like a fortress. Its commemoration stone said it had been built in 1864 and its dark brickwork and small high windows all supported its severe appearance. Inside the walls were covered with green and yellow tiles accompanied by a faint smell of bleach. The visitor entered through the blue swing doors into an area with a counter and benches for the public to use on one side. Behind the counter was a door leading to the Charge Office and from here another door led to a corridor with six cells. Behind the Charge Office were the canteen and a spare room used for interviewing witnesses. There was a yard at the rear of the station which was used by police vehicles and those fortunate enough to own a car; the majority of the staff, including myself, however, used the bicycle shed in the far corner.

On my first morning at the station I bumped into the station cleaner, known to all as Auntie Lilly. She was a little wiry woman about sixty years of age with bright brown eyes, dressed in a grey smock-type garment with a cigarette jammed between her teeth, which did not stop her humming continuously. She cooked breakfast for the morning shift and also lunch when necessary and had been cleaning the station for over thirty years. The next person I introduced myself to was the Station Officer, Ronnie Holliday, who was another fixture of the station staff. A bright, cheerful, middle-aged constable with a large brown moustache and a smart bearing, who had served in the army during the war and wore the medal ribbons to prove it. He had a habit of speaking out of the corner of his mouth, which gave the impression that everything he said had to be treated in confidence.

The third person I met was my section sergeant, Howard Nelson. He was a red-faced burly man, who like most officers had long acquired a nickname, which in his case was Lord Foulmouth, a name he had brought with him from the A Division on promotion to sergeant and his transfer to our Division. The nickname illustrated the fact that every second or third word he uttered was followed by a 'Christ' or 'bloody', but if he became really stressed or angry his choice of language became even more Anglo-Saxon. I found out that there was a strange twist to his personality in that he was married to a woman who was a staunch Primitive Methodist, who did not believe in the use of swear words and insisted on this being observed by her two daughters and her husband, the sergeant. This arrangement was the source of much amusement by the officers at the station, but the truth was confirmed by his friends who said that when in the company of his wife and during the course of twenty years married life they had never heard the whisper of a swear word from the good sergeant in her presence. Whenever this fact emerged in conversation, Ronnie Holliday used to say, 'God works in mysterious ways,' which left everybody smiling and nodding in agreement. Notwithstanding his presumed Jekyll and Hyde personality the sergeant was well liked and in my case seemed to have taken a positive interest in my welfare. I am not sure why; like most of the older officers he had seen war service, in his case with time in the Navy, and perhaps my service in the Marines had struck a chord.

On my first morning I paraded with the rest of the Section in a large room which had a table in one corner. There were nine constables including myself, lined up in the process of producing pocket books and staffs. I noticed that four of these officers were 'old stagers' each with police service in excess of twelve years. I later found that all of them were looking for a regular day job to take them out of the pressure of shift work. These jobs were either divisional jobs, such as Lost Property officer, Cycle officer, who would repair police bikes or roles in the city centre such as court staff for the Magistrates and Crown Court, or perhaps a day job in Police Headquarters. Other inside shift work jobs at Divisional Headquarters were also sought, such as clerks, station officers and reserve men, who looked after prisoners. There were four other constables with service up to ten years. These officers had reached a stage where they would be hoping to secure a transfer to a specialist department within the Force, such as CID or the Traffic Branch. However, given the economic boom, which was a characteristic of the time, many of them would leave the Force to take up a better paid job in Civvy Street. Finally there were two probationer constables, myself and Eddie Stone, who was senior to me having already completed twelve months' service.

Listening to the members of the Section and their hopes for the future it began to dawn on me that the role of the beat constable in the city seemed to have two very different and contradictory ways when assessing its status. On one hand the senior officers of the City Police and the members of the public were continually singing its praises. There was much talk about how important it was to have the bobby on the beat keeping in touch with the community. On the other hand listening to experienced beat constables, most of them seemed to be trying to escape from this supposed ideal job, aiming for specialised policing or for the older members a release from shift work and working the streets. After listening to this I decided to keep quiet, gain experience and see how I would assess the role. Mealtimes developed into a routine. We were given forty-five minutes for our break and there were two periods allocated. Half the relief came in early and after their allocated time went back on their beat to be replaced by the remainder. Usually odd-numbered beats came in early, whilst even numbered came late, but on the night shift things were different and the difference related to the availability of card players. Somebody in the dim and distant past had introduced to the Division a form of three handed Whist and it was this requirement which governed who came in early or late. Fortunately because my beat was the furthest away from the station I was always able to come in early for my break and in any event once I became a competent player I found it easy to take part in the games. Most of the card players were the older members of the Division and at night the predominant colour after the dark blue of the uniform was grey in line with the colour of their hair, together with the dark-coloured NHS framed glasses which were mostly worn. These older officers were big solid men, many over six feet tall, who grasped their playing cards in large hands. There was little conversation during the game and many mugs of tea were consumed from large white jugs during this time. I found that card games were a staple of policing, whether it was in the station or crouched in the back of police transport van waiting to be turned out for a public event, whether it was a procession or public demonstration.

After settling in I wondered if as a new boy there would be some sort of initiation process which seems to be common in most organisations. I expected that there would be something to watch out for and I was not to be disappointed. On the second day of 'afternoons', Ronnie asked me to sort out a dispute between neighbours in Edward Street involving a Mr Shackleton at number 10. This street was a small cul-de-sac of terraced houses near Princess Park. I knocked on the door, which was opened by an old lady who peered out suspiciously. Going into the house it seemed as though the furnishings and decoration had not been touched since it was built. I was ushered into the kitchen and met the other occupant, a man of a similar age, who turned out to be Mr Shackleton; they told me they were brother and sister, who had lived together since their parents had died.

Mr Shackleton complained that his neighbour next door was causing trouble by directing noise through the wall to the annoyance of himself and his sister, who nodded vigorously in support. I couldn't hear anything and assumed that the noise had been switched off, but no, the man insisted that it was still going on and invited me to join him by kneeling on the floor and placing my ear to the wall. I took off my helmet and knelt in the dust alongside Mr Shackleton and his sister, trying my hardest to hear a sound but without any success. The other two still seemed to be convulsed with the noise and I made one more attempt, but I could not hear a thing. I drew back stood up and put my helmet back on; I had now come to the conclusion that these two were as we used to say 'away with the fairies'. Mr Shackleton looked at me and said that many policemen had come to the house but no one had been able to stop the noise. At that point the penny dropped and I realised that I had fallen into the trap that Ronnie had set. I told them both that I took their complaint very seriously and would speak to their neighbour to resolve the matter. I went next door and after talking to the woman neighbour found that this was a long running dispute which had been going on intermittently for many years without any happy resolution being found. When I returned to the station there was general laughter at my account, since most of the officers had also had a similar experience with the Shackletons. For the next two months the initiation process continued with me being required on the 'morning' shift to visit the local butchers to get off cuts of bacon and sausages, known as 'wrap ups', which Auntie Lilly fried for a communal breakfast. But it didn't stop there, on 'nights' I was sent to the local bakery to collect a selection of cakes and buns for the night shift to consume. These tests finally came to an end for me when a new probationer arrived and with relief I handed over the poisoned chalice to him.

One of the advantages of working on the D Division was that it enabled me to watch Somerford City Football Club. Their ground was situated on the Division between the districts of Belltown and Hathersage and because they were in the First Division the police supplied a lot of manpower during home matches. I had become a City supporter many years previously not withstanding that my father had never been interested in football, unlike is younger brother Len who was an avid fan of City. However, my father kept up to date with local affairs including football and had a basic knowledge of most of the members of the first team, who were playing for the club at the time. He demonstrated this ability when he and I were on the number 68 bus going to see his sister, my Auntie Helen who lived near Princess Park. I was about seven years old at the time and it was just before my father bought a car, after his promotion to general manager of the hardware store he had joined after returning from the war. We were both sitting on the top deck when the bus stopped near the junction with Bristow Street and Great King Street. A man got on and climbed onto the top deck and sat immediately in front of us. He was a big fellow with broad shoulders and he seemed to fill most of the seat. On seeing him my father turned and asked me in a loud whisper if I knew who he was. I had no idea and looked back at him with a blank expression; he smiled and said that the man was Arthur Jarvis, Somerford City's goalkeeper. I remembered Uncle Len telling me that Jarvis was the best goalkeeper in the country, so I reminded my father what his brother had said. Whilst this conversation was going on between us Arthur Jarvis turned round in his seat and confirmed his identity, giving me a broad smile and offering his hand to shake. As he engulfed my hand I realised what huge hands he had and at the same time I thought he was the most important person I had ever met. I basked in his smile and told him I was a City supporter, which was not true at the time, but resulted in me badgering Uncle Len to take me to see City at the first opportunity. Len took up the challenge and I used to go with him on home match days and stand with his friends in the Main Stand. I always looked forward to half time when I was given a cup of Bovril and sometimes a meat pie. All these memories conspired to keep me as a City supporter up until the present day.

Policing football matches was conducted in two ways; the senior constables, who were always club supporters, policed the inside of the ground, the other officers controlled traffic and spent most of their time outside the stadium dealing with home and away supporters. As a junior constable the best I could hope for was to perform traffic duty outside the ground and once everybody was inside join them in the stadium and find a space at the top of the main stand and watch the match until fifteen minutes before the end of the game when I was required to make my way out of the ground and resume traffic duty once more. At least I got a flavour of the match, but there were games when last-minute goals could make all the difference and then I was impatient to find out how the game had ended. In those days most of the fans stood and watched the game; in City's case ground capacity could reach eighty thousand fans, but the Division had a system for dealing with such numbers and I don't remember any major problems. In fact there was a joke amongst the City fans that the main job of the police sitting around the ground were not there to look after the supporters, but to keep an eye on the police officers at the top of the Main Stand who were the people usually making most of the noise.

After I had joined the Division I put my name down for football duties and the first match I policed was a grudge match involving a rival team whose supporters who could always be relied on to cause trouble. In these circumstances we met the away fans at the main city centre railway station and escorted them by foot to the ground in a column. As this was the first time I had taken part I was told to wear either my cape or raincoat, but no explanation was given for this instruction, which left me mystified because the weather was fine and not particularly cold. We met the fans outside the station and we set off together with a couple of police horses in support at the front of the column. Most of the supporters had been drinking and all of them started to chant a variety of songs, none of which could be described as tuneful, and as we got nearer to the ground the volume increased together with the insults aimed at the Somerford City supporters. We conducted them to the turnstiles and let them enter the stadium and at that point I made my way to what had become my usual spot up in the Main Stand. Sergeant Nelson was coming up behind me and on passing mentioned he could see that I had been in 'the wars'. I had no idea what he meant at the time and smiled vaguely in acknowledgement. On this occasion I was able to watch the whole match as we let the home fans away first and after they dispersed I went to collect the away supporters for the return trip to the station. As their team had lost the match their mood was quiet and sullen and we returned to the station without mishap and I was glad to see them depart. I returned to the station and when I took my raincoat off I realised the reason for the sergeant's comment as the back of my raincoat was covered with spittle. I arranged for it to be cleaned and found that I was not the only one whose raincoat had been affected in this way as a couple of other officers had also received the same treatment.

Some beats had a particular responsibility which the beat holder was required to undertake, and my beat had a 'very important job' which came round once a month on 'nights'. It required the beat officer to turn up to the docks just after midnight, usually on a Wednesday, to meet the arrival of the Guinness boat from Dublin and collect a crate of Guinness which was then conveyed back to the Harrison Street station to be consumed by the officers on duty. The presentation of this gift had arisen in recognition of the actions of a now retired PC 'Big' Jim Flannigan.

The story went that Big Jim was patrolling past the main dock gate when he was summoned by a member of the Docks Police because of trouble on the wharf following the arrival of the Guinness boat. Flannigan was the largest policeman on the Division (which in those days meant he must have had the stature of a man mountain). He made his way to the scene to deal with the situation, which involved a group of dockers fighting some members of the crew. Once 'Big Jim' had decided to sort out the situation, in a matter of minutes one man had been tossed down into the water of the dock and two others were unconscious on the ground before order had been restored. The captain of the ship was so appreciative of Flannigan's actions that he presented him with a crate of Guinness, telling him that a crate would be forthcoming every time the ship docked, and this tradition had been carried on over the years and it had now become my responsibility to undertake as the beat constable. There was a further point which was always made as a postscript to the story and that was Big Jim was teetotal, never touched alcohol, but that had not stopped him accepting the gift for the benefit of the rest of the section.

In order to carry out the task I had to borrow the station cycle and make my way to the docks, meet the ship and after thanking them for the crate, place it across the handlebars and cycle cautiously back to the station. On the first occasion I cycled round the back streets, avoiding the main roads. I had managed about halfway back to the station when a man came out of an entry in front of me and waved me to stop. He told me there was some trouble in Alma Street, which was the next street along. I walked to the next corner and saw a few people gathered in the street. Parking my bike along the wall and placing the crate nearby I walked up the crowd. It turned out that there had been a party in one of houses and people were dispersing to go home. I returned back to my bike to find that the crate of Guinness had disappeared. I hunted around for a while, but there was no sign of the crate or the man who had stopped me. When I returned to the station I had to confess what had happened and once the groans had finished I then had to put up with the laughter at my expense. Thereafter during my time on this beat I varied my route each time and managed to bring the crate back safely to the station, to the satisfaction of all concerned.

I was to find that there was a lot of tedium to police work, but occasionally being at the right place at the right time and having a degree of persistence can work wonders and it happened a couple of weeks after my first football experience. I was on 'afternoons' and was leaving the station to start my first job of the day which was to be outside St Paul's Primary School to see the kids across the street. Three thirty and all the children had been safely conducted across the main road and it was now time to get on with a couple of jobs I had been given by the Station Officer.

I turned the corner into Duke Street and on the opposite side saw a black dog in a heap at the side of the road close to the pavement. In those days road accidents involving certain animals, especially dogs, had to be recorded, under the Road Traffic Act, and this seemed to be my first job. I wandered up to the animal, but it was clearly dead and I saw that it was wearing a collar. The dog tag was worn but I was able to make out a name which appeared to be 'Hands' together with number 16. I pondered for a moment, was this the name of the dog or the owner? It wasn't clear so I set about trying to find the address of the owner. I knocked on the first house nearby without result. Nothing from the next two, but the woman who came to the door of the fourth house, said the dog was local, but did not know the owner. Armed with this information I carried on down the street and eventually secured a positive result just at the end of the street. The old man who answered from the last house said that he thought the dog was owned by a man who lived alone in Cooper Street, just round the corner. I had a flash of inspiration and asked if he lived at number 16? He nodded, saying he thought the man was called Sam Hands.

Around the corner I found the house, but there was no reply. I hung around for a few moments wondering what to do next, perhaps Mr Hands was out and as the time was close to six o'clock, he could have been at the pub. Before I could begin my enquiries the door to number 18 opened and a man stood in the doorway about to leave the house. He stopped on seeing me and I asked him if he knew where his neighbour might be. "He doesn't drink," he said, answering my query about the pub, and turned back inside and shouted for his wife. A few moments she arrived and I told her about the dog. She seemed surprised, but agreed from the description I had given her about the dog that it was probably his animal, but had no idea why it was dead on the road. She said that it only went out with Mr Hands. It was about this time that an alarm bell started to ring in my head. I asked her about her neighbour, his age and habits, had he gone out, did he have any friends, was he still in the house? She told me that he was getting on, over seventy she thought; he had been a bus conductor and had retired about ten years ago. He was a widower as his wife had died about a year after he left the buses. He was a quiet man who kept himself to himself, walked the dog each day and went to church every Sunday. She said she had seen him early this morning when she had brought in the bottles of milk, they had exchanged greetings and he had walked off with the dog. He did not have visitors much, although she remembered a car outside the house, when she went shopping for her husband's tea a couple of hours previously. The car had gone when she returned. Before leaving I asked her if she could remember any details about the car, had she seen it before? She shook her head, she couldn't remember seeing it before and it may have been black, but other than that she had no more details to give.

I knocked on the door again, but to no avail. I had now come up against a problem which besets most police officers at some time during their careers, namely when to act and when to stand back and let the tide roll on. I tried to weigh up the situation, it was possible that some friends might have come round and taken Mr Hands out and the dog might have inadvertently escaped somehow, perhaps chased the car and been run over in an accident. It seemed possible, but unlikely. I asked the woman if I could look round at the back of the houses. She led me through the kitchen, into the yard and through the back gate into the entry at the rear. Fortunately the gate next door wasn't fastened and I went into the yard. The place was untidy, but I was able to see through the window. The glass had not been cleaned for ages. Peering through the dust and grime I could make out the kitchen table, but the room seemed untidy, but not normal untidiness, since I began to realise that chairs had been knocked over and there were plates and cutlery on the floor. The inner kitchen door was open, but the table, which was directly under the window blocked out any further views of the room.

The untidy state of the kitchen appeared to be recent, maybe Mr Hands was ill, perhaps he had suffered heart attack, and had fallen creating this mess. There was only one course of action left; I decided to break into the house. If I got it wrong Sergeant Nelson would have me writing reports forevermore and any hope of a police career would disappear in the damage I was going to cause in gaining entry to the house. Breaking through the back door took more effort than I anticipated by which time I had gained an audience, as the woman next door had summoned a number of her friends to watch my antics. The door gave way and I followed it into the house; almost immediately I saw the old man on the floor. He was lying half in the hallway leading to the front door. I went over, but he was not breathing and I noticed that there was blood around his head. I suddenly realised that the wound looked as though he had been hit by a weapon and at that moment the thought of murder entered my mind. The neighbours were now all murmuring quietly by the open door. One of the lessons from the District Training Centre rushed through my head about preserving scenes of crime, so I asked them to leave and secured the back door as well as I could.

The next job was to inform the station, there was a phone box on the next corner and I persuaded the woman from number 18 to dial 999 and inform the police of what had happened. She smiled and said she had always wanted to ring 999. "It's just like the films," was her parting remark as she left to make the phone call.

I waited what seemed an eternity, but was probably about ten minutes, when a car pulled up and two men got out; the Day Crime Patrol had arrived. I realised that I was facing Detective Sergeant Albert Davies and Detective Constable Herbert Jackson, who were collectively known as 'Darby and Joan'. It was never clear to us who was Darby and who was Joan and no one ever had the temerity to ask since both men were over six feet tall and in the words of Sergeant Nelson, as 'rough as a bear's arse'. Their nickname came from the bickering which took place between them and which related to their wartime service, since Davies had been in the Coldstream Guards, whilst Jackson was a Grenadier Guardsman. Before joining the police my service with the Marines had made me aware of the great rivalry between both regiments, which these two detectives appeared to have developed into a fine art. They listened to my description of what had taken place, examined the scene and called their boss, Detective Chief Inspector Reg Carter; I found out later they had turned up because the neighbour who had made the 999 call had been a bit garbled through excitement and the message relayed to the CID did not make clear whether she was reporting an accident or a murder and the DCI wanted to be sure as to what had happened. The two detectives complemented me on securing the crime scene, told me they would be in touch with me later to sort out my statement and suggested I complete my report concerning the dog accident.

I had completely forgotten about the dog and went to arrange for the removal of the animal's body. When I arrived at the scene a man was standing nearby looking at the dog. It turned out that he had seen the accident whilst on a passing bus. He said the car involved had been a black Austin Cambridge with two men inside. The dog had been chasing the car and when it reached the corner it seemed as though the driver had deliberately run over the dog. He couldn't remember the number of the car, but knew it contained a letter N and numbers 236, saying that his wife used to live at 236 High Lane. I wrote the information down in my notebook and went back to Mr Hand's home to tell the detectives, who had already arrived. When I returned the place was overrun with scenes of crime officers, who seemed to be photographing and fingerprinting everything. In the middle of this mayhem was the large figure of DCI Carter, directing operations. 'Darby and Joan' had disappeared. Looking at the scene I knew that Carter's deputy was a thin weedy character called Detective Inspector Corbell Watson, who was usually close at hand to convey the Boss's instructions and take notes. Sure enough I found him in his usual position and gave him the information I had collected. He gave me a wan smile and said that he would inform the 'Boss' and told me to leave it with him. I was now feeling a bit peckish so I returned to the station for my refreshments. I was eating my sandwiches when Sergeant Nelson popped his head round the corner of the door and said that a member of the public had just reported seeing a black dog dead in the street. He fixed me with his bloodshot eyes and asked wasn't I supposed to be dealing with this? No peace for the wicked, I thought, and promised that I would sort it out again... The dog was eventually disposed of and the two men in the car were caught and convicted. It turned out that they were relatives of Mr Hand's who had heard, wrongly as it turned out, that he had come into some money, and had visited him to collect their share. There had been an argument between them which led to blows and resulted in the death of the old man.

I later made my first appearance at Crown Court as a witness to a murder trial. The Crown Court was located in a new building close to the Magistrates Court in the city centre. I arrived there before 10am and wandered round getting my bearings. The police canteen was on the first floor and I went up there hoping to catch Mr Carter and his team. As I walked along the corridor I could hear the sounds of laughter and I found them in the canteen, all sitting at a large table with the 'Boss' at the centre of the conversation. I stood at one side trying to gauge what was going on, but I was spotted by the DCI who beckoned me over. He told me I was first on in the Witness Box, but not to worry since I was setting the scene and provided I kept to the facts in my statement, the Defence would not try to trip me up; all their efforts would be directed at him and other members of the team. He told me that I had done a good job which had provided the information leading to the arrest of the murderers and said that if all went well he would write me up for a Commendation.

The case started at ten o'clock and half an hour later I went in the Witness Box, took the oath and gave my evidence. There were no challenges from the Defence and I sat down and watched the rest of the trial. Proceedings went smoothly until the DCI went into the Box and at that point the defence counsel started to question Mr Carter very closely, in particular asking the detective if it was true that he had assaulted the prisoners during the interview sessions. Mr Carter denied the accusation and I formed the impression that both men, the barrister and the detective, were going through the motions and these verbal attacks were part of the trial and expected by both sides. Later that afternoon the prisoners were found guilty and sent to prison for life.

I went with the CID staff for a celebratory pint and the following day was back on duty. The DCI kept to his word and later through his good offices I was awarded the Chief Constable's Commendation for Good Police Work. This helped my future career, but that's a tale for another time. Thinking back that black dog did me a good turn, perhaps he also should have been given a commendation.

Another quality which I found to be important in police work was local knowledge. My knowledge of the area was pretty limited but as I settled into the job and became accepted on I found that the more experienced officers began to give me information about people and places. For example they told me about a family, who lived on my beat, called Knuckles, who had been involved in crime over many generations. There was one member of the family, Father Alfred Knuckles, the parish priest of St Gerard's Catholic Church in the north of the city, who appeared to have escaped a life of crime, but the rest of his relatives all had convictions for drunkenness, disorderly behaviour and crime. Ronnie, our station officer, claimed that when he joined the police, the family had a reputation for criminal behaviour which stretched back to before the First World War. Initially I had little contact with them until a break-in was reported at an off licence on Harper Street. I went round, took the details from the manager and examined the scene. The thief or thieves had forced open a door at the rear during the night, silenced the alarm and then stolen a large quantity of sprits. As I wandered round the shop I saw a mark on the wall by the rear door. It looked like somebody had recently thrown some water about and splashed the wall. I mentioned it to the manager but he had no idea what had happened, saying that it must have been one of the staff members. The mark was drying out and did not seem of any significance and since I had all the details for a crime report I left the shop to inform the CID.

About a few weeks later there was another break-in at an off licence near the docks. I had just arrived at the station to have breakfast, but instead found myself retracing my steps to my beat and on to shop. Upon inspection at the scene the circumstances seemed very similar to the previous break-in at Harper Street. Once more the thieves had entered via the back door, silenced the alarm and taken sprits from the shop. I examined the back door and noticed a splash mark on the wall nearby. I pointed it out to the manager, but he shrugged his shoulders and said he had no idea where it had come from. There were some other members of staff present and I put the same question to them and again no one was able to give an explanation, in fact I could tell they all thought I had lost my marbles. I went back to the rear of the shop and looked at the mark for inspiration and suddenly decided to smell it. Thinking back that seemed to be the only thing left for me to do in the circumstances. After a couple of sniffs I thought I could smell urine and I asked the manager if he could smell anything. He looked at me in surprise and then bent down and smelt the mark. He straightened up with a puzzled expression and said that it seemed that somebody had pissed on the wall. I could see he was going to take it up with his staff so I told him to keep it to himself for the time being because I was now beginning to wonder if the thief or thieves might have been responsible.

I returned to the station where Auntie Lilly was making breakfast and tucked into bacon, egg and sausage with the rest of the morning relief. Ronnie was there with another old constable Norman Sharpe putting the world to rights. I sat opposite them and waited for a break in the conversation. Eventually they both paused and I jumped in with an account of the break-in and in particular the mark on the wall and the accompanying smell. There was silence whilst both men digested the information and I took the chance to mention the previous break-in at the off-licence in Harper Street. Norman looked at Ronnie and asked him if he remembered Harry Knuckles, and then went on to say, wasn't that his trademark? Ronnie smiled and nodded saying that Knuckles had been a prolific house breaker, but he thought he was still in prison, since Knuckles had gone to prison for a long stretch after his last court appearance. Norman said that he could have been released early for good behaviour and Ronnie laughed saying that good behaviour was not something he associated with the Knuckles family, but he agreed to check it out.

It turned out that Harry Knuckles had been released early about six weeks previously and although he had promised to mend his ways the temptation to resume his regular career proved too hard to resist. Unfortunately for him he had not been able to dispose of all the bottles of spirits he had stolen and when our divisional CID went to his house there was enough evidence to convict him. I found out later that he had this compulsion to relieve himself after he had committed a crime which led to the splash marks I had found in the shops.

CHAPTER TWO

Time was marching on and the end of October heralded the start of preparations for the fifth of November. This was a busy time for the fire brigade and to a lesser extent for the police and the local authority. Few houses in Belltown had gardens and families and neighbours looked to using any spare ground which could be made into a bonfire site. Most of the areas selected, which were usually called crofts, were the remnants of bomb damage from the Second World War. Many of them had been cleared by the local authority in preparation for a building programme which was going to provide new council housing for the residents. This promise had been around for many years without any signs of movement and the local community had decided that as usual the corporation had lost interest or more likely run out of money. We were asked by the council and the brigade to keep an eye on bonfire preparations which would need to be moved because they were in a dangerous position or could disrupt traffic.

With this in mind I walked around my beat looking for possible sites which might cause a problem. Within a few minutes I found the first location, which left undisturbed could certainly pose a big problem. I had turned the corner of Barlow Street and Harper Street and saw on the opposite side a group of children aged about seven or eight years building a bonfire right up against the wall of the end terrace house. This operation was being directed by a girl of a similar age who was urging her friends to find more material to build the bonfire even higher up wall of the house. I went up to the group and took the leader to one side, whilst the rest stopped working and edged closer to see what was going to happen. She seemed to me to be an intelligent girl who clearly knew what she was doing and when I asked her to tell me why she was building a bonfire in this location, she looked up at me and said that her grandmother lived in the house and she didn't like her grandmother. I was initially taken back with her reply; I wondered what on earth her grandmother had done to deserve this course of action. I told the rest of the group that if they wanted a bonfire in the location they would need to move it into the middle of the croft. After a lot of muttering they started to rearrange it. Once this was underway I took their organiser, who I now knew was called Agnes Fellows, to the house to see if her grandmother was in, but there was no reply. We then walked to her home, which was not far away and fortunately both her mother and granny were together having a chat and a cup of tea.

On the way round to her house the girl's mood had changed and Agnes was now crying whilst she explained that she had become angry when her grandmother had not bought the birthday present of a doll she had initially promised and which Agnes had desperately wanted. As a result the girl, in a fit of pique, had decided that the location of the bonfire seemed a fitting response to her grandmother who had failed to provide the special present she had expected. She told me that she loved her granny and wished she had never thought about moving the bonfire. I decided that Agnes had learnt a lesson and that I would try and help her out of a difficult situation. I give both women a brief description of had happened, saying that the bonfire was too close to the house. I did not mention that I knew whose house it was, leaving them to work out what had happened. I noted that they both recognised the location, but said nothing; after a cup of tea I left them to sort out the problem.

One of the side effects of collecting bonfire material in the area was that it sometimes revealed interesting relics from the past. On the Saturday afternoon prior to the fifth all was quiet in the station and I was completing a Missing Person Report. I finished the work and put it in Sergeant Nelson's tray for approval and drifted into the front office to have a word with Ronnie before returning on my beat. As we were talking the public door to the reception area opened and shut and Ronnie, followed by me, looked into the area, but there was no one to be seen. Ronnie turned to me that said it was probably the work of the wind, at which point a small dirty hand came into view from below the counter and placed what looked like a hand grenade on the counter. Ronnie instinctively shouted, 'Get down!' and we both hit the floor in record time. Nothing happened and we slowly got up and looking over the counter saw the face of a small boy, aged about five, smiling up at us. He said that he and his friends had found it whilst searching for firewood; he had then taken it home to show his mother, who had told him to hand it in at the station. He told me where he had found it, but said that he and his friends had made a good search around without finding anything else.

After carefully removing the dirt we both examined it and found that it was certainly an old make of grenade; Ronnie reckoned it was Second World War vintage with the firing pin still attached. We had no idea how it had come to be found in the area and Ronnie thanked the boy and rang the Army Bomb Disposal Squad to collect it. To keep it safe he put the grenade in one of the station fire buckets, which as well as sand was normally used as a receptacle for cigarette ends. I left the station just as one of the PCs was bringing in one of the local drunks who he had arrested for causing trouble with the queue at the bus stop near the church. The drunk was a frequent visitor to the station and was very reluctant to be placed in a cell to await the return of Sergeant Nelson who would charge him with being drunk and disorderly. This reluctance was so difficult to overcome that it needed the three of us to get him into the cell, after which he started to shout and kick the door in anger. I left the station and went over to search the area which the boy had said he and his friends had found the grenade, but to no avail, so I carried on to complete a couple of outstanding enquiries.

About an hour later I returned to the station to have my refreshments and found that the drunk was still shouting abuse at the police in general and

Ronnie in particular. I could see that Ronnie was getting fed up with the noise and before I could ask him if he wanted a cup of tea he suddenly picked up the fire bucket with the grenade still visible and marched off down the cell corridor. I followed after him to see the fun and I wasn't let down. The drunk was watching Ronnie through the open hatch in the cell door. Ronnie put the bucket in front of the door where the drunk could see it and pointed at it with his finger and then in a loud voice told the prisoner in no uncertain terms that if he didn't stop shouting he would personally chuck the grenade into the cell. The prisoner calmed down and Ronnie left the bucket in place before the Army Bomb Disposal Squad turned up and took the grenade away with them for disposal.

After bonfire night my family held a party for my brother Peter who had taken up the ten pound offer and decided to emigrate to Australia. Immediately after the party I returned back to work on 'nights' the worse for wear and requiring to catch up on my sleep. One of the benefits I had gained from service in the Marines was the ability to take brief snatches of sleep or 'combat naps' as they are now called, and I hoped that if things were quiet in the night I might be able settle down for a couple periods during the shift but I was doomed to disappointment. During the first half the alarm went off at the local Co-op store and together with the crew of the divisional van and a dog handler who turned up with a large Alsatian dog called Sabre, we all went to the premises. We searched the outside of the premises both front and rear but found nothing suspicious and eventually the key holder turned up and opened up the store. The handler let the dog in, but again nothing was found at which point the divisional van took off at high speed. That left me with the key holder and the handler and his dog, which was a long-haired animal which kept on looking at me and barking loudly, showing an impressive set of white teeth. The handler came over and asked me if I would go and hide in the store since his dog needed to find someone or he would be unhappy for the rest of the night. He assured me that this was common practice which made me wonder whether this had prompted the sudden departure of the van crew. His request didn't fill me with much enthusiasm, especially since the dog now seemed to licking his lips in anticipation, but there was nobody else at the scene and I very resultantly agreed to volunteer.

I entered the store and started to look for somewhere which might offer some protection against this big animal, which seemed very eager to hunt me down. I noticed a sign indicating public toilets and hurried towards them hoping that they would provide adequate protection from Sabre. The gents' toilets had a urinal and a separate toilet cubicle which I decided to use as an extra measure and entering it closed and bolted the door behind me. I waited with ears alert for the sound of the dog, for what seemed like an eternity. Nothing happened for a while and then I heard the soft padding of the dog's paws. Suddenly without warning the door shook and the animal started to bark furiously and I thought that the toilet door was going to give way under the weight of the dog's attack. There was a shout and I heard the handler entering the room, the dog stopped barking and then his handler told me to come out, thanked me, telling me that Sabre had enjoyed the exercise, which was more than could be said for me and I left the shop and resumed patrolling my beat.

After refreshments I left the station and located a spot behind some shops to have a quick snooze. The gate at the back of the local butchers was open and I went into the yard and found a dustbin by the adjoining wall to the next shop took off my helmet, sat on the dustbin and leaned back against the wall to doze off. It only seemed a moment when I felt a foot on my left shoulder and woke up to find someone climbing over the wall behind me. I pulled myself off the dustbin and the man fell off the wall and bounced off the dustbin at my feet. I saw that he was also carrying a bag, the contents of which spilled on to the floor. On seeing the contents I realised that he must have broken into the photographic shop next door, since there were cameras and films all around. I took him to the station and charged him with shop breaking, but I couldn't say in my evidence that I had been asleep before his arrest; instead I altered my evidence to say I had heard a sound from the shop and had gone to investigate. My prisoner had no idea what had happened and since he pleaded guilty my secret was safe, but there were no further opportunities that night to catch up on my sleep.

During winter time I found another location, which was warmer and allowed me to have a quick snooze on 'nights'. At the northern end of my beat was a private bus garage which I used to visit and find the back seat of a bus to have a rest, usually after 5am. This system worked well until on one occasion when I must have been very tired and my automatic combat nap set in my brain for twenty minutes, failed to work. I woke up with a start to find that that the bus I was on was in motion and we were heading into the city centre and the time was just before 6am. I got up in a rush and headed for the front of the bus, pressing the first bell I could find. The bus screeched to a halt and I nearly fell to the floor causing the driver to turn round to see me scrambling to my feet, helmet in hand. He said he nearly had heart failure when the bell had sounded and I apologised leapt off the bus and found myself opposite the Town Hall. As luck would have it there was another early bus opposite and I jumped on board before it headed back towards Harrison Street.

It was about this time I had my first assessment interview with my inspector, Albert Murdoch. He was a lanky individual with a leathery complexion whose driving ability was the stuff of legend. Because inspectors were required to cover a fairly large area they were given a black Morris Minor to get out and about. Nobody had ever seen our inspector ever get out of second gear; on nights you could hear his car grinding its way around the area. He had a confident, down-to-earth approach to his work and caution was not something he had any time for in dealing with incidents. He used to say that you had to get stuck in while the trail was still hot; 'don't let it get cold' was one of his pet phrases. I met him in his office for the interview and he read to me what Sergeant Nelson had written about my progress up to date, which was satisfactory and as a result the rest of the interview consisted of him recounting various episodes in his career and giving me his assessment of the Marines, who he had dealt with during the war, whilst in the Army.

The build up to Christmas commenced with some of the probationer constables, including myself, being drafted into the city centre to help out with traffic duties, given the increased volume of traffic and people in the area, during this period. In those days it meant donning white oversleeves and gloves and manning busy traffic junctions for eight hours at a stretch, to be relived occasionally by city centre officers. This did not happen often since most of them told us they had more important jobs to do, such as visiting various shops and stores and coming out with parcels, which would require them to return to the central police station. They worked different shifts to us so I was never able to see what was in those parcels, although those of us drafted in had a suspicion that these officers were making the most of the Christmas spirit. However, before returning to my division I did eventually find out what was going on as the result of a mistake.

The Friday before Christmas I was on point duty and ready to retire, when the door opened in the pub opposite to where I was directing traffic and a man came out of the premises with a parcel under his arm. He beckoned me over and asked me if I knew PC Brady; he then told me he was the licensee and asked me if I would give this officer the parcel. Apparently this licensee had been previously called away due to family illness and had not been able to see the officer and wanted to wish him the season's greetings. I had come across Brady who was a large fat individual, who seemed to spend all his time lurking around the station. He must have led a charmed life since during the three weeks I had been working on this division I had never seen him out on the streets. I told the licensee I would try and locate him as I was just returning to the station. When I returned the place was deserted, except for the Charge Office staff and when I asked them if they knew the whereabouts of Brady, they told me that he had gone home. I knew that this was my last day of attachment to the city centre and would be returning to Harrison Street so I opened the parcel and found a bottle of whisky. My three weeks on traffic duty had not been entirely wasted.

Just after Christmas the station held a party for the officers' children and selected members of the public, these included the children of local licensees, shopkeepers and the vicar. The entertainment varied each year, in the past one of the sergeants, who looked like Tommy Cooper, the comedian, performed magic, the vicar could be tempted to play the banjo and the licensees had formed a barbershop choir. This particular year Inspector Murdoch had arranged for the local zoo to provide some animals to entertain the children. I was told to collect them and jumping into the inspector's car, the inevitable Morris Minor, I headed off for the zoo. I went in via the private entrance to be met by the zoo keeper, a little wizened chap, called Seamus Walsh, who had a chimp on his shoulder who he introduced as 'Albert'. On the ground nearby were a number of boxes containing the animals; I could see a snake, an armadillo, something that looked like a rat and also a parrot. I helped them all into the car and Seamus elected to get into the back seat with 'Albert', telling me that the chimp had an urge to drive cars, when he was seated at the front. At this point I should have realised that 'Albert' was capable of causing trouble, but without thinking I drove off to the station. We were about halfway on our journey when I suddenly felt a furry hand grasp my right ear and start pulling my face to the right. I asked Seamus to sort out 'Albert' and then I remembered the inspector telling me that the zoo keeper was deaf. I tried to wriggle free, but 'Albert' had a firm grip and was not letting go. By this time my eyes were watering and my face was being turned towards one hundred and eighty degrees and the only option was to stop the car and get Seamus to deal with the chimp. Fortunately there was not much traffic about and after shouting at the zoo keeper he extracted my ear from 'Albert's' grasp and we resumed our journey without any further problems.

On arrival we took the animals up to the Social Room on the first floor and to a great roar of approval from the kids Seamus introduced each one in turn and after doing so let them loose. The next minute there was bedlam with the snake wrapping itself around the neck of one child, the armadillo was chased under the table, the parrot was swinging on one of the light fittings and the rat had disappeared. 'Albert' was busy eating all the leftover party food, surrounded by a group of admirers, whilst Seamus had been given a beer by the inspector and the two of them were shouting at one another at the back of the room. I subsided in a corner, having grabbed a sandwich before 'Albert' had got to work on the plate. About an hour later the party ended and I helped Seamus collect the animals and I drove him and his animals back to the zoo; by this time 'Albert' was asleep and snoring loud enough to wake the dead.

New Year's Eve was a busy period for us at Harrison Street. We used to mount special patrols in areas where there was a history of troublemaking and I had been given Elizabeth Street. I was to patrol the street which had two pubs, the Bull's Head at one end and the Admiral Rodney at the other, from 10pm to 2am. The night started off without much trouble and then after midnight a crowd erupted from the Bull's Head and suddenly piled out into the street, with at least half a dozen men fighting in the middle of the group. It was more than I could handle on my own so I ran to the back of the pub and asked the landlord to ring the station for some assistance. With help on the way I walked slowly round to the front of the pub to see the divisional van approaching at high speed. It pulled up nearby and out of the vehicle strode Chalky White and his colleague Bert Henson. These two officers occupied a special place on the Division for the very calm and determined way they could sort out trouble and violence in its various forms. They were big tall men, who could conduct a conversation between themselves across the roof of the Austin J Type police van; they both had about ten years' service with Chalky playing as second row for the police rugby team, whilst Bert was anchorman on the police tug of war team. I knew that currently Chalky was hunting for a new partner for the second row to replace his old one who was now absent through injury. He had approached me after hearing that I had played in the Navy and I had promised to turn up at the next training session in the New Year.

They opened the van doors and within a short period of time were filling the back of the vehicle with drunken rowdy prisoners. I managed to provide a couple of my own prisoners and then Bert put the last one in the back and asked me to close the van doors as he was about to drive the vehicle to the station. I was just about to do so when I noticed a movement and looking down saw a small brown dog on the pavement trying to jump into the van. Turning to the last man placed in the van I saw that he had what looked like a dog's lead in his hand. I realised that Bert had been a bit too enthusiastic in his efforts to stop the fighting, so I gestured to the man to get out of the van. I helped him out and before he could say anything promptly told him off for getting too close to the incident, giving us the impression he was involved in the fighting. He thought for a moment, looked up at me, nodded and then scuttled off with his dog.

Road traffic accidents were not a big problem for the police in Belltown, as very few people owned a car. My father, as a manager of a hardware store, was the first in our family to own a car, which was a Ford Popular. Every weekend the family car was lovingly cleaned by my father, after which my parents would go for a ride, all dressed up, especially when visiting relatives. His brother, my Uncle Len, who lived near my beat, never owned a car and continued to use public transport, to and from work, only venturing out to use the train when taking his family for their annual holiday to Blackpool in the summer. The other option to corporation buses was to use the bicycle, which was still my mode of transport. I was riding my green Raleigh Lenton Sports model from my parents' address to and from work, generally the traffic was slight during the time of day I was on the road and unless it was raining it was a good way to travel. The result of all this lack of traffic was that from a policing perspective, traffic accidents were few and far between for us to deal within Belltown and generally were the preserve of the Traffic Department.

My first serious road accident occurred early on in my service. It involved a heavy lorry which got lost, having arrived at the wrong destination and causing a great deal of damage in the process. It was the middle of a winter's afternoon, grey, miserable and raining when I heard a loud bang and then a crash from a nearby street. I walked towards the noise and found that a lorry had reversed into a terraced house in Edward Street. Looking at the scene it seemed that the driver had backed into the house and was now trying to extricate the vehicle. As he did so I realised how poorly constructed these homes were and that the adjacent houses were in danger of collapse. I rushed over and told the driver to stop moving the lorry, since the house seemed to be resting on it. After he stopped the lorry I started to contact the inhabitants and find out if any of them had been injured. The only occupant of the damaged property was a woman, who fortunately was in the kitchen at the rear and escaped round the back on hearing the crash. I got the other neighbours out on either side and found I had collected three young children and four women. Nobody was injured, although the woman in the kitchen was understandably shaken; the driver of the lorry seemed in a daze, wandering round his vehicle saying it should never have happened. By now a number of bystanders had arrived, including the vicar of St John's Church, who I remembered played the banjo at the children's Christmas party. I asked him if he could look after the women and children until the safety of their homes could be confirmed and he took them off to the vicarage. I then went to the corner shop and contacted the station; Ronnie agreed to inform the council to help and secure the houses. He also told me that the Traffic Department would send a vehicle examiner and Sergeant Nelson, who was in the station, would also attend.

It turned out that there were two Edward Streets in the city, one on my beat and the other, a much larger street, situated in an industrial area to the north. The lorry should have gone to the latter but by mistake had ended up in Belltown. Eventually the city housing department housed one of the families, whilst the others were looked after by nearby relatives. The lorry was taken to a local Corporation bus garage to be examined by our Traffic Department and later by a Transport Ministry examiner, but was found to be well maintained. I was given the Accident Report to prepare and it was now my job to find out what had caused the accident. The driver Leonard Wrigley, a middle-aged man, came from the Midlands and seemed a sensible chap. He had no traffic convictions and had been a driver for the haulage company for many years. I found that he had picked up the load of steel piping late in the morning and because of some administrative problems had experienced a delayed start to Somerford. After arriving in the City he had stopped to ask for directions and unfortunately he had been given the wrong location. I took a statement under caution from Wrigley who said that his foot must have slipped off the brake as he was making the U-turn. I examined his footwear but could see nothing out of the ordinary. I could only find one witness to the accident, a passing milkman, who told me that he had seen the lorry reversing in the street, mount the pavement and then it seemed to speed up and hit the front of the house. Talking to Wrigley and considering the circumstances it seemed to me that once he realised he was in the wrong location he had panicked and that this had led to the accident. I put a file together and suggested that Wrigley be prosecuted for Dangerous and Careless Driving, although I wasn't sure that the actions of the driver amounted to Dangerous Driving. My file was passed on to the Police Prosecutions Department which was located on the first floor of police headquarters and about a week later I was summoned to see the chief inspector in charge.

The role of the Police Prosecutions Department in those days was to initiate proceedings in relation to most criminal cases, including licensing offences. In practice most serious crimes, such as homicide were referred directly to the Director of Public Prosecutions in London, who often sent their own staff to handle the case. The rest of the cases were left to the police, although in the City many of the important ones were given by the Prosecution Department to the City Legal Department to provide representation in court. The Prosecutions Department handled the rest, except for the very minor cases which were dealt with by the individual officer by way of arrest or by summons. As a result by now I had prosecuted some of my own arrests or summonses, such as drunk and disorderly or obstruction of the highway which gave me some basic knowledge of presenting cases and questioning witnesses. This particular police role lasted until the middle of the nineteen eighties when the Crown Prosecution Service was formed and took over responsibility for all criminal prosecutions.

Chief Inspector Wilfred Scott was a cheerful, slim, well-spoken officer, who appeared to have a pencil permanently attached to the top of his right ear. The Department also included a number of both police and civilian staff, who worked in a big open office, which was full of stacks of files, piled high in different locations. Scott said he was satisfied with the contents of the file and went on to ask me about the character of the milkman, my only witness, querying how he was likely to perform in the witness box. He then told me that the haulage firm were employing a legal firm to defend Wrigley and that he, Scott, would prosecute in this case. During our conversation the chief inspector said that if Wrigley's legal team approached this case in the right manner, pleading guilty to Careless Driving and asking for Dangerous Driving to be withdrawn, the magistrates would probably agree, because the police would have no objection. When I queried what he meant by the 'right manner', he laughed and said that some solicitors from outside the City, especially those from London, sometimes got up the nose of our magistrates and could prejudice their own defence case. Scott finished off by saying that I would get to know the date of proceedings in a month's time. In the event the case went in accordance with the chief inspector's prediction in that Wrigley was convicted of Careless Driving, fined and disqualified from driving for twelve months.

By now I had made friends with a number of officers at the station; there were two other probationer constables, like myself, and a couple of other younger officers, who had passed through their probationer period. One of them was an affable character called 'Lord John'. He was given the nickname because of his southern accent and the fact that he owned an old black Armstrong Siddeley limousine. It was a beautiful car, which he kept in immaculate condition. When we were working on 'afternoons' we would meet up after finishing duty and climb into the car and 'Lord John' would take us to the 'Golden Lion' where we would enter through the back door and spend time drinking after licensing hours had finished. Lord John's friend George had a crush on the bar maid at the pub and spent most of the time chatting her up, although from her manner in response to his attention it wasn't clear to me that she felt the same way.

Just before Christmas it was the licensee's birthday and we drank a lot of beer before climbing back in the car. We all lived on the south side of the city and 'Lord John' dropped us off near our homes. My parents lived in a Victorian terraced house which was three storeys high. My parents used the front bedroom on the first floor and my brother Peter had used the bedroom on the same floor at the rear. I used the bedroom on the third floor, which was called the attic, and on this occasion I entered the house and without putting the lights on, silently and slowly climbed the stairs. I was counting the stairs as I went up and completed the first flight without difficulty. I turned the corner and started up the second flight, still concentrating on counting the stairs. I thought I needed one more step to reach the top, but I had miscounted and as I tried to carry on up I lost my balance, fell over on my back and gathering speed went back down the stairs. As I reached the first landing the linoleum helped me continue to increase speed and I sped into my parents' bedroom still on my back. The light went on and my mother shot up looked down at me and woke up my father, who raised an eyebrow in my direction. I scrambled to my feet, apologised to both of them and headed off back upstairs to my attic to get some sleep.

CHAPTER THREE

With Christmas out of the way I was over halfway through my probationary period and had now gained a better idea of what police work was all about. When I first arrived at Harrison Street, Sergeant Nelson had given me some advice which always stayed with me. I remembered him saying that to be a good policeman you had to like people, but you must not be soft, because if you were they would try to take advantage. Liking people, he said, means that you can exercise your discretion that the law gives you to better effect, and that's what I tried to do throughout my police career. Having gained experience I now found that report writing was no longer the problem it had been at the start. I knew what was expected when putting pen to paper and as a result the sergeants no longer exercised the same amount of scrutiny.

There were a couple of problems to police work that I was experiencing; firstly there was the negative impact that the rotational shift work had on my social life. I had met a few girls but either I or they were not really interested in developing any long-term relationship and I was still looking for the right one to come along. The other difficulty I found was that the shift system gradually caused the friends that I had made from schooldays to fade away; most of them had regular day jobs in the city centre and over time we drifted apart to be replaced by friendships made with work colleagues. It seemed as though all the features in policing were conspiring towards restricting social contact with the outside world. I was also still living with my parents and although my mother had now settled down to coping with the vagaries of my rotational shift system I was still causing her the occasional upset when I returned home late at night suffering from an excess of beer. In particular I was trying not to wake my parents up at two or three o'clock in the morning, but was not always successful. One example comes to mind when I returned home late one night after a session in the Golden Lion with the intention of being as quiet as possible. I crept into the house and into the kitchen, took my boots off and then looked for my slippers, which I had bought to reduce the noise when I went upstairs to bed. I couldn't find them and went down on my hands and knees on the floor crawling round the kitchen, desperately looking for them. I must have been making a lot of noise when suddenly the kitchen door opened and I saw my mother, who had been woken up by my antics, standing there like the Archangel Gabriel, in her night dress. She asked me what I was doing and instinctively I stood up, unfortunately I was under the kitchen table at the time and all the knives, cups and saucers set for breakfast cascaded onto the floor. I was now faced with trying to hide my drunken state whilst carefully replacing the utensils on the table. Many years later my mother remarked that she was very impressed that I had been able to set the table without falling over, since she was well aware of the state I was in.

My main ambition during this time was to save up and buy a car, as my only form of transport was still my bicycle to get to and from work. However, I was making slow headway in saving up and buying a car seemed a long way off. I had seen the car, a second-hand Sunbeam Alpine that looked just right, and I hoped that another couple of months would be all that was required to make the purchase. If I could manage that I thought things would change for the better.

I was beginning to realise that licensed premises and licensees played a significant part in law enforcement as well as providing beer for thirsty police officers. In the policing calendar Friday and Saturday evening were set aside every week for visits to local pubs by the sergeant, accompanied by a senior constable. The system required each pub to be visited once a month and the sergeant went round each licensed room to satisfy himself that all was in order and that the premises were being run properly. After which he and his colleague generally retired to the back room behind the bar with the licensee and had a quiet pint, which also included being given a packet of cigarettes. There were about fifty pubs supervised from Harrison Street station, which meant that about twelve had to be visited during the evening of the two days and I grew to admire the ability of these experienced officers, whose capacity for drinking large quantities of beer and keeping a clear head, were legendary. In order to satisfy the police requirement for paperwork each pub visit was entered by the sergeant in the Visit to Licensed Premises book together with observations about the conduct of the premises.

My first experience of major disorder in a pub involved a wedding celebration which got out of hand at the Crown Inn on Commercial Street. The pub had number of large rooms on the first floor which were used by the locals for social functions. I knew about the wedding, which was a big affair involving two local Irish families, with about one hundred guests expected. Sergeant Nelson and a PC made an early call at the pub and found the place busy, but in order. About ten thirty I was patrolling the top end of Commercial Street when the divisional van came towards me with Bert and Chalky on board, together with Sergeant Nelson, who gestured for me to get in the van. They stopped and going round the back of the vehicle I found that the interior was full of officers who told me that fighting had broken out at the Crown.

When we arrived at the pub all the lights were on and many people were gathered around, both on the street and inside the entrance. As we all got out of the van and went inside I could hear a lot of noise and the sounds of violence. At the time I was a fan of the western film star John Wayne and the sight which met my eyes reminded me of many of his films. There was a large brawl involving half a dozen men taking place near the front entrance, whilst another man was tumbling down the stairs head over heels from the first floor. We separated the contestants by the entrance and those who refused to quieten down were bundled into the van.

The next step was to move upstairs and it was

about then that I realised that some of the women guests were also fighting on the floor above. On reaching the first floor I found that some tables and chairs had been broken and that I was wading through broken glass together with food and drink which had been scattered around. The two women fighting were found to be the bride and her chief bridesmaid. After they had been separated, and this was not easy, the premises started to calm down. Chalky took the bride to one side and I conducted her bridesmaid down the stairs and into the lounge at the back. By this time she had recovered and told me that the trouble had started when she found out that the bride had been having an affair with the best man, who was her boyfriend. Apparently somebody mentioned it at the bar and she overheard the conversation, ran upstairs to challenge the bride who admitted it, and the fight then started between them. In the process other arguments took place and within a short time the whole pub was in an uproar. Neither woman wanted to take the matter further and Sergeant Nelson brought the two fathers of the bridal couple together and left them with the licensee to settle the bill for the damage which I could imagine would be quite a sum. Several weeks later I saw the newlyweds and from their behaviour I got the impression that things had been patched up.

Generally the relationship with pub licensees and the police was good and I got to know them all on my beat over time. However, when new licensees were appointed the odd problem could arise. One particular instance comes to mind and it started when I was making a 'point' about quarter past five in the evening on the main road out of the city. I watched the green corporation buses go past, one after the other, all jam-packed with people on their way home after work, most of whom would be reading the local paper, the Evening News. However, on this occasion most of them were staring intently at me, initially I couldn't understand what the attraction was until I noticed a man coming towards me from the nearby pub, holding a pint of beer in his hand. He had a smile on his face and I realised that he intended to give me the beer. I gestured him to stop and told him to get back into the pub with the pint as fast as his legs would take him. When the time for a visit from the sergeant had passed I waited for a few more minutes and then went round the side of the premises and into the pub to find out what was going on. It turned out that a new licensee had taken over and having seen me standing outside he had poured a pint and said to one of his staff that the beer was for me, thinking that I would come in and he could then introduce himself and vice versa. Unfortunately his remarks had been misinterpreted and one of the locals had dashed out with the beer. It allowed me to spend some time on the premises getting to know the new landlord and his beer, before resuming patrol.

The winter months gave way to spring and parading one afternoon as Sergeant Nelson was coming to the end of his read up he pulled out a piece of paper and announced that Sir Oswald Moseley was due to visit the city to hold a meeting with his supporters on the following Saturday. As a result of this visit and with the expectation of trouble our Division had been asked to supply officers to assist the C Division, where the meeting was to be held. Many of the older constables were aware of Moseley's effort to create a fascist state before the Second World War and suggested that we let the public vent their fury on the ancient blackshirt. The sergeant grinned and then began to read out the names of those officers selected and I heard that I had been included on the list. The instructions were to report at ten am at our Divisional Headquarters, which meant that I had been taken off the afternoon shift on that day and that in turn meant a possible night on the tiles.

As I was leaving the station Ron shouted over that there was a call waiting for me. Somewhat surprised, I picked up the phone and found that I was talking Charlie Brooks. He had also been selected for the demonstration on Saturday and wondered if I was free on Saturday evening to go to a party given by a policewoman, who was celebrating her twenty-first birthday. In those days the Policewomen's Department was run as a separate unit from the rest of the Force, controlled by a woman superintendent, Miss Garside, who was known to keep a beady eye on her charges. It was generally reckoned within the Force that the women were 'a better class of person' from the male members, who according to a previous chief constable were members of the artisan class. The policewomen worked different shifts, had a restricted police role, being responsible for women and children who came to the notice of the police, and had other limited responsibilities. Up till now I had not had many dealings with them, so the party might improve this deficiency; who knows, I thought this could be my lucky day. So I told Charlie to book me a place at the party and I would be there if he would provide a lift, which he agreed to do, knowing I was still without my own transport.

The rest of the week passed without incident and Saturday morning arrived with me in an excited frame of mind, firstly going to my first major public demonstration and then followed by a party. I arrived at Divisional Headquarters on time and after having my name ticked off on the list I then hung around with the rest of the officers waiting for transport to arrive. It eventually came in the form of a large green bus, which rumour suggested had been acquired from the nearby US airbase. When I think back now it is easy to see how the police have changed their response to major outbreaks of public disorder. In those days there was no special riot gear issued; no flameproof overalls, protective helmet, Tasers, mace, special extendible staffs, shields, not forgetting shin pads and kneepads and of course specially protected vehicles.

On that particular day I was dressed in ordinary uniform, the only additional gear I was wearing was an unofficial cricket box which one of my colleagues, who had some previous experience, suggested might be a good idea to wear. In those days if trouble was expected policing relied on supplying large numbers of officers to control the event. Police training instructions stressed the importance of the use of cordons rather than aggressive tactics which were common in Europe where police forces routinely used water cannon and tear gas. There seemed to be an unofficial acceptance by both police and the demonstrators that extreme violence would not be used and the only specialist units available were police horses, the use of police dogs was never considered. These methods had been in use since the start of professional policing and were over one hundred years old; of course occasionally public order became so extreme that other nearby police forces were asked to supply additional officers and in the past the army had been called out to assist, but such incidents were extremely rare.

Off we went to the C Division; there were about fifty of us, under the command of one of our chief inspectors, who was universally known as 'Wizzo' because of his previous service in the RAF and his matching moustache. C Division Headquarters was a large red-brick building in the form of a square. We entered the courtyard and I could see that three sides of the building comprised of married officer accommodation, whilst the fourth side contained the operational offices into which we were ushered. We ended up in a large hall which already had contingents from the other city divisions; there must have been a couple of hundred officers in total all waiting for a briefing. The Chief Superintendent of the C Division started the proceedings by telling us that an open-air meeting had been organised on some open land where Moseley would address his supporters. He went on to say that the mounted branch would be available to give active support if necessary and then used a map of the district showing us the area which had been allocated to each division. Finally he finished his briefing by saying that a large number of demonstrators were expected from all over the country and they would make every effort to prevent Moseley from speaking, and it was our job to keep both sides apart and ensure violence was kept to a minimum.

We marched to our appointed area which was about ten minutes from the station and were shown the street we were to cordon off near to the open ground that was going to be used by Moseley. It was some two hours before the speech was due to be delivered and the district was very similar in composition to my own Division, with its series of rows of terraced houses. There were a few people about and those that were there seemed to be locals who had turned out to see the 'fun'. The Traffic Department had closed off the area to traffic and we formed a loose cordon across our street and waited. Looking over towards the croft I couldn't see much going on, there was no sign of Moseley; perhaps, I thought, hopefully, he wouldn't turn up. The crowd began to increase and I found out later that many had arrived at the city centre by train and had walked the couple of miles or so to the scene. When I turned to look at the croft again I saw that more of his supporters had gathered and that a car had pulled up nearby with a number of men getting out, one of whom I assumed must have been Moseley. The noise and pressure from the crowd increased and time seemed to speed up. I noticed that someone had hoisted up a large red banner bearing the words 'Anarchist Society' and the pressure against the cordon was increasing by the minute. We had our backs to the crowd trying to prevent them moving forward, but we were slowly being pushed towards the meeting place. In the struggle my helmet had been knocked off, which I found to be one less thing to worry about. I looked up and saw in front of us a tall man wearing a dark pinstripe suit, wearing a bowler hat and carrying a black furled umbrella; he was shouting something at us like 'hang on lads'. A flash of recognition took place in my mind and I realised I was looking at our chief constable; the next moment he dashed off and seconds later two police horses appeared round the corner and headed towards us at a brisk trot.

At that time the City Police had a large Mounted Branch with about forty horses and I had visited their headquarters during my Induction Course. One of their sergeants had taken us round their stables explaining their role and allowing us to inspect the horses, which to my untutored eye, seemed to be to be very large animals. He told us that a couple of them each weighed nearly a ton and that they were highly trained, especially in dealing with public disorder. He explained that in these situations the usual technique was for the horse to be turned ninety degrees to the crowd and lean sideways into them with a pushing motion which forced the crowd backwards. Whilst I was thinking back to that visit to the stables I found myself trapped between the excited crowd and the rump of a large brown horse. I could smell leather and a strong sweaty horsey aroma and I realised that I was being pushed slowly backwards into the demonstrators, who were also gradually being moved back. As I went backwards I could feel resistance from the people at the back who were still trying to move forward and then a surprising thing occurred; I felt the horse's stomach start to ripple and the next moment it gave an enormous fart. The air seemed to have turned blue and the accompanying smell was awful, it seemed to be everywhere, clinging to us like a cloud. I lost interest in holding back the crowd and felt a strong desire to escape and fortunately members of the crowd had much the same idea. In a flash the street was full of people running down the street keen to leave as much distance between themselves and the stench with the remains of the police cordon coughing and spluttering. This incident effectively finished the demonstration in our part of the district and when I recovered I found that Moseley had left the scene and his supporters had drifted away leaving the area to revert to normal.

We returned to the coach to be driven back to our Divisional Headquarters. I reported the loss of my helmet and in true police fashion was required to complete a long-winded report of the circumstances. I was then given a temporary helmet and told to report to the clothing store the following week for a new issue. In the event I had not seen the last of my old helmet since it turned out that the member of the crowd, who seized it, was about to enter St Paul's Central Railway station to return home when he was spotted by a PC who arrested him. I made an appearance at the City Magistrates court where the man was fined and my helmet, which was slightly the worse for wear, was returned to me.

I returned home I got ready for the party, which included picking up a bottle of Cinzano and a party size can of Red Barrel which I hoped would fit the bill. Charlie turned up and made some sarcastic comments about my dress sense, which made me realise that I had still not come to terms with drainpipe trousers and coloured shirts which now seemed to be the order of the day. Anyhow it was now too late to do anything about it, the partygoers would have to accept me in my dark grey suit and tie. Charlie was a cheerful extrovert type who had always had a way with women, starting from his early exploits at school, so I wasn't surprised that he had made contact with the policewomen's department. I told him he was not helping me get into the party mood, but he laughed and off we went in his car.

We spent the journey with Charlie giving me an up-to-date account of which policewomen were likely to come and whether some nurses from the local hospital were also expected to arrive. As he carried on I started to brighten up since my experience with girlfriends to date had been mixed. I had taken a few girls out during school days, but I suppose my first proper girlfriend was a librarian who I got to know during my initial training course with the Marines in Plymouth. She was a good deal older than me and taught me a lot about women; we had fun together, but I knew it wouldn't last. The next time I had a narrow escape which occurred in Malta. My unit had been transferred there to join the 3rd Commando Brigade and I started to go out with a Maltese girl, who was working in the Brigade Admin Office. She was a lovely girl called Maria, who was twenty-one years old and lived with her family near the base. I was one of the few Marines who had a Maltese girlfriend and in those days taking her out also meant taking out her elder sister and on other occasions her auntie, since it was normal, in those days, to be accompanied by chaperones. I preferred her sister as she had her own boyfriend and as a result Maria and I could exercise a bit of freedom, but there was no such luck with her auntie, who took her responsibility very seriously and would not allow us to get out of sight. Our relationship moved on when I was invited for Sunday lunch with her family. Initially I wasn't too concerned since I had eaten there before, but when I reached her house and went through into the courtyard I realised that the situation had changed. I found the place to be full of her relatives, many of whom I had never met before. I was ushered to the table and we all sat down and then during the meal I was asked a variety of questions; where did I come from, was I going to stay in the Marines, what did my father do and many others along a similar line. The penny dropped and I realised that I was being sized up as a possible husband for Maria. I eventually left and returned to the base and fortunately for me a week later I found out that my unit was being shipped to Cyprus to help deal with EOKA. A short while after the *Ark Royal* docked at Grand Harbour and I left the Island for Cyprus and did not return to Malta until I had a family holiday there many years later.

We arrived at a Victorian terraced house where the birthday girl, Pauline Wilson, shared a flat with two other policewomen on the middle floor. All the lights were on in the house and I could hear the sound of Herman's Hermits 'waking up one morning' wafting down the street. I followed Charlie up the stairs and found most of those present were police officers, many of whom I already knew. The girl whose birthday we were celebrating turned out to be a red-faced stocky young lady with short-cropped blonde hair. She gave me a kiss and then we went into one of the corners of the room where two other women were standing talking. I recognised one straight away as Barbara Lewis, a jolly bubbly girl who was Charlie's current girlfriend. I knew she was training to be a primary school teacher at the local Teacher Training College. The other girl, who I had never met before, was introduced as Helen Broadbent, who turned out to be a policewoman working on my Division. She was a tall, slim, attractive woman with blue eyes. I formed the impression that she was a quiet type, obviously very different in personality to Barbara. Surprisingly upon introduction she stuck her hand out and I automatically shook it hoping that I had not been too vigorous in my response. She smiled slightly and said that she had heard all about me, giving me pause for thought, but Charlie had not let me down so I relaxed and got us both a drink. We spent some time getting to know one another and I found that her family came from London and that she had moved north when her father, who was in the insurance business, had got a high-powered job in Somerford. She lived with her parents in Oakham, which was a wealthy suburb in the south of the city. She had a brother and sister, who had gone back south and she had been a policewoman for nearly three years. I rattled through my history, conscious that my home background didn't match hers; in fact the only thing we seemed to have in common was the police service.

We danced and jived during the evening, ate sausage rolls and sandwiches, finishing off by shouting 'happy birthday' when the cake appeared. The party was drawing to a close and I realised that Charlie and Barbara had disappeared leaving me without a lift. Helen could see the expression on my face as I was now trying to find a solution to the lack of transport and she asked me what the problem was, and reluctantly I put her in the picture. She told me not to worry as she had a car and would drop me off on her way home. On the way we talked about the party and as she stopped outside my parents' house I summoned up courage and asked her if we could meet again. She paused then smiled saying, 'Of course,' adding that she was on 'afternoons' the following week and that I knew how to contact her at the station. I turned to thank her for the lift and before replying she leaned across and kissed me, which I was happy to reciprocate with great enthusiasm. I got out of the car in a surprised state and she drove off with a wave of the hand. As I walked up the steps to the front door I decided that the gods had been kind and I now had girlfriend, but there was still a problem to be solved in that the pressure was now on for me to get a car. I had saved up some money and with a loan from my father and another one from the bank I was able to buy a car, which I had my eye on for a while; it was a second-hand light blue Sunbeam Alpine. On my first long trip out with the car, Helen and I spent a very enjoyable weekend in the Lake District.

Time marched on and once again I was on 'nights' and finding out that a week of night duty had a particular routine. Usually Monday night was quiet with the locals recovering from the weekend and the first day back at work. After that as the week moved on the workload increased with lots of clubs staying open until 2am when customers would drift out onto the streets, causing trouble. I remember a particular Monday night. I had just finished a hit and run traffic accident report and was leaving the station when Ron Holliday asked me to go to a domestic disturbance in Francis Street. This street was not on my beat but as the regular officer George Flowers was busy at a house fire, Ron asked me to attend. He told me that this was a regular occurrence, usually involving the couple who lived at number thirteen. According to Ronnie these incidents arose through the actions of Ted Mason who lived with his common law wife at this address, who regularly beat her up and seemed to be terrorising the neighbourhood with his antics. He went on to say that he would arrange for the divisional van to attend when they were free to give me some support.

At the Police Training Centre we were told that whilst on foot patrol we should never walk more than three miles an hour, but on this occasion I thought I had better speed up since at one o'clock in the morning nobody would be bothered. I turned into Francis Street and spotted the house straight away, since there were some neighbours hanging around the front door. I slowed down and found the front door open and from inside I could hear angry shouting. I strode in and made my way along the passage and stood in the doorway of the kitchen. In front of me were a man and a woman, who were busy shouting at each other. He was a short stocky fellow who had his back to me, whilst his wife was a small thin woman whose face was covered with blood. She noticed my arrival and looked up at me and the man, who I took to be Mason, turned round. As he did so I noticed a photograph of him in army uniform, wearing a red beret of the Parachute Regiment on the mantelpiece behind him. Before he could say anything I seized the initiative and asked him if he had been in the Paras; he looked surprised and then realised I had seen the photograph. The tension in the room began to subside and I heard the bell of the ambulance as it turned into the street and asked his wife if she needed to go to Casualty and have her face treated. Before getting a reply I then asked Mason if he had hit her. Mason shrugged his shoulders and said that she was his wife and he could knock her about if he wanted to when she caused trouble. For the first time Mrs Mason interjected saying, 'Common law wife,' as though this meant something special. I didn't answer either of them and instead helped the woman to the waiting ambulance and returned to confront Mason.

I had enough experience by now to know that in these situations once you made a decision to act in a specific manner there was no going back, and I was angry with Mason and felt that he should not be allowed to get away with his behaviour. I suspected his wife would not go as witness against him for this type of assault as that seemed to be the usual response from women in this situation unless the injuries were very severe, which meant in practice that husbands or boyfriends were rarely prosecuted. As I returned and entered the kitchen Mason told me to get out of the house because he wanted to get some rest. Looking at him I suddenly had an idea; if I could goad him into attacking me I reckoned I could lay him out; he seemed tough, but he was overweight and I thought he had slowed down from his days in the Army. I remembered the advice I had been given by the older constables at the station when dealing with violent members of the public. Firstly it was a cardinal rule not to hit them in the face, whether using a staff or a fist, unless it was absolutely necessary, and secondly if you did need to hit the individual you should always arrest him for disorderly behaviour, and if he were to complain afterwards about excessive violence being used the matter should always be brought to the notice of the magistrates who could usually be relied upon to support the officer in these situations.

I went up to him and told him I thought he was a coward hitting a defenceless woman and if the Parachute Regiment got to hear about it they would disown him. Before I could carry on with my description of his behaviour and ancestry he suddenly rushed at me shouting abuse. I dived out of the way and moved round his back and with one hand seized hold of the collar of his shirt and with the other grabbed hold of his trouser waist and with a rush manhandled him out of the house and into the street. He tried to turn and I thought, *He is going to have another go at me,* and he didn't let me down. The neighbours watched with interest as he wrenched himself out of my grip and aimed a punch at my face. The Marine training and reflexes kicked in and I ducked and hit him hard in the stomach. He stopped and sank on his knees onto the pavement, just as the divisional van turned the corner and came to a stop nearby. I hoisted him into the van and we went to the station where Sergeant Nelson charged him with police assault, keeping him in the cells for a morning court appearance.

When the dust had settled and the paperwork was completed I went round to Somerford Royal Infirmary and to the Casualty Department to see Mrs Mason. She had been treated and apparently the injury was limited to a blow on the nose. I told her that I had arrested her husband for police assault and asked her if she wished to press charges against him for the injury he had caused. She made it clear that she did not want to take the matter further. She seemed a nice woman and I was at a loss to suggest anything else, other than she might consider leaving him. She looked at me and said that normally her husband was as nice as pie, but that at the moment he was under pressure at work and this fact plus the drink had got the better of him. Given what I had been told by Ron at the station, I found this explanation difficult to accept, but she seemed satisfied with the way I had dealt with the situation. I told her if that if he assaulted her again she was to ask for me and I would come round and have a word with him; looking at me, she smiled and said she would bear it in mind.

The City Magistrates Court was a large Victorian red-brick building in the city centre, and the normal practice was for officers attending court to go down into the basement to book in. There was no natural light at this level and as a result the atmosphere was gloomy with an environment that suggested nothing much had changed from the time it had first opened for business some hundred years ago. To get into the holding area it was necessary to approach a barred gate, identify yourself to the police gatekeeper and enter into the main area, which was busy and noisy, with uniformed, plain clothes and CID officers, plus probation officers, defendants' solicitors and admin staff to name but a few, all going about their business. At nine thirty all the prisoners appearing that day would be lined up and identified to the various arresting officers, who would take their prisoners to one side and ascertain what plea they were going to make, whether they had engaged a solicitor and if there were any other offences they were prepared to plead guilty to or as it was known in the 'trade', TIC or 'taken into consideration'. This latter feature was mainly a concern of CID officers who were anxious for prisoners to admit additional offences which would then be used to improve their detection rates. As time went on and I gained more experience I saw the importance of TICs to the CID and the way pressure was used on prisoners who would in some cases be prepared to admit to anything in order to keep a particular detective off their backs.

Usually the first prisoners dealt with in court involved those arresting officers who were working 'nights', after which those officers who were working 'afternoons' were called up. I waited until 11.30am when I was called before the court to give my evidence; unbelievably Mason had no previous convictions and he pleaded guilty. He admitted he had been drinking, saying that he would apologise to the officer for causing so much trouble, after which he was fined. I managed to keep my face straight in court while he was giving his explanation, but when I took him to the Fines Office I told him I had seen his wife and asked her to let me know if he caused any more trouble because I would make it my business to return and this time I would sort him out properly. He seemed to have been thinking over the events of the previous night because he asked me why I had made a comment about the photograph of him in the uniform of the Parachute Regiment. I explained to him that as a Marine Commando I had worked with them in Cyprus; he nodded in response, saying that he should have taken more notice of that remark. I could see that the rivalry between the paras and the commandos had surfaced in his mind and he confirmed it when he then claimed that if he had been ten years younger he would have sorted me out.

I looked at him and decided that it was not the time to engage in an argument and simply replied, 'Perhaps.' But thinking about it I doubted that he would have come out on top if we had a fight when he was in his prime.

One belief which was common amongst the community in Belltown, was that common law marriages offered women a degree of protection and was one step above 'living over the brush' as cohabiting was known locally. As part of our police training we were given no advice about the legal status of common law marriage and as a result we accepted the community's view. However many years later that I found that the community's beliefs were wrong. Did my threat work with Mason? I think so because I don't remember receiving another call from Francis Street and the neighbours said that things at the Masons' house seemed to have settled down, but in any case my thoughts were now elsewhere, thinking about my impending visit to have a meal with Helen's parents.

My relationship with Helen seemed to be developing at a nice and easy pace and during the previous six months we discovered that we liked rambling in the countryside, dancing and when shift work allowed we would find suitable country pubs to have a drink and a meal. I had introduced her to my parents and whilst my mother made every effort to make her feel at home, I thought my father seemed a bit wary, although I never challenged him at the time. I had met her parents on the occasional basis when I had driven round to pick her up at her house and whilst they were polite there didn't seem much warmth in their attitude towards me, but I hoped that this would improve as I got to know them over time and when Helen asked me to have an evening meal with her parents I thought this would be a good opportunity. In the event, however, I was to be sadly mistaken.

On arrival I was ushered in and it soon became clear to me that her father didn't see me as an asset to the family. We discussed my background and when we came to my service in the Marines I found that her grandfather had been a colonel in the Corps, which allowed me to admit that I had reached the dizzy heights of Marine First Class. I did mention that if I had signed on for a further tour I would have been promoted corporal, but this possibility made little impression and passed him by. By now her father was getting into his stride with the further announcement that he had seen service in Europe as a captain in the Hussars, by this time I was having a hard time controlling my temper and restrained myself from expressing surprise, since by now it seemed to me that during his time in the army he should have reached the rank of general. As the evening wore on I could see that Helen was beginning to look worried and so I limited myself to nodding my head with the occasional smile through gritted teeth. We moved into the dining room where I began to realise that it was now the turn of Helen's mother to test my knowledge of the etiquette of dining. I was on slippery ground in this situation because I had not much experience and so I kept a close eye on the others when it came to the use of fish knives and forks, not forgetting when to have red and white wine with particular courses of food. Her mother apologised for not having any beer in the house, which she obviously thought would be my tipple of choice, which was correct, but I suspected she was making a negative point to the rest of the family at my expense.

The evening couldn't finish soon enough for me and when Helen saw me out she gave me a quick peck on the cheek, promising to get in touch. But I never saw her again, since the next thing I knew she had resigned and left the City Police post haste. I later found out from Charlie's Barbara that Helen's parents had never supported her decision to become a policewoman and their attitude may have helped her initial decision to join the City Police to spite them, since I knew that her relationship with them had been stormy and difficult. In the event they found a way to persuade her to resign by offering to fund a course for her at a London art college, which she decided to accept and off she went leaving me in a dejected state. When I told my mother she was upset for me, but my father tried and failed to hide a triumphant grin, saying that all along he had known that Helen wasn't right for me, claiming that she was not of my class and we would have never have made it work. I was despondent since although I acknowledged the substance of his remarks I had hoped we could have overcome those issues, but obviously I was wrong and the class issue had been more important than I thought. Fortunately being a basically optimistic character I soon recognised that I should now take the advice of a popular song at the time and 'pick myself up and start all over again'.

CHAPTER FOUR

All the incidents I had dealt with so far had physical explanations which in turn required the production of facts from which a criminal case could be established and presented in court. I was gaining knowledge in what to look out for if incidents of larceny, housebreaking, drunken or violent behaviour came my way. But there was one unusual event I was involved with which to this day I cannot explain with a rational and forensic approach.

It all started on 'nights' when I was entering the station to have my refreshments. Before I could get into the canteen Ronnie told me that he had received a call from a Mr Roberts from a public telephone kiosk saying that there was some trouble from at number twenty-one Carlton Street involving the Featherstone family. He went on to ask me if I would take a look as there was no one else available. I trudged off back into the night; fortunately Carlton Street was at the back of the station and I was soon at the house. The front door was open and I could hear a young girl crying at the rear. I followed the sound, walking along the hallway and into the kitchen. The room looked as though it had been subjected to a hurricane – chairs had been tipped over and a large piece of furniture which I thought was probably a dresser had fallen flat on the floor. There were broken cups, saucers and plates flung across the floor and standing in the middle of the room was a young girl, aged about eleven or twelve, in her night dress, crying softly. In one corner was a woman who I took to be her mother, fearful and white-faced with shock. When I entered the kitchen it was as though I had broken a spell, because the girl stopped crying and her mother rushed up to hug her. I noticed that her father was in an opposite corner on my left and upon seeing me he seemed to come alive. All the adults were also dressed in their night clothes.

Looking at the scene I had assumed that there had been some sort of domestic dispute which had got out of hand. The story the Featherstone family recounted, however, made me realise that I had completely misjudged the situation. They were all in bed asleep when their daughter, Alice, had woken up and feeling thirsty had gone downstairs to make herself a drink of water. As she approached the kitchen she heard the sound of a breaking plate. She pushed open the door and as she did so felt a current of air as though one of the windows was open. She switched on the light and felt something fly past her and smash against the wall. By this time she was frightened and stopped in the centre of the room just to see the kitchen dresser suddenly fall away from the wall towards her. She was now terrified and stood in the centre of the room crying and shouting for her parents. They both came down to see cups and saucers falling to the floor; everybody was now petrified and they stayed there until I opened the door and strode into the kitchen.

I looked at the windows but they were all securely shut and there were no signs that anybody had broken into the room. I then helped pull the dresser upright and found it was a heavy piece of furniture and not something that Alice could have moved easily. By now her mother had filled the kettle, which was on the stove, and she made us all a cup of tea. I asked them how the front door came to be open but none of them could offer an explanation. The situation appeared to have quietened down and I returned to the station. I recounted the events to Ronnie and he suggested that it might have been caused by a poltergeist, which I later found was supposed to be a spirit which manifests its presence by acts of mischief such as throwing furniture about. Ronnie and one of the older constables remembered a similar set of circumstances many years previously which also involved a young girl. Within a couple of weeks the Featherstone family had left the area. Efforts were made to tackle the problem when the Parish Priest of St Joseph's Catholic Church, Father O'Connor, was asked to conduct a service at the house to exorcise the evil spirit, but it was plain that nobody was anxious to occupy the premises. As a result the house remained empty for nearly two years before it was demolished as part of the council area clearance programme. I made enquiries to find the Mr Roberts who had made the initial call, but he did not live in Carlton Street and none of the neighbours could help in locating him. I was never able to explain the events during that night and maybe it was a poltergeist, since nothing else came to light.

We got a new addition to our ranks at Harrison Street after Christmas in the form of PC Ian Johnson, who returned to uniform duties after a spell in the Plain Clothes Department. Ian was a quiet amiable character with a good sense of humour and a reputation as a good police officer, who quickly became friends with me and Charlie. As well as these important characteristics he also had one significant possession which put him head and shoulders above his workmates: namely he had acquired a large number of GCE 'O' levels whilst at school. I had three GCEs – maths, English and woodwork – but this paled into insignificance alongside Ian's collection. To understand the importance of this achievement it is useful to look at the policy of the Recruiting Department of the City Police, who simply aimed to appoint large fit men, who could read and write and who were not colour blind. In general policing did not attract recruits with good academic backgrounds and no attempt was made by the City Police to address this failure. The Department did not see the point of recruiting men with academic qualifications, since at the time it was believed that all that was required to make a good police officer was basic common sense. Nobody in the City Police possessed a degree and the general consensus was that such a qualification was a waste of time.

As I got to know Ian I soon realised that here was a man who had thought about policing as a career and seemingly had mapped out his way to the top. He was waiting to become an aide to the CID, which was a method to assess his suitability as a detective by giving him a six-month attachment to the local CID divisional office. If all went well he wanted to transfer into the

Commercial Fraud Squad for a few years before moving onwards and upwards. He had already passed the Promotion Examination to sergeant and I couldn't imagine him staying with us on the Division for long. Listening to him as he explained the possibilities which policing offered and in doing so he opened my eyes to what a future police career might bring.

I was back on 'afternoons' discussing a change of duties with Sergeant Nelson in the Charge Office when I was introduced to one of the districts well known characters. PC Jackson had just brought in a young lad called Sammy Holt who was twelve and had become a resident of our local authority children's home, about five years previously, as a result of his parents splitting up and leaving Sammy on the doorstep of the local vicarage. Sammy was a frequent escaper from the Home and on this occasion had been caught trying to hitch a lift, without paying, on one of the Corporation's buses. The sergeant told me that as soon as he went into care he had taken up a life of crime, gaining convictions for theft, shoplifting and housebreaking. He was currently languishing in the local authority boys' home whilst the authorities decided whether he should be sent to an Approved School or given his age move him to Borstal. This decision seemed to be taking a long time as it appeared that neither of the above institutions was in a hurry to receive him, which resulted in many of his detractors in the area suggesting that the Tower of London would make a better location. Given his frequent contact with the police it soon became clear to me that the two officers he liked to deal most were Sergeant Nelson and Ronnie Holliday, since he always asked for them upon his arrival at the station. He was a small thin child with a perpetual worried look on his face; he rarely smiled and seemed old for his years. If he was in a good mood or if one of his two heroes were about he could be usually be persuaded to admit to committing crimes of one sort or another. Whenever he was captured the local CID were informed and a detective would turn up and many crimes would be cleared up, and the detection figures improved accordingly. Listening to him I formed the impression that although some offences had been clearly committed by him there were many others which had been committed by others, but this discrepancy did seem to bother Sammy or the CID.

On this occasion the sergeant asked me to ring the Home to collect Sammy, as our divisional van was tied up. He then told the boy that I would look after him until he could be collected by a member of staff, which was usually Monica Thompson, who was the assistant to the Matron of the Home. Sammy looked at me suspiciously as a new 'boy' at the station and asked the sergeant whether I had been in the army. Nelson smiled at the youngster and nodded in confirmation, telling me that Sammy only had time only for ex-soldiers, since in his eyes they were the only ones who could be trusted. At the time this sort of remark was not considered worthy of further examination. Sammy had never complained about his treatment at the Home and in those days a certain amount of corporal punishment by staff was accepted as a means of controlling disobedient children. Within the police and wider community there was no suggestion of widespread misconduct whether sexual or physical abuse occurring in Children's Homes and such remarks by the boy did not raise any suspicions.

I rang the Home and arranged for Sammy's collection, after which I gave the lad a cup of tea. About half an hour later the bell at the public counter rang and I went through the Charge Office and into the public reception area and saw a middle-aged woman who introduced herself as Monica Thompson. I fetched the boy, who nodded when he saw her and the pair of them left the station.

Some weeks later I was on 'nights' and making one of my points wondering whether Sergeant Nelson would turn up. Ian Johnson had been given the beat adjacent to mine and I knew that his point was not far away. I hung on for a few moments but there was no sign of the sergeant so I crossed over the street and saw Ian nearby. We went into a shop doorway and started to arrange a meeting the following week at a local pub we used, when we heard shouting from the back of the shops on his beat. We both made our way towards the noise and turning a corner saw a number of residents gathered outside a house which was on fire. The flames were on the ground floor and seemed to be coming from the rear. Seeing the blaze we rushed up to the scene and were told that that an old lady in her seventies called Mrs Crabtree lived at the address. One of the locals had run off to the nearest phone box to call the fire brigade, but it was not clear if Mrs Crabtree was still in the house. A couple of the local men had tried to get in without success and we both set about the front door with a vengeance. It quickly broke down and a huge cloud of smoke and heat roared out of the doorway. The neighbours suggested that the old lady was likely to be in the kitchen since she rarely ventured upstairs because of problems with her knees. We were both wearing greatcoats and tying handkerchiefs across our mouths we lowered our heads and rushed along the corridor and into the kitchen. We found the woman sitting in a chair, as we had been told; she was awake and appeared terrified. By now the heat was intense and we picked her up and dashed back out of the house, sitting her down on the pavement away from the fire. I joined Ian with Mrs Crabtree, who was now recovering from her ordeal, having been given a glass of water by one of her neighbours.

I went to get some water for Ian and myself and went back to join them. Suddenly she looked up at us and asked if her dog had also been collected from the house. I looked at Ian, but neither of us remembered seeing the animal, which Mrs Crabtree said had been lying close to her feet in the kitchen. Seeing that the dog had not been rescued the woman started to cry, pleading with us to recover her pet. Ian looked down at her and before I could say anything had rushed back to the house and dived through the door into the smoking inferno. I dashed after him, but it seemed to me that the fire was burning more fiercely than ever and there was smoke everywhere. I pulled my handkerchief out over my face and took a deep breath and was about to run along the corridor to help Ian, when I heard a crash and saw the stairs suddenly collapse in front of me and smash into the passage, sending sparks and burning debris towards me. There was no sign of Ian and my route into the kitchen was now blocked. I turned and stumbled out of the house into the arms of the local Station Fire Officer; the fire brigade had arrived at last, together with an ambulance. I told them what had happened and they led me back to Mrs Crabtree. I sat down beside and tears started to fall downs my cheeks, I couldn't believe what had happened, I knew everybody was looking at us in silence. I started to cough uncontrollably, I didn't know what to think it was all too dreadful to contemplate, my friend was gone all because of Mrs Crabtree's pet dog.

In those days there were no offers of counselling, police officers like the military were expected to handle traumatic incidents in their stride. That doesn't mean to say that people within the Force were not oblivious to the problems that such events can cause, after all many of the older officers had experienced dreadful scenes in warfare and had seen comrades die in battle. By now Sergeant Nelson and turned up with Inspector Murdoch; they both wanted to know what had happened and I spent some time putting them in the picture. Mrs Crabtree was being taken to Casualty and the sergeant asked me if I needed to go, but I declined the offer saying that miraculously I had not been burnt. He told me to return to the station and I was glad to get away from the scene. I arrived at the station to find that Ronnie, who must have already been told of the incident, was awaiting my arrival since he placed a mug of hot tea in my hand. He later told me that I had turned up in a uniform that was covered in dirt and with a face submerged in grime and soot from which two blue eyes peered out at him looking dazed and confused. We sat in the canteen and the tea started to work wonders as I began to relax and explained what had happened. He then told me about his experiences during the D-Day landing and how he had seen many of his friends and comrades fall to German fire. I could appreciate what he was trying to do and later thanked him, saying that

I never knew he had a sensitive soul. Other members of the Section were turning up and I found myself developing a shortened version of events, concentrating more on Ian's exploits than my own part in the tragedy. Sergeant Nelson returned and told me to retire from duty and take a couple of days off; I wasn't sure that was what I wanted to do but I nodded and went home.

The first night's sleep passed off without any problems, but thereon after I started to have regular nightmares, usually relating to fires and burning buildings. It must have taken about a month before things started to calm down, but even after that I still experienced the occasional bad dream. I woke up the morning after the tragedy to find that I had become a hero with a picture of Ian and myself in the newspapers. I didn't certainly feel like one, in fact I initially couldn't get over the problem that I was alive and Ian had died. When I later met Ian's parents I thought that they might have resented the fact that I was still alive, instead of Ian, but that wasn't their response to my ill-disguised anxiety. His father was a vicar and he and Ian's mother, were both anxious to hear my account of what had happened and afterwards said that Ian's actions did not come as a great surprise since dogs had played an important part in their family life, being much-loved members of the household. They pressed me to keep in touch with them on a regular basis which I did over the following years.

When the fire brigade had completed their examination of the cause of the fire their conclusion did not cause much of a surprise. They found that Mrs Crabtree had been sitting near the fire smoking a last cigarette of the day before getting already for sleep. Unfortunately the old lady had fallen asleep whilst smoking and the cigarette had fallen out of her hand and set alight the rug by her fireplace. They told me that she was very fortunate that Ian and myself had been able to get to her before she suffocated. The skeleton of the dog was found near to her chair and Ian's remains were found at the entrance to the kitchen; it seems that he was trying to retrace his steps but the collapse of the stairs into the hall prevented his escape.

I stayed at home for a couple of days and when I returned to the station found that the inspector and the sergeant had decided to keep me inside performing station duties with Ronnie. This lasted for a week and then I saw Inspector Murdoch who asked me how I was feeling. He told me that Ian and I had been put forward for a medal and that in addition the chief constable was going give me a Commendation for Brave Conduct. I told him that things were settling down, which wasn't quite true, but I was fed up with station duties and wanted to get back on my beat again. He agreed to let me resume beat duties and before I left told me that it had been decided to have a service of remembrance for Ian at the cathedral which I would be expected to attend. About a month later the invitation for Ian's memorial service arrived and I had to attend a practice service the day before. The actual service for Ian was well attended and went ahead without a hitch. The local bigwigs were present including the lord mayor and the chief constable; I was placed on the front row next to Ian's parents and I was glad when it finished. It was a fine end to a dreadful affair and after some small talk with 'the great and the good' I slipped off home to have a quiet pint at my local and offer a silent toast to my lost friend.

It was good to get back on 'nights' and as I wandered on to the west side of my beat my sprits picked up. This area was mainly comprised of commercial properties and a small slice of the city's dock area. I didn't have any responsibility for the docks as they had their own Docks Police, however on 'nights', whenever I could I would make a point of meeting up with one of the docks officers, who I had got to know. The Docks Police were a small unit of about one hundred men; their current chief of police was a retired superintendent from the City Police. They wore police-type uniforms, but the uniform jacket and trousers were not usually the same shade of blue, which the City Police dubbed sports coat and flannels and was an indication of the limited resources available to them. They tended to be older in age than the regular police and many of them were ex-dockers who had suffered minor injuries at work. Their knowledge of the criminal law was scanty and their role was mainly that of watchmen. They worked twelve-hour shifts which for the individual member tended to be either permanent nights or days. The dock officer I knew was called Herbert Grimshaw and his job was to man the western gates and during the night he supervised loaded vehicles, which were entering or leaving the docks. He made use of a small office by the gates and always had a kettle on the gas stove situated in a corner at the rear, which meant that when I called round to see him, we would go into the back of the office and have a cup of tea. The tea was made in a large white jug which was so strong that I felt it could be used to strip paint. It was a welcome relief in the middle of the night when everything was quiet and we would settle down to have a natter for ten minutes.

On this particular morning we were sitting in the back of his office enjoying a cup of tea when there was knocking on the side door. Herbert opened it and we saw a young docker who told us that the body of a man had been found in the nearby eastern dock. We went round and saw the body in the water; it was difficult to make out any details other than he appeared to be fully clothed. Herbert looked at me obviously waiting for instructions and I told him that our first job was to get the body out of the water and onto the dockside. We got a long pole and guided it to some nearby steps after which we went down and lifted the body out of the water and onto the quayside. In the light it seemed to be the body of a man in his thirties wearing a suit, shirt and tie, *An office worker perhaps*, I thought to myself. Herbert decided that the man was probably a 'jumper' who had most likely leapt off the nearby road bridge to commit suicide, which had happened on several occasions in the past. I thought he was probably correct until I noticed a bruise-like mark on the side of his face which made me suspect that he might have been attacked, although as Herbert suggested it might have happened during his fall. We went back to Herbert's office and I phoned the station. I didn't mention the cup of tea, simply telling Ronnie that Herbert had reported the matter to me and we had recovered the body. Ronnie told me to hang on and then returned to the phone saying that Inspector Murdoch, who was in the station, would come and have a look at the scene.

A few moments later the black Morris drove onto the quay and the inspector got out. I put him in the picture, saying that it might be a straight forward case of suicide, but also pointing out the bruise for inspection. I knew that Murdoch had been in the CID before his promotion and I watched his examination of the body with interest. He looked at the body and I helped him turn it over, then he examined the hands and said it was probably suicide, but he would contact the Night Crime Patrol and asked them to have a look when the body was in the mortuary. I asked him why he had paid special interest in the hands and he told me that any cuts or bruises could indicate that the individual had been fighting, which might suggest his death was not a suicide. After a search we recovered some money, a wallet and a driving licence, and papers which I carefully entered into my notebook; the inspector noted the details and initialled the entries as correct. Meantime an ambulance had turned up and the inspector told me to go with them to the Casualty Department where the duty doctor would turn out and pronounce death, after which I knew that the body would be taken to Central Mortuary for a coroner's inquiry to be held to establish the cause of death. He added that with a bit of luck the Night Crime Patrol would be waiting for us at the mortuary.

The Night Crime Patrol consisted of two detectives, one of whom was a sergeant, their job was to go to all scenes of crime which were reported during the night on the Division. They investigated the scene of each incident and usually questioned witnesses and any prisoners who had been arrested. At the end of their shift they provided a report and their information was then given to the day CID staff with a request for additional material if the incident needed some follow-up work. The Day Crime Patrol fulfilled a similar function during the day.

We arrived at Casualty where the body was left in the vehicle until the duty doctor appeared, gave it a quick examination and confirmed death, after which we set off for Central Mortuary. I had visited the premises a couple of times before and when we arrived we were met by the mortuary assistant, Mr Moon. He was a small man with big hands and ears, but was strong enough, since I had seen him handle bodies in the past without much trouble. I helped him take the body out of the ambulance and into the building and found that the Night Crime Patrol had already arrived. Both detectives were wearing trilby hats, which was a badge of office in those days. Detective Sergeant 'Lucky' Jones was a neat, tidy individual who was coming to the end of his service. He had gained his nickname after serving on the battle cruiser HMS *Hood*. He had a lucky escape as a result of leaving the ship for other duties a month before it was sunk by the Germans. His colleague, Detective Constable Arthur Mole, was another 'old soldier', who was also approaching retirement.

Mr Moon removed the clothing from the body and the two detectives examined it, but there were no obvious signs of violence. Mr Moon said that the pathologist was already booked in to examine another body later that morning and this one would be added to his list. I showed the detectives the property which Mr Murdoch and I had previously taken and we examined it in more detail in the better lighting at the mortuary. The driving licence was made out to a

Frederick Allsop, with an address on the north side of the city, and there was a library card in the same name. I handed over the property to Mr Moon to be returned to the family at a later date. Although we hadn't found a suicide note the facts still seemed to indicate that the death was a suicide, but final confirmation would await the pathologist's examination and report. We left the mortuary and I hitched a ride with the squad back to the station. On the way back DS Jones decided to give the road bridge near the eastern dock a visit to see if there was any evidence to support the suggestion that the man had jumped from this point, but we found nothing. Both detectives believed that Allsop's car would be parked up somewhere in the vicinity of the bridge and told me to mention this possibility to the morning staff.

I handed over the information to the morning sergeant and reported off duty. When I returned the following night the facts about the suicide had now been established. It turned out that Allsop, who was a married man with a family, had been arrested in one of the gents' toilets in the city centre, having been caught having sex with another male when he was arrested and as a result was charged with committing the offence of male gross indecency as it was known in those days. After his release from police custody it would seem that he had picked up his car and driven round for some time before deciding to commit suicide, without returning home. As DS Jones had suspected his car was found near the bridge parked in a lay-by. The pathologist's report confirmed that he had only been in the water a few hours and the bruise on his face must have resulted during his fall from the bridge. One of the morning staff told his family, a task I was glad I had missed.

Coincidently I was back on a job near the main dock gates a couple of weeks later. I was having breakfast when Ronnie received a call from a woman living in London, to say that she had been trying to get in touch with her elderly uncle, who lived alone, but could not establish contact. Ronnie suggested that her uncle might have gone out shopping or out on some other errand, but the woman was insistent that they had this arrangement to get in touch each week at a particular time of day and her uncle could be relied on to receive the call as agreed. The address she gave was on the main road and was one of a row of Victorian terraced houses, which were the remnants of a previous housing estate that had been knocked down to make way for the dock expansion at the beginning of the twentieth century.

I finished my breakfast and went round to the address, ringing several times, but there was no reply. I walked round the back, but the premises seemed secure and there was nothing to indicate anything was amiss. I knocked next door, but again there was no reply, I then tried the house on the other side with success as this time a young woman opened the door. I told her of the reason for my visit and asked her when she last saw the elderly resident, who Ronnie had told me was called Mr Robinson. She thought for a moment and said that she had not seen him for a couple of days and had been wondering whether to get in touch with his niece in London; the same woman who had got in touch with Ronnie. She told me she had a key to the premises which I asked her to give me so I could check on the house to see if everything was in order. She agreed and after I had opened the door we both entered the house. There was a musty smell as we walked along the hallway, which looked dirty and dusty. I looked into the front room which was sparsely furnished, but with no sign of Mr Robinson. At the end of the corridor we stopped and I opened the door into a large room, which must have been the dining kitchen. In the room all I could see was newspapers, neatly piled high up to the ceiling, row upon row with a small corridor in the middle leading into the centre of the room. As I stepped in through the door I could now smell something in addition to the all-pervading musty atmosphere. Just to be sure I told the neighbour to wait at the door and followed the passageway into the room. I was now following a path through the newspapers and after turning left I came to the fireplace, which was empty of coal, and there sitting in an armchair, close by, was an old man. At first glance he seemed asleep, but when I examined him I knew that he was dead and that he had been in that condition for some time as his face seemed puffy and the smell was awful. I went back to the doorway and told the woman what I had found and asked her if she would ring for an ambulance.

When the ambulance arrived the crew alighted with the stretcher and we are all in the hallway before entering the room when we realised there was a problem in that the corridor through the piles of paper was too narrow to allow the body to be carried on the stretcher. It wasn't safe to move the paper so I helped the crew carry the body through the room and into the hallway, after which we placed him in the ambulance. The neighbour locked up the house and I told her that I would inform Mr Robinson's niece of the circumstances, after which it was another journey to Central Mortuary via a stop at the Casualty Department for the duty doctor to confirm death. I gave all the details to Mr Robinson's niece and then completed the report for the coroner. I found out later that he had died of natural causes about three days before I found him and that it had been a peaceful death.

The nightmares following Ian's death were not so frequent and I felt I was beginning to settle down to my normal cheery self again and the darkness had lifted. I was at last taking an interest in women again, together with football as well as having a pint of beer. The end of the probationary period was in sight with about three months to go; Charlie and I talked about the future which seemed straightforward in that both of us had decided to make policing a career. We had not properly planned out what we were going do, but we were now giving it more thought.

I had now moved on to the evening shift and found that on the following Friday I had been selected to assist the Plain Clothes Department in a raid they were undertaking at an illicit drinking den in Hathersage. This district was about a mile further south from Belltown and was divided into two distinct halves, the northern part nearest to Belltown was the Division's red light area, whilst the southern end, a more respectable area known as Hathersage Village, to differentiate it from the more notorious end of the district. The 'Village' was very different to the rest of the Division in that it was semi-rural with a number of large detached houses, clustered around a small village, together with a couple of small farms, on the banks of the River Star which formed the city boundary with our county constabulary neighbours.

The northern area of Hathersage was different to Belltown; it had been built at a later date and was mainly comprised of larger terraced red-brick Edwardian housing, with small front gardens and cellars. The population was also different; as well as the usual white element there was a substantial black community, almost entirely drawn from the West Indies, who had arrived after the Second World War, together with a smaller number of Sikhs and an even smaller number of Africans from West Africa. In addition to normal police work other additional activities such as prostitution, drugs and illegal drinking had become a feature of the area. This meant that policing responsibilities now included a need to control a range of sexual offences, including brothels and immoral earnings, together with offences of criminal male homosexuality as well as unlicensed drinking dens and drugs taking. From a policing perspective it was an exciting environment to work in and one which I hoped to move into when my two-year probationary period had been completed.

In order to police the specialised nature of crime in Hathersage the Division had formed a specialist squad to deal with the problem. This unit should have been called the Vice Squad, but because the Watch Committee and the chief constable refused to admit publicly that such a situation existed, this squad was known officially as the Plain Clothes Department. It consisted of a small unit of a dozen constables with a sergeant in charge, and officers were limited to a stay of twelve months in the department. Officially the need for this restricted time period was explained as a means of ensuring a regular turn of manpower, but everybody suspected it had been implemented to prevent corruption in the squad. Police pay in those days was not high and many officers found it necessary to supplement their wages either looking for extra paid work such as in painting and decorating or in the building trade, or through bribery and corruption. In an area like Hathersage where drugs and sex attracted money it wasn't difficult for unscrupulous officers to direct a part of that money into their own pockets. Although to be fair I did not come across any overt corruption during my time on the Division.

On the evening in question I had been told to report at Divisional Headquarters at 10.30pm and I made my way to the Parade Room on the first floor. It was full of Plain Clothes officers and some male and female uniform officers. We didn't have long to wait before a side door opened and in strode the Plain Clothes Sergeant 'Gorgeous' George Whittaker with Inspector Murdoch. The sergeant, who was a dark, heavyset man, had gained his nickname because of his success with women. Unlike most of the men present he was on his second marriage and was a snappy dresser. Overlooking his dress code I was at a loss to see how he qualified for such a nickname, but perhaps he had hidden talents. Sergeant Whittaker went through the roll call of the thirty officers present and then described the operation in further detail. We were to raid a 'shabeen', as unlicensed drinking dens were known locally; in this case it was in a converted cellar in one of the houses in Churchill Street. As a uniformed officer my job was to guard the front door and prevent anybody leaving the premises unless approval was given by the sergeant, who made it clear to me that nobody was to escape. The others were to question the punters as the 'customers' were known, whilst the Plain Clothes staff were to seize the drink and any drugs as well as question the owner and staff. The van crew were to provide backup and secure any prisoners. It being a Friday night, the sergeant estimated that there could be up to one hundred drinkers on the premises. We were then all herded onto the green bus and set off for Churchill Street. The bus stopped in a side street nearby and we followed the sergeant down an alley which brought us out near the 'shabeen'. The music and noise from the premises was very loud and I wondered what the neighbours made of all this activity.

I was in the front group with the Plain Clothes officer who was carrying a lump hammer and as we neared the house we broke into a run, along the path through the garden and down the steps to the door. The sergeant who was close behind was in possession of a search warrant and I supposed he would announce our presence to the doorman and inform him of the warrant. In practice I found that things operated very differently from what I had been expecting. Ned Gibson, the officer with the hammer, raised and hurled it at the door with a mighty swing. The next moment the door seemed to explode off its hinges and came to rest on the floor of the cellar. I stood to one side to allow the others to storm over the door and into the 'shabeen'. It was the first time I had been to this type of premises and I found the place to be dark and dingy. Upon our entry the noise was tremendous and then the music stopped and I could hear beer glasses and bottles clattering to the floor with shouts of alarm from the punters who were being questioned.

The door was still on the floor and I thought it was now time to tidy up and so I lifted it up to place it out of the way. You can imagine my surprise when I saw the door man still lying underneath. He was a large black man, whose eyes were still rotating trying to come to terms with what had happened. I helped him to his feet and asked him if he was alright; he shook himself and nodded. Out of the gloom Sergeant Whittaker appeared, smiled at the scene and took the doorman away, leaving me to carry on clearing up. A few moments later a man came up to me and tried to leave the cellar, I grabbed hold of him and held him against the wall, telling him that nobody was going anywhere until I had been given the all clear by Sergeant Whittaker. He protested saying he was a member of the A Division who had been helping with this operation and made a second attempt to leave. I got hold of him and said that if he made any further efforts to leave I would arrest him for being drunk and disorderly. He looked at me and shot off back into the cellar. Eventually Whittaker appeared with the man in tow, confirming that he was a police officer and telling me to let him leave. After he had gone I reminded the sergeant that nobody had told me that there was a police officer in the cellar taking observations on our behalf and the sergeant nodded saying not to worry as it was an oversight on his part, but he did not think my actions had blown the officer's cover.

Many years later I remember hearing the story of the 'shabeen' raid from a uniform inspector, who turned out to have been the same officer from the A Division I had argued with on the premises. It was the first time since the incident we had met and we had both moved on since then as I had become an inspector in the Complaints and Discipline Department, which is now usually known as the Professional Standards Department. I said that I had not heard the story for a long time and admitted that I was the officer responsible for threatening to lock him up; we had a laugh and shook hands.

As things settled down in the 'shabeen' my next task was to conduct the prisoners to the divisional van waiting outside. I noticed that the small grey van used by the Plain Clothes Department had drawn up behind it and that it was being loaded with crates of beer and spirits by members of that department, one of whom waved to me with a bottle of beer in his hand. The prisoners to be transported numbered about a dozen, half black, the rest white, including a couple of women. Their offences ranged from possession of drugs, licensing offences and in the women's case being wanted for prostitution on outstanding warrants. I helped the van crew to put them in the van and then jumped on board and we drove off back to Divisional Headquarters.

As we pulled into the Divisional station yard I saw a number 78 all-night bus parked straight ahead. All the lights were on and a number of the passengers had got off and were standing round in the yard watching what was happening inside the bus. I helped the van crew to take our prisoners into the Charge Office and returned to the yard. Inside the bus I could see a fight in progress on the bottom deck, involving Sergeant Clarke, the Charge Office sergeant and further along the bus was another fight involving a constable. I got on the bus to help out; Clarke and the man, who had his back to me, were exchanging blows with gusto. I got hold of the sergeant's sparring partner by the back of the coat and wrenched him back. He lost his balance and I dragged him off the bus, by which time he had fallen completely and I was able to deposit him on the ground. Sergeant Clarke had followed us out, grabbed hold of his assailant and frog marched him off to the Charge Office, leaving me to return to the bus. As I got back on board I noticed, for the first time, that the bus conductor was stretched out on the floor between the two bouts of fighting although he appeared to be coming round with a dazed expression on his face. I helped him to his feet and then went further up the bus to assist the PC, who I now recognised as Ted Shaw, the station clerk. He seemed a bit worse for wear in that his nose was bleeding and his opponent seemed to have the better of the exchange. I pulled Ted back and thumped his opponent in the face causing him to stagger back, which enabled me to drag him off the bus before he could recover. Ted and I took him into the Charge Office which looked like a scene from bedlam with Sergeant Clarke slowly establishing a sense of order. By now the bus passengers were attempting to follow us into the Charge Office to see the fun but Sergeant Clarke returned to shoo them into the Waiting Room to await the return of the bus crew.

I returned to the bus and took the conductor into the canteen to get him a cup of tea and was surprised to find his driver was already there drinking from his own cup. The atmosphere in the room between the two men suddenly began to get very tense and I found myself acting as a referee as an argument broke out between them as the conductor accused the driver of cowardice. Things eventually calmed down and I found out that the fight had started between two drunken men, which the conductor had tried to sort out without success. As the bus was passing the station at the time the driver had taken it upon himself to drive into the yard, park the bus and run into the station to inform the staff. The Charge Office sergeant and his clerk had rushed onto the bus to deal with the matter and fortunately we had arrived shortly after to give them additional help. We got the crew and passengers back on the bus and off they went to finish their journey.

Two weeks later I had an appointment to see Inspector Murdoch who told me he was completing the final report for my probationary period, my two years were up. He said he was very satisfied with my progression and would forward the report to the divisional commander, Chief Superintendent Fairbanks, to confirm my appointment as constable. 'Dougie' Fairbanks was a keen supporter of the police rugby team and because I was still turning out to play for them on a regular basis I had got to know him pretty well. I found him to be a kind man who attempted to hide this side of personality by being a stickler for discipline and urging officers to 'do the things right and not let down the City Police' which was one of his frequent bits of advice. As an ex-army officer, he had risen through the ranks by serving mainly in the chief constable's office, which looked after force administration, but nobody saw him as an office boy, since he had gained operational experience at every rank. When I saw him a week later he congratulated me on confirming my appointment and then we spent the next half an hour discussing rugby and the upcoming match with Staffordshire Constabulary.

Mr Murdoch had also told me that I was being transferred to Hathersage Village as part of a move to gain further experience. I would not be working in the village but would be given a bicycle beat on the southern edge of the division. He finished off by saying that this district, which was a wealthy, leafy, suburban area, was far different from my work in Belltown and would add to my knowledge of police work.

CHAPTER FIVE

Although I wasn't aware at the time my move to Hathersage Village was part of a divisional reorganisation to increase the size of the beat boundaries in an effort to compensate for the shortage of staff. This area had been chosen because of its suburban nature and its lower levels of crime which made it easily adaptable to the increased use of motorcycle and bicycle beats, which in turn reduced the number of police officers covering the area. No attempt was made to publicly inform the residents of the changes that were being made, although we were not prevented from explaining what was happening if they asked us and since very few them seemed to notice, everything went ahead without any adverse reaction from the public. The section retained one constable on a foot beat in the centre of the village to reassure the public of our commitment to community policing whilst the rest of us were told to keep ourselves visible and active at all times. The beat motorcycles used were a form of scooter, which allowed officers to cover an area equivalent to four foot beats in the past, whilst cycle beats usually corresponded to two foot beats. In practise these changes meant that the twelve constables who had originally policed the Hathersage Village section were now reduced to eight. As well as manpower changes on my Division I later found that that further reductions were taking place on the other divisions within the city. What I was experiencing was the effects of manpower loss within the City Police, becoming the start of the process which was to lead to quite drastic changes in the future, which will be highlighted later in the story.

My new beat was bounded on the south side by the River Star, which was also the local government boundary between the City and the County. On my side there was a distinct rural feel about the place with a couple of small farms situated alongside the river. My beat was a large rectangle with the northern end close to Hathersage Village. The village was a prosperous bustling place with a good variety of shops; as you went north from the village towards the city centre the housing changed in character, moving from some large detached houses, through to semi-detached red-brick Edwardian houses with gardens front and back, and eventually ending with the small terraced streets at the commencement of Belltown. There were three police stations in Hathersage; a small one in the village, which I used, a red-brick Victorian station in the centre of the area, and a larger station, in the red light district, which acted as the Divisional Headquarters.

I reported at Hathersage Village station on the first day of my transfer on the 'morning' shift. The station officer was another old constable called Alf Cotton, who was a fat untidy man, who looked as if his breakfast had missed his mouth on a couple of occasions and come to rest on the front of his tunic. The sergeant was out of the station at the time and Alf suggested I find a bike and spend some time getting to know the area and report back in an hour's time when the sergeant was expected to return. Alf then showed me round the station, which was small and compact, comprising a public office, canteen, interview room and toilet. The bicycle shed was in the yard at the back and I went round to select a bike. Police cycles in those days were large heavy black machines with brakes that squealed. They were made for officers who were at least six feet tall, which made me wonder how the smaller members of the Force managed to cope. I eventually found one which seemed in reasonable condition and set off with the beat book, which Alf had given me, to familiarise myself with the area. These books had been recently introduced and contained basic information such as beat boundaries, the four points to be used for visits for supervision purposes and a section at the back listed as 'away from homes'. This last item was a new responsibility for me which I had not come across before in that it contained information provided by the householder giving dates and times when their house would be vacant. This situation usually referred to periods of absence whilst on holiday and required the beat officer to check the property, at least once during his tour of duty to see that everything was in order. I reflected that this form of police service was not provided to the residents of Belltown, possibly because they rarely if ever went on holiday, or perhaps it was thought that they had nothing of value to steal. In any event it provided the first of a number of differences as to how the two areas were policed.

Going round this new beat was a matter of getting used to the new environment I was now faced with, which was very different to what I had been used to in Belltown. There seemed to be more traffic about, lots of detached houses and a distinct absence of noise. I didn't see many pedestrians and there wasn't much activity of any sort taking place. Eventually an hour passed and I decided to return to the station where I met my new Section Sergeant Thomas Fairbrother. He was a fair-haired man, about forty, who had recently transferred to the City Police from the neighbouring County Force. He seemed a decent straightforward officer who was still familiarising himself with the new customs and practices of the City Police. As an ex-county policeman he suffered from the fact that as the City Police felt that they were a cut above the County Force, the officers at the station were not making it easy for him to settle into his new job. As a result I formed the opinion that as he and I were in similar positions, both being newcomers to the section, I was not going to get much advice from him concerning the local knowledge of the area, which meant that I was going to have to find this out from other sources. My first port of call was Alf, who gave me some good background information, including the fact I did not have any school crossing duties, since there was only one school in the village and this was the responsibility of the village officer, Harry Cornish, who I met later that day. Harry was in his thirties, married, with about ten years' police service. He had spent most of his time policing the village and turned out to be an invaluable source of local information;

he and I quickly became friends.

As I got to know Alf I found he was a man of few words and almost entirely devoid of a sense of humour. It came as a bit of a surprise when at the start of my first period on 'afternoons' Alf asked me to attend an incident at Laburnham House on Hillside Crescent. The caller was a Mrs Margaret Armstrong-Chalmers who had apparently spotted an intruder in the back garden. On giving me the message I noticed that Alf's face was contorted into what might identified as a smile. Since I had never seen such an expression before on his face I could not be sure and thought nothing further about it. When he asked me to attend I thought it a bit odd because the road was on Harry's beat, but I assumed that he must have been engaged on another job so I cycled to the address. Laburnham House was a large detached property overlooking the river and I propped my bike near the front door and rang the bell. The door was answered by a tall attractive woman, about forty years of age, who smiled and asked me in. She turned out to be the caller and I followed her into the lounge. I noticed that she was swaying slightly as we went into the room. Before I could ask her about the intruder, she said that I must be a new member of the station staff, since she knew all the officers who worked there. As she spoke I formed the impression that she was used to getting her own way and as the conversation continued I smelt the undertones of drink. All mention of the intruder had disappeared and now she said she wanted me to follow her upstairs to sort out a more immediate problem.

We went upstairs to her bedroom, during which

she told me that she and her husband had separate rooms. When we arrived she said that she was having trouble with the zip of her dress and could I assist? At this point the penny dropped I now knew why Alf had smiled when giving me the message from her. She had turned her back to me and it was decision time. I did not have a girlfriend and in fact women seemed to have dropped out of my life at the moment, perhaps now was the time to get back into gear. With a flourish I dealt with her zip and she immediately stepped out of her dress. She turned round giving me a good opportunity to admire her figure, after which she unbuttoned my tunic and within moments we were in her bed. About an hour later, after a very enjoyable and energetic time we were having a drink in her kitchen and during our conversation I realised that this was an impersonal arrangement as far as she was concerned. Thereafter I visited her on a Wednesday afternoon (when her housekeeper was taking time off) on a number of occasions for about six months. During this time I found that I was one of a small band of officers from the station, who also 'enjoyed' her company.

She said little about herself during my visits but I got to know that she had two grown up children living in London; her husband was into property development and they both had freedom to do as they wished. I never saw her drunk, although on many occasions she had been drinking when I visited. I eventually identified the other officers, one of whom was Harry Cornish, who was also looking after her housekeeper. Harry had the inevitable nickname of 'shagger', which he accepted with pride. This unusual arrangement could not last forever and when

I returned after completing a training course I found that the house was up for sale and the Armstrong-Chalmers were in the process of a divorce. Margaret had moved down to London to be near her children; her husband, who I had never met, was about to marry his secretary and had moved elsewhere. The other matter which stayed in my memory was that she always wore a pearl necklace which I never once saw her take off, regardless of what was taking place between us.

Another job I remember spending time on whilst I was policing Hathersage Village, which did not come my way whilst I was in Belltown, was acting as a messenger for hospitals conveying information about injured or dying relatives to the residents. The first time I was given such a task involved a hospital in the Birmingham area who asked us if we would contact a family member to inform them that a woman relative was dying and was anxious to see them. It was early in the morning on a Saturday and I cycled to Mount Road and found the house. After knocking repeatedly on the door, it was opened by a young man, who appeared to have just woken up. I gave him the message and in return he gave me a baffled look, saying he had never heard of the woman concerned. I apologised and said that the hospital must have given us had the wrong address, at which point I heard a woman's voice from upstairs telling him to get back to bed. I returned to my bike and started to pedal off back to the station to check out the details with the hospital. I had only reached about one hundred yards from the house when I heard shouting behind me and stopping and turning I saw the same man, together with a woman, both running in their pyjamas and bare feet, obviously trying to catch me up. I stopped and waited whilst they caught up. It turned out that the hospital patient was the young woman's mother, which may have explained the memory loss of her husband. I gave them both the message again and his wife thanked me and explained that her husband must have been half asleep when I had called and that they would visit her mother later that day. I promised to let the hospital know of their intention and returned to the station.

It was round about that time that Charlie and I started to talk about the future. As we were now regular constables we were able to take the promotion examination to sergeant. Promotion in those days required the passing of two different sets of national exams. The first was the educational part consisting of papers in maths, English and general knowledge; the second part was the law exams dealing with crime, traffic and general duties. These exams were not easy, with a high failure rate, and tended to favour the ex-grammar school boys, of which there were only a few, rather than the secondary modern school candidates, who usually had a limited experience of examination techniques. We decided to obtain samples of the syllabus together with previous educational exam papers to try and familiarise ourselves with the subjects. At the time there was no effort made by the Force to assist with passing the examinations and consequently we were left to make our own arrangements. We spent many happy hours revising the subjects, which I found hard work, but gradually we built up a routine and the information began to stick in the brain.

We sat the exams and waited for the results, in my case with some trepidation, however, to my great surprise I passed and so did Charlie. Soon after I went on a driving course and on completion I felt I had taken my first step forward, since the qualification allowed me to drive uniform vans and other divisional vehicles such as CID cars and Plain Clothes vehicles. I was still on my cycle beat at Hathersage Village, but I now found that I had become a reserve van driver, which extended the scope of my duties. The end of my probationer period had seen a gradual reduction in supervision by my sergeants with the general acceptance by supervisory staff that I could be left to handle most incidents without assistance. I was beginning to get used to the change in status and with it less supervision from the sergeants leading up to an increase in confidence on my part.

I was back on 'afternoons' having finished the driving course and returned to the station, and was completing a report before retiring from duty. Alf was ready to go home when the phone rang with a call from the British Transport Police at the City's St Paul's Central Railway station. It seemed that the driver of the London train had stopped at the next station further south in the county and called in to say that he thought he may have hit someone as his train had passed over the River Star. Going at speed and in the dark, he could not be sure but thought that someone had jumped in front of the train just as he entered the bridge on the City side before crossing over the river. The BT Police asked us if we could check the scene to confirm whether such incident had taken place and if so they would mount a full search in the morning to recover the remains. Sergeant

Fairbrother was summoned and put in the picture; the 'night' relief who were taking over from us were short-handed and the sergeant asked for volunteers from my shift to provide a search party with the incentive that 'time due' would be made available.

I volunteered without a second thought and it was only later when I was walking along the lane to the railway line did the thought strike me as to whether the demons I had experienced after Ian's death might make a return visit. In the event they didn't which I took as a positive sign that I had now finally got over the problems of the past. Before we left the station the sergeant had contacted Inspector Murdoch who agreed with the decision to make an immediate search since it was important to establish where the accident had occurred. Because the river was the boundary between my own force and the County Police if the accident had happened on their side they would be informed and asked to take over. I and three other officers together with the sergeant got in the van and I drove them to the scene.

The first job was to contact to local signalman in the box next to Hathersage Village station to ask him to make the track safe for us for an hour or so while we searched the area. When this had been completed we went to the river and climbed up the embankment and onto the railway track. It had just finished raining and the area was dark and very silent. Armed with a couple of canvas bags and torches we made our way south along the track towards the bridge. In order to lighten the mood we reminisced about memorable journeys we had made on this line. Harry Cornish and his family made regular journeys to see his mother-in-law, who lived in London. Jeff Webster, who was an avid Somerton City fan, recounted a journey to Wembley to see the Cup Final and I related a visit with my family to the 1951 South Bank Exhibition.

We followed the curve in the track and then stopped talking as the bridge came into view, but initially we couldn't see anything out of order. As we moved along it nothing came to hand; perhaps the driver had imagined the incident or maybe it was an animal. We reached over halfway and if anything was spotted now we could legitimately hand over to the County Police. Just before we reached the other bank I saw a lump at my side of the track and we hurried over to see what it could be. It turned out to be the sleeve of a gent's raincoat and inside was the remnants of an arm, but there was no part of the torso and there was no hand attached at the end of the sleeve. By now we had left the bridge and we could see another larger lump which turned out to be part of the body, wearing the remains of same raincoat and a man's suit. It was obvious that the man had thrown himself in front of the train as it had left the bridge and not as the driver had remembered the incident. We could not see any other remains on the track which probably meant they were in the undergrowth further away, and a search by the County Police in daylight would have to be mounted to recover them. We walked back with the parts of the body we had found and told the signalman the result of our search, adding that we would contact the County Police and leave them to decide what further steps to take. We returned to the station and I went home. The following day I found out that the man was a local solicitor who had been caught embezzling a client's funds and had decided to take his own life before the law took its course.

The crime rate on the section was pretty low; we used to get some offences of shoplifting and the occasional burglary, but about a month after the railway suicide we started to have what amounted to a crime wave. It started with a number of break-ins on my beat and then Harry Cornish's patch started to erupt. I came in on the 'morning' shift and found that there had been two break-ins on my beat which had happened the previous day. I went round to have an inspection of the locations, both on Clifton Drive, where the backs of the houses overlooked the river. The houses were large detached properties a couple of house lengths apart from each other and in both cases the crime had been committed whilst their occupants were away at work. Entry to the houses had been from the rear, forcing open the back door. Initially I thought that the thief or thieves had approached from the riverside, but the fences looked undisturbed, so I decided that this approach appeared unlikely. Money and jewellery were the common items stolen from the houses, although from one house a carriage clock had also been stolen.

When I returned to the station for breakfast Harry told me that he had also had a break-in on his beat and there seemed many similarities in the methods used to the break-ins on Clifton Drive. We spoke to Jimmy Redburn, the detective constable covering our area, but there were no fingerprints at the scene and no further information had come to light. I prowled around my beat, talking to the locals and going over the scene again to see if I had missed anything, but nothing turned up. No further incidents happened for the next two weeks and then another couple of break-ins occurred this time on Harry's beat; again, the items stolen were limited to money and jewellery and in both cases the break-ins had taken place during the day when the owners were away and the properties were empty. Once more access had been gained from the rear; the locations were similar and all the factors seemed to point to the actions of the same thief or thieves.

We decided to discuss the matter with Jimmy, but he was away on 'a course' and the detective officer who was covering his patch in his absence didn't seem too enthusiastic to get involved with us. We decided to put our heads together and formulate a plan. Whilst agreeing that the break-ins seemed to be committed by the same individual or individuals, what was the significance of the two-week break between the offences taking place? The only conclusion we could come to was that the thief or thieves must have a regular round and we needed to take observations in the next two-week time period. We discussed this proposal with Sergeant Fairbrother, who agreed with our idea and said we could alter our shifts and that in order to help he would sanction some overtime. We made our preparations; we decided to initially concentrate on Harry's beat, which seemed to offer more possibilities of success, and identified two possible observation sites. Our next task was to persuade Divisional transport to loan us a small van which we could use for a couple of days during the week in question to move about the area.

On the first day we had mounted our operation I

went to DHQ and picked up the van early in the morning and collected Harry. We were both in 'civvies' and we drove onto his beat and selected the first observation point, which was on the junction of three roads, and parked up. We watched the milkman finishing his round and the early commuters heading for the station. The weather was fine and we settled down to our observations; the grocer's lad appeared on his cycle and soon it was time to eat the sandwiches and the flask of tea that Harry's wife had prepared. A van from the local furnishing shop passed us, but nothing happened to arouse our suspicions. I left Harry to have a wander round on foot and then drove over to inspect my beat, but found nothing out of the ordinary; if anything there was even less happening on my side. I returned for Harry and we spent some more time keeping the area under observation, but eventually we called it a day and returned to the station and put Sergeant Fairbrother in the picture.

Day two started with Harry and I parked up on his beat at a second site which we thought offered us a better prospect for success. Once again we saw the milkman and this time the Corporation dustcart made an appearance, and then just before lunchtime round the corner came a horse and cart with two men on board; they seemed to be working as rag and bone men. I looked at Harry and we both raised our eyebrows since we had not seen these men in our area before and we watched them both at work with interest. They slowly went up the road shouting their presence in loud voices. We noticed they would stop and knock on the doors of each house and when somebody answered, they were either given clothing or else sent on their way empty handed. We slowly followed, keeping well back, and as they got to the sixth house they knocked on the door, but got no reply. We saw them swiftly move round the back of the premises and I drove the van into the driveway and we both leapt out and followed them round the back. I was impressed by their speed and efficiency since by the time we reached the back door they had broken in and leaving the kitchen had made their way upstairs. We ran upstairs and found them in one of the bedrooms ransacking the room. They were arrested after a struggle and we took them to the station after which I returned to search the cart and found money and items of jewellery hidden under some sacking. The only outstanding problem was what to do with the horse and cart. Fortunately Alf, our station officer, had a contact with the local council who arranged for its collection; the horse in the meantime was tied to a nearby lamp post, spending time eating the grass verge.

It turned out that the thieves were brothers and members of a well-known family of Irish Tinkers called Flynn, who had recently moved into the area from the north of the city. One of them was married and they were all now living together in a council house in a small estate at the edge of the village. We informed the Day Crime Patrol and DS Monty Evans and DC Jackson had arrived at the station. Monty was a boisterous character, who had recently returned to the City after a spell with the Regional Crime Squad and was full of stories relating to the investigation of major crime and of the criminal underworld. Whilst he was drawing breath I told him it must be a major let down to return to the sleepy world of Hathershaw

Village. Monty who could take a joke, didn't bat an eyelid, telling me that he would be clearing up the villains in the village once he had taken his coat off. We searched the men and found a bunch of keys, as a result of which Monty asked Herbert Jackson and myself to go to their address and see if there was any other stolen property in the house.

The estate consisted of a small row of post-war terraced housing; the brothers' house was an end terrace with an extended front entrance, which I assumed allowed them to tether the horse and park the cart. We knocked at the door which was opened by a plain young woman, who admitted being Mrs Flynn. Herbert told her that her husband and his brother had been arrested. We entered the house which was clean, although sparsely furnished. I went upstairs whilst Herbert covered the ground floor. At the back of one of the wardrobes I found a box stuffed with cash and in the other bedroom one of the drawers also contained a bundle of cash wrapped in a man's sock. The two amounts of money seemed similar in value. By this time Herbert was in the garden searching a shed and found a tin containing some wristwatches. We collected the property together and showed it to the woman, but she said she had never seen it before and had no idea how it came to be in the house. We didn't believe her but we decided not want to press the matter at this stage and left to return to the station.

Initially under questioning the men claimed that the money had been earned through their work as rag and bone men, but when the watches were identified as stolen property they altered their story and admitted that they had stolen them. They were then both charged with housebreaking and theft. We found that they had previous convictions for similar offences on the north side of the city and had moved over to our side where they presumably hoped to make a fresh start in their life of crime. They would not implicate the woman in the crimes and she was never charged. Both men pleaded guilty and as a result I was not required to give evidence at court. They were sentenced to six months' imprisonment. I later found that after release from prison they upped sticks and moved on to pastures new in the Birmingham area.

It was now time to progress my career in the police and having passed the Education exam for promotion I was now fired up to take the Law exams. I arranged to see Charlie to sort out how we were going to overcome the next obstacle and due to our success the first time it occurred to me that we should make similar arrangements to study the law syllabus. Charlie seemed distracted with the idea and I quickly began to realise that he had other problems on his mind. I asked him what was going on and he said that he and Barbara had decided to get married. This did not come as a big surprise to me since they had been going out for about two years and I knew from talking to them both that marriage was now on the horizon. He went on to say that they had recently set the date for next June and he wanted me to be his Best Man. Given what he had said it seemed to me that studying for the exam was going to take a back seat and that we should wait until after the wedding. Charlie agreed with me and we put the law books away for the time being. Before we parted Charlie said something to me which did not seem important at the time, but when I looked back later did appear to indicate that Barbara was forming the opinion that the police service was not a suitable career for her husband-to-be. It seemed that they had a discussion about 'the job' with Barbara highlighting the negative aspects of policing whilst Charlie emphasised the positive aspects including that after their marriage, he would be receiving an enhanced rent allowance to help for the cost of maintaining their new home. I found out later that he didn't tell her that in those days if the officer wished to get married he had to seek the approval of the Force and provide details of his wife-to-be's background as part of the process. In addition the Force also required the location and type of the house to be assessed for approval before rent allowance would be given.

I remembered that Harry Cornish had performed the role of Best Man on a couple of occasions and hopefully he would be the most likely person to give me suitable advice. I explained that I was not a natural funny man and had difficulty telling jokes. He said not to worry since I was good at telling stories and I should keep the speech simple by gathering a few funny incidents from our mutual schooldays and any suitable stories from our time in the police which involved Charlie. He suggested that I concentrate on a few mistakes Charlie had made so far during his career in the police, such as the time he tried to capture a lost dog, which had escaped into a greengrocer's shop and hidden under a display of vegetables. Charlie was not going to let the dog escape and made a great effort to capture the animal, getting his fingers bittern in the process. In doing so he upset the vegetable display which led to him being overwhelmed by a large quantity of potatoes and carrots. In the ensuing uproar the dog managed to slip past Charlie and disappear. This particular story had quickly been passed around the Division to the embarrassment of my friend. Armed with this advice I felt I could put down something suitable and started to draft my maiden Best Man's speech.

Whilst I was gathering information for the wedding I was posted for a couple of weeks as Divisional van driver. This time I was working with Edgar Walters, who was a tall thin man, who suffered from a complete absence of hair from his head and face. In an effort to cover up this problem and improve his appearance he had taken to wearing a wig which did not fit very well on his head and looked, according to Harry, like something Edgar had found in his Christmas cracker. The whole effect when Edgar was on duty in uniform made him looked very odd at times, since when he wore his helmet the artificial hair would start to slip sideways, giving him a lopsided look. He refused to accept he was wearing a wig, referring to this apparel as a hairpiece. As a result of his efforts the matter generated so much laughter and jokes at work that eventually he was forced to stop wearing the offending hairpiece. I found out later that he continued to wear the hairpiece after work, since I remember seeing Edgar and his wife shopping in the city centre with his hat over the hairpiece which didn't seem to improve his looks to any great extent but obviously must have been of some comfort to him.

Edgar and I were on 'afternoons', it was quiet and

IN THE 'NICK' OF TIME

we were parked up, watching the rush-hour traffic heading south from the city centre. It was a good time to have a hidden cigarette. Time passed and then we received a call from Headquarters Information Room asking us to go to the Star River ford were two County Police officers were asking for assistance to rescue a cow which had fallen in the water. This was an unusual call and we drove round to the ford to find out what was happening. When we arrived I had to hold back laughing at the scene; in the water was a large brown cow, which seem unconcerned and was swimming about without any apparent difficulty. Nearby was a small dingy with two county officers close to the cow trying to place a rope about her neck. Fortunately at this point the river was not fast flowing and nobody seemed to be in any danger, and then for no apparent reason the cow changed tack and turned towards the dingy and seemed to rear up as though she was trying to get into the boat with the officers, who had now managed to get the rope round her neck. As she did so the dingy overturned and the officers joined her in the water. Edgar and I went down to the water's edge and he turned to me and said that since I had been in the Navy perhaps I could suggest a solution.

By now a large crowd had joined us on the bank enjoying the situation and offering advice to the County lads, who were now trying to get back on board their craft. The cow on the other hand seemed to have lost interest and had turned towards us with the rope trailing in the water nearby. The river did not seem too deep and I ventured out to see if it was possible to get the rope, as the cow was still moving towards me. However, it veered past me and I turned to see that the farmer had appeared and was now standing on the bank next to Edgar shouting at the cow. An ironic cheer went up from the crowd when the farmer picked up the rope and he and Edgar pulled the cow onto dry land. It was at that point that I began to realise how cold the water was and made my way back on to the bank. The two County lads were also returning to our side of the river. The farmer shouted his thanks to us and took out a small bottle of whisky from his pocket. On seeing this I thought that I also could do with a dram to warm me up and went over to him with the County officers close behind. Before anything could be said the famer turned and tipped up the head of the cow and poured the whisky down its throat. The three of us stared aghast at what had taken place, but the farmer seemed unconcerned and smiled at us, saying that his cow liked the odd tot of whisky when it was cold. I was lost for words and turned away to leave the County officers to sort the matter out. We drove back to my place and I got changed still muttering about what had happened.

A short time later, still on 'afternoons' we were summoned to DHQ to collect a prisoner and take him to Kirkbrook. The town was on the east side of the city with its boundary running alongside C Division. It was a small borough and had a reputation of being an insular place, which kept itself very much to itself. I had been to the town on a couple of occasions and knew that it had a borough police force which numbered about two hundred officers, who followed the spirit of the place by keeping very little contact with the City Police. Thinking back, I remembered that we had a Kirkbrook constable on our course at the District Training Centre, who had been given a police uniform, together with a bus inspector's hat to wear. He had been told that they had no helmets in stock and were waiting for a new consignment to arrive and in the meantime they had supplied with this headgear to make do whilst he was at the Centre. Not surprisingly he had to suffer considerable ridicule from the rest of us, but to be fair to him he weathered the storm without complaint.

We collected the prisoner and placed him in the back of the van, and Edgar jumped in with him and off I drove to Kirkbrook Police Headquarters which was in Victoria Square, at the side of the town hall. We were told to contact our Force radio when we reached the Square and the double doors at the rear of the building would be open in time to receive us. The town centre was dark since many of the street lights were not in operation. I drove into the Square and after giving our position to the Information Room went round to police headquarters just as the gates were opened. They shut behind us when I moved into the yard and turned the van round so that the rear doors were facing the Charge Office. On seeing us a number of borough officers came out into the yard and lined up at the back of the van, forming a corridor leading to the Charge Office. I got out and opened the doors, allowing Edgar to alight with the prisoner. The prisoner was left to walk between the officers, receiving what appeared to be a traditional welcome, by being beaten by each officer in turn as he made his way to the Charge Office. After a few steps he broke into a run in an effort to avoid too much punishment, soon running as fast as he could into the building. Not a word was said by the borough officers who simply nodded at us and returned to the building. I followed them in to get a signature for the prisoner and his property from the Charge Office sergeant and returned to Edgar, started the engine and drove the van out of the yard.

As we moved out of the Square I asked Edgar if the beating the prisoner had been given was standard practice by the Borough Police. He nodded and said that he had seen it before when he had delivered other prisoners in the past. He went on to say that his wife's uncle and family lived in the town and when he had discussed policing issues with him, her uncle's response was to say that the Borough Police were regarded by the townspeople as an 'army of occupation'. Edgar looked at me and said, 'Nobody has a good word to say about them.' I pondered what he had said about public attitude to policing and compared his observation with the City Police. It seemed to me that we had the support of most of the community and whilst we were prepared to use violence when necessary, if we could dissuade people from causing trouble, with the option of arrest if they refused, that approach was the preferred option which the community accepted as a reasonable. I drove along the dark and dingy streets, glad to leave the Borough, not knowing that a number of years later I would return on a more permanent basis.

It was about this time that the officers who had joined prior to the war started to retire and the first on our division was Sergeant Howard Nelson. He had his retirement 'do' in the White Hart in Belltown and I went up there to wish him well. He was a keen fisherman and we had all contributed to buying him a new fishing rod and tackle. Unlike many police retirees he was not moving to a seaside town or down to the West Country, which seemed a popular destination for many retirees at the time, but had taken a new job in the town hall as a member of the security staff. The chief superintendent, who had joined around the same period as Howard, made some funny remarks recounting some personal experiences that they had both shared and Howard, who was not noted for his public speaking, made a short reply of thanks. I felt I was fortunate to have had Howard as my first sergeant since I had learnt a lot from him as to the role of a sergeant, firstly in how he was able to get the best out of his subordinates and just as importantly how to deal with and keep the public on side. I recognised that most of his approach had been gathered from his experience in the Forces, but the rest came from his personality, which was kind and generous with a hard edge which came to the surface when the occasion demanded. Some six years later I attended Howard's funeral; for officers of his age it was not unusual to die after five years of retirement. Twenty-five years of shift work and six years of war service took its toll on even the toughest of constitutions and Howard Nelson was no exception to the rule.

I completed my period of van duties and was back on my bicycle beat with the sun shining. It was late morning and I was returning to the station for my break. As I was cycling past the village shops Mr Patel, the owner of the local newspaper shop, waved me down. He was holding his hand to his head and there was blood seeping through his fingers. I stopped and he told me that a man had entered his shop and produced metal bar from under his coat and demanded the contents of the till. Mr Patel initially tried to resist the intruder but the man had struck him over the head and then taken the till contents, after which he said that the thief had run out of the shop and turned left towards the railway station. He gave me a brief description of his assailant and in particular mentioned he had what seemed to be a couple of shaving cuts on his chin. I told him to get some assistance for the wound and I left him and cycled along the street, but couldn't see anybody about; perhaps the man had parked a car around the corner, but there was nothing to see, so I carried on to the station.

On impulse I went into the railway building and found a train already in so I walked along the platform looking into the carriages and spotted a man who resembled the description given by Mr Patel, especially in relation to the shaving cuts. Going over to the carriage I asked him to get out, but he refused, which resulted in me trying to pull him out, whilst he made desperate efforts to resist. By now both the train guard and the station staff had come to my aid and between the three of us we pulled him out on to the platform. I forced him face down on to the platform and handcuffed him; at the time I was surprised by the level of violence, but after all this resistance on his part I was pretty confident I had got the right man. I hauled him to his feet and frogmarched him into the station master's office. I used the station telephone to ask Alf if he would arrange for the divisional van to pick us both up. I sat the prisoner down and told him that the handcuffs would stay on until he calmed down. He was of average height, but powerfully built with short cropped hair; he reminded me of my old colour sergeant. He had dark brown eyes which were currently filled with anger and hatred which seemed to be directed towards myself. I couldn't explain his behaviour towards me but there was obviously something going on with him which had escaped me. I asked him his name, but he refused to answer and turned his face away so I searched him and found a lot of loose cash in his pockets together with some ten bob and pound notes which looked like the remnants of the change taken from Mr Patel's till, but there were no personal items such as a wallet or driving licence. I still thought the degree of violence and his strange behaviour towards me signified that something else was going on, but at the time I had no explanation for his conduct.

The van came fairly quickly, they must have been in the area, and I got in with him and we went to the village station, leaving my bike at the railway station. We put him in the interview room and I told the Day Crime Patrol, after which I rang the shop and spoke to Mr Patel's wife to put her in the picture. Mrs Patel was a small excitable woman and she then seemed to take about five minutes telling me about the trials and tribulations which her husband had faced. When I eventually got a word in, it turned out that she had patched him up and he was in the back of the shop having a cup of tea. I returned to the interview room and found the prisoner had been taken to DHQ by the CID who had left a message asking me to arrange for Mr Patel to be taken to their office. I asked Alf what had happened but all he knew was that the Day Squad had turned up, took one look at my prisoner and whisked him out of the station, giving Alf the message for me to pick up Mr Patel. I went into the yard and found a van which wasn't being used and went off to collect Mr Patel. I found that he was back on his feet and didn't seem any the worse for his experience. Overriding his wife's objections, he followed me into the vehicle and we drove to DHQ and then up to the CID office.

The office seemed busy with a lot of extra detectives I had never seen before and who I later found out were members of the Serious Crime Squad. I looked around and then DS Jones appeared and took Mr Patel away with him. I was still trying to find out what was going on when I saw Jimmy Redburn and he explained what had happened. He told me that the Squad had been keeping a gang of bank robbers under observation and had found that they were making plans to rob the District Bank on Commercial Street, Belltown this particular morning. They had taken up positions in and around the bank and had captured four out of the five members of the gang, but the fifth member, George Brady, the gang leader, made his escape. It seems that he had made his way to Hathersage Village and had robbed Mr Patel, because he wanted cash to buy a ticket, to enable him to get a train to London, but had been foiled before he could leave the area. I could now understand why he was so angry having been caught by a plod on a bicycle, who just happened to be passing at the wrong moment as far as he was concerned. I told Jimmy what had happened, including the fact that he wouldn't talk to me, and Jimmy laughed when he heard of my account. He told me, 'That man's a professional criminal and he only speaks to detectives, it would ruin his reputation with if his fellow criminals if they found out he had been caught by a uniformed copper on a bike.'

I hung about waiting to see if I was needed to take Mr Patel back to his shop and as I waited was told that an Identity Parade was going to take place in the main parade room on the floor below. I had never seen such a parade before, which is the responsibility of the uniformed staff to organise, supervised by the duty inspector, who conducts proceedings. At this point Inspector Murdoch appeared and seeing me in the CID office told me to help the Charge Office staff find a number of suitable male members of the public for the line-up. I thought at the time that finding about a dozen men, who would agree to volunteer, might be difficult, but I was wrong and we got our volunteers without any problem and gathered them in the parade room. They were a mixed bunch as far as having a passable resemblance to my prisoner was concerned, but that didn't seem to bother the inspector. Brady was brought in and asked if he had any objections to the line-up, but he shrugged his shoulders, in fact I don't think he even looked at them. He selected a place and settled down to wait and shortly afterwards the witness, Mr Patel, appeared with the inspector. The inspector asked him to examine the line to see if his assailant was in the line-up. Mr Patel had no hesitation in picking out my prisoner after which he was led out and the rest of the line-up were dismissed, except for Brady who was later charged with a variety of offences. I then went back upstairs to wait for the witness and a few moments later I was driving Mr Patel back to his shop. I was never asked to give evidence at Brady's trial and assumed he pleaded guilty to the offence involving Mr Patel, perhaps Jimmy was right and my appearance at his trial would have ruined his reputation in the criminal underworld. I wondered what Brady would have thought if he had known that it was only Mr Patel mentioning the railway station in his directions to me during our conversation that led me to go there and eventually find him.

CHAPTER SIX

The next important officer to retire as far as I was concerned was Inspector Murdoch, but before he did so he rearranged the duty roster and once more I found myself on the move. This time I had been transferred to a foot beat at the north end of Hathersage, moving from the leafy suburbs to the busier end of the 'red light' district. The beat was a square bounded on one side by a busy main road, Fox Lane, leading to the city centre; unlike Belltown most of the other streets were red-brick Edwardian terraced houses. The local population were a mixed group of white and West Indian residents, with a small Sikh community. The area consisted of a couple of night clubs on the main road, together with an evangelical chapel, packed every Sunday with mainly black worshippers. On the Lane was a fish and chip shop, which also specialised in curried meat pasties, which I grew to like, soon becoming a firm favourite of mine.

The first resident of the area I came into contact with was Clarence Dawson, a tall, thin, black man; he was married with two children and had moved to the UK from Jamaica in the 1950s, becoming a bus driver for the City Transport Department. We stopped to talk one evening shortly after I moved onto my beat, and I found he had been a policeman in Kingston. I asked him what his job had been like in Jamaica and we soon started to compare notes. It quickly became obvious that he thought the British style of policing was too 'soft' as he put it, insisting that the police over there were required to be much tougher on the locals. He pointed to fellow West Indians and told me that these 'boys' get away with anything. 'You people don't know what's going on,' was his explanation to my query as to his comments. We talked over the differences and I realised that colonial policing was very different in its methods when compared to the British system of policing.

At the end of our conversation he invited me into his home, which was nearby. I was introduced to Sheila his wife, and his children. I'm very glad I met them because over a period of time they opened a window into West Indian culture which proved very important to me in understanding what was going on in the community. I would not class them as informants in the police sense, but I stayed in touch with them for nearly ten years until Clarence died of a stroke and Sheila returned to make her new home back in Jamaica. Shelia's mother had come over with them, but her husband had stayed on the island. When I queried his absence Clarence explained that his father-in-law had no intention of coming over since he was a 'wandering man'. I had no idea what that meant until I later learnt that he had a number of woman friends, who needed his attention and obviously didn't want him to leave.

His son, Clarence Junior, was an apprentice electrician who was shortly to have his twenty-first birthday party and they asked me to join them. His daughter. Leonara, was four years junior to her brother, was a cadet nurse at the local hospital and she seemed a serious young lady, who was obviously going to make her mark within the nursing profession. Clarence Junior stayed in the area and over time developed a small electrical business; his sister on the other hand moved to London, married and established a family in South London.

The twenty-first party was a happy, noisy affair with loud West Indian Reggae music bouncing around the house. There were some white neighbours and lots of friends and relatives. I had bought a bottle of Jamaican rum as a present, not knowing that Trinidadian rum was more highly rated by Clarence and his family. I thought my presence as a police officer might cause a problem, but it didn't seem to, maybe Clarence hadn't told them and I never let on. I was introduced to curried goat during the evening, which had been prepared by Clarence's brother; it was all a new experience but I got into the swing of things and enjoyed every minute. Eventually I left with a piece of birthday cake and a kiss from Leonara, who had lightened up a great deal during the course of the evening. The following morning I managed to get to work in one piece but kept a very low profile for the rest of the day, nursing a sore head.

I gradually settled down on the section, getting to know the rest of my colleagues. The section sergeant was Tony Fellows, recently promoted officer, who was by far the youngest sergeant I had so far encountered. He was a calm, sensible man with a good sense of humour, who preferred to use Christian names rather than collar numbers. The station officer was another elderly constable called Tommy Hardy; he always had a pipe stuck in his mouth and seemed to know the residents of entire neighbourhood by name, including in many cases their parents and grandparents. I found out that he had joined the police pre-war and was one of the few members of the Force who had not been called up for military service, remaining in the City Police throughout the war. He was a cheerful soul who had a house-proud attitude to the station, since if there were no members of the public about he could be found sweeping up and keeping the place tidy.

I started my tour of nights and for the first few days walked round getting to know the lie of the land. I found that certain streets were used by the local prostitutes, most of whom were white, to pick up clients in cars. I also identified houses used as shabeens, frequented by the locals and outsiders who came into the area, looking for sex as well as late-night drinking. On the whole there did not seem to be too much trouble on the streets, since the women looked on their role of prostitute as a job and a lot of their clients seemed to be regulars, looking for particular girls. The main places where trouble could be expected were in the night clubs, especially at weekends, and my first experience came when we received a call from the owner of the Congo Club, situated at the northern end of the Fox Lane, to say that there was a man causing trouble on the premises. The owner, according to Tommy, was a large fat man called Batty Hendricks who had the reputation for managing a well-run establishment, with a licence to drink until 2am; he also had a juke box and served food. I went round to answer the call and climbed up some steps to the first floor. There was not much noise, which surprised me, and I went past the doorman and into the premises. The club was not busy, there may have been about a dozen customers, but I still couldn't see any signs of trouble. I went over to the barman and he directed me round the back to a door marked 'office'.

Going into the room I found a large black man, who I took to be Batty, together with a member of staff and a white man who was sprawled across a chair, smelling of drink and looking the worse for wear; I also noticed that he had a black eye. Batty told me that whilst the man had been standing by the bar he had leaned over and tried to grab some money out of the open till whilst the barman was serving a customer. Batty who told me that he habitually sat on a stool at the end of the bar and when he saw what was going on had grappled with the man and together with the barman had hauled him into the office. With a straight face he went on to say that the black eye had been caused whilst they struggled to get him from the bar area. He confirmed that no money had been stolen and, not surprisingly, the barman agreed with his version of events. I asked them if the man was a regular customer, but they told me that he was a stranger and Batty said that he would be barred from entering the club in future. I told Batty that the best I could do was to charge him with attempted larceny, on the understanding that both he and the staff member would be required to attend as witnesses. I was hoping Batty Henricks would see the light since the Night Crime Patrol would not thank me for taking this man to the station and submitting a report of crime which in their eyes was a non-event. Batty thought about it and after moment said that perhaps the matter could be sorted out between himself and the drunk. I turned to the man and asked him if he understood what had been said, he looked at me and nodded, initially relieved that he was not going to see the inside of a police station and then I saw the look on his face change as he realised what could happen. We both knew he was going to learn a lesson from Batty, but I had more urgent matters requiring my attention and left the club.

I was to learn a lesson of my own in the way we kept crime figures down in Hathersage later on during that period of 'nights'. I had returned to the station about 2am for a meal when a well-dressed man in his thirties rushed into the station complaining that he had been robbed of his wallet. I stayed in the front office as Tommy asked him where the crime had taken place and the man explained that he had been visiting an address in Hanover Road. I noticed Tommy's eyes move upwards and he asked the caller for the number of the house. The man said number 37, at which Tommy smiled and asked him if he was aware that this house was a well-known brothel. The complainant started to calm down and I could see that he was reassessing the situation. Tommy then wanted to know the circumstances of the robbery and the man told him he had picked up a prostitute in his car whilst driving around the area, and that she had directed him to this address. They had entered the house and went into a room on the first floor, a price had been agreed and he had taken off his clothes and placed them on a chair by the bed. After they had finished he put his clothes back on and left the house. Whilst he was looking for his car keys he realised that his wallet was missing and he returned to the house, but after repeating knocking at the door could not gain entry and at this point decided to inform the police.

Tommy listened to his account in silence and told the caller that if police took formal action and arrested the thief, the case would go to court and the press might get hold of the story. It was the type of incident that attracted them and they would probably publish the circumstances, said Tommy sagely; the public like these sorts of stories. Would the caller be prepared to be the subject of such publicity? The question hung in the air for a few moments whilst the man thought it through. By now I could see that the caller was having second thoughts; by the look on his face it was obvious that he wished he had never told the police or even gone to the house. He said he was sorry he had mentioned the event, but Tommy suggested a solution; if the man reported the matter as lost property he would ask an officer, looking at me, to go round to the address and see if the property could be recovered. The caller now looked resigned to the inevitable and asked if he could go with me to that address. I looked at him and told him that if he caused any trouble he would be locked up, saying that I wanted him to be quiet and just be there to identify his wallet, if we were lucky enough to find it, which in the circumstances seemed highly unlikely. Before we left the station Tommy said he would ask the divisional van to attend as backup, if they were free.

Number 37 Hanover Road was an unlit terraced

house and I went up to the front door and knocked loudly, as the police van pulled up. I carried on knocking, getting louder with each blow; suddenly the door opened and we were confronted by a worried-looking woman. Before I could say a word the van driver, Chalky White, strode past me and started talking to the woman, who he obviously knew. She stood aside and we went up the stairs and into the room indicated by the complainant. The room was empty and in darkness and after putting on the light we made a quick search for the wallet, which we found under the bed, devoid of money. Looking at the circumstances the thief must have been either under the bed or perhaps in the wardrobe and had searched the clothing whilst the man and the woman were occupied in the bed. We all left the house and I told the man the lost report would be torn up and he would have to regard the missing money as something to be charged to experience.

My time at Hathersage was full of surprises and perhaps one of the best came when Sunny Churchill rushed into the station about 2am one morning and told Tommy that his wife Pearl was in labour and about to have their first baby, and asked if Tommy would summon an ambulance. I had just come into the station with a fellow constable, Robert 'Rob Roy' Macgregor, whereupon Tommy said he would ring for an ambulance and asked us both to go back with Sunny, who lived around the corner, and try and offer whatever help was needed. Sunny rushed us round and his description of events seemed correct as Pearl was making a lot of noise and seemed to my non-expert eye to be in the last stages of labour. Rob Roy told us he would deal with the situation, proudly announcing that he had delivered loads of lambs at his parents' farm in the wilds of Scotland, assuring us that the birthing process between sheep and humans was pretty similar. Sunny did not look reassured at the prospect, but resigned himself to the inevitable as Rob Roy took off his tunic, rolled up his sleeves and got down to work. I remembered that in the films people were always getting hot water ready to be used so I put the kettle on and found some clean towels. By then Pearl was well advanced and the birth had started, with still no sign of the ambulance. Sunny appeared to be going into heart failure, either because he couldn't believe in Rob Roy's ability to do the job and perhaps in his eyes the whole situation seemed to be heading towards a complete disaster, and by then I had a lot of sympathy for him. In any event there was no stopping Rob Roy who took charge and to everyone's surprise seemed to know what he was doing. The first baby was born and then a few moments later a second baby appeared to the astonishment of everyone. I had been present at the birth of twins and suddenly Sunny was all smiles and we congratulated both him and Pearl. Fortunately for everyone the ambulance appeared and Pearl and the twins, a boy and a girl, together with Sunny, who still looked in a daze, were rushed off to hospital. Later Sunny told Rob Roy that the baby boy had been named after him in recognition for his efforts. He also told me that if it had been two boys the other son would have been named after me, although in truth my part in the event was minimal.

Another unusual event also took place during this tour of 'nights'. I was walking back to the station for refreshments and had just turned into Fox Lane when

I noticed that there was a couple in front of me. They were about one hundred yards away with the woman walking in a determined fashion, slightly in front of the man who seemed to be following on whimpering to himself. Before I could catch up they had turned left into the station and I followed them inside wondering what was going on. They went into the public office and Tommy was there to meet them; being nosey, I followed on after the pair. The woman turned out to be Doris Roberts, a local prostitute, and she told the following story.

She had been walking along the lane and went past this man, who was standing in a shop doorway, wearing what she described as a 'flasher's mac' which was a long raincoat. As she went past the man she said that he had opened the bottom of the coat displaying his 'crowned jewels', as she put it to us. She told Tommy she was enraged at what she saw and on impulse decided to turn the tables on him by turning back and telling him she had never seen such a large 'one' before. With a happy smile he opened his raincoat again and she promptly seized his male member and matched him off to the station, which was shortly after I saw them both. Tommy and I had a hard job keeping our faces straight whilst she was recounting her story and at the same time looking at the man who later gave his name as Walter Evans. I told Tommy I had followed them up the Lane after Doris had seized Evans in what looked like a vice-like grip. It was decided that I would charge Evans with the offences of Indecent Exposure and Breach of the Peace with Doris as the main witness and we would keep him in the cells until morning court. By now Evans had calmed down and after we had ignored his protests could see that he was not going to get any sympathy from Tommy and myself and without a word followed me into the nearest cell.

Doris turned up at court the following morning looking very respectable in a plain dress and wearing a limited amount of makeup. I briefed her as to what to say in her evidence, especially since Evans was not employing a defence solicitor. I told her not to mention her occupation but instead to concentrate on Evans exposing himself to her and her emotional reaction in response. I suggested that she did not need to mention that she had 'man' handled him to the police station. I went on to suggest that she explain that I arrested Evans after she had told me what had happened, again not referring to where the arrest had taken place. I made it quite clear to Evans that he should plead guilty and say as little as possible if he wanted to avoid becoming the laughing stock of the City, since the press would have a field day if they found out what had taken place. I need not have worried because as we went into court I saw the bench of magistrates and I knew that Evans did not stand a chance. The chairman was Mrs Potts with two male colleagues. Mrs Potts had a reputation of having 'a hang them and flog them approach' to dealing with crime, especially indecency. Although Evans' plea of guilty probably saved him from the maximum sentence the court could award him he was not going to get off scot free. I gave my evidence which was a brief account, describing the events, as I could see that the court was not interested in my story and wanted to hear Doris's account as the Magistrates began to see it was of more importance. She did not let them down with a very lurid description of what had taken place. I managed to restrain from bursting into laughter during the trial although listening to Doris's version of events I found it very hard not to break into a smile. Evans, who had no previous convictions, looked resigned when he had to suffer a further severe telling off by Mrs Potts, who as chair, remonstrated at him at great length informing him that no decent woman, looking at Doris, who nodded in agreement, should have to put up with such outrageous behaviour. The case progressed even better than I had hoped and Evans was fined ten pounds and given another telling off by the Chair, making it clear to him he would go to prison if he came before them again for the same offence.

Initially I did not have any dealings with the Sikh community who kept themselves to themselves. I had, however, come to recognise a couple of Sikhs, one of which was Ranjit Singh, who preferred to be known as 'Ronnie'. Ronnie, who worked in the city centre, was the youngest son of the local coalman; he was in his mid-twenties and still lived with his parents. Unlike the rest of his community he was clean shaven, did not wear a turban and instead had a short back and sides which was the usual men's haircut of the day. He was an excitable fellow who liked a drink and found it easy to get into an argument. Apparently his parents were trying to find a suitable girl for him to marry, but unsurprisingly in my eyes, had not met with any success.

It was a Saturday morning and I turned into Renshaw Street in which the Sikh temple was situated in an end terrace house. I walked slowly towards the temple, when there was a burst of noise and out of the temple entrance ran Ronnie followed by a Sikh, wearing a bus conductor's uniform, waving a large gleaming sword. Ronnie turned left and came up the street towards me with the sword carrier and a large crowd of Sikhs following. By now Ronnie had spotted me and was shouting for help. When he reached me he grabbed my arm and said he was going to be killed. I told him to calm down and stand next to me by the wall. The conductor rushed up and I told him to put the sword down and tell me what had happened. He explained that at the morning religious service Ronnie had started an argument at the back of the congregation and on hearing the disturbance the temple chairman had walked over to him, took off his turban and placed it on the floor in front of Ronnie, requiring him to leave the temple. Ronnie had stared at the chairman and then down at the turban and in a fit of anger had kicked the turban towards the front of the congregation which resulted in an uproar by the worshippers and Ronnie's swift departure from the building.

Fortunately tempers were beginning to cool down and I told them I would arrest Ronnie for Breach of the Peace and that the matter would be dealt at the station. I asked the conductor if he would contact Ronnie's father and ask him to come to the station. I then told him to put the sword away and turning round, handcuffed Ronnie in front of the crowd. This seemed to satisfy everybody and they left the scene, drifting back to the temple. Ronnie and I left the scene with him grumbling at me for putting the handcuffs on, leaving me to tell him that I had done it for his own benefit since the crowd wanted his blood and I had to show them that I was going to deal with this matter seriously. As we walked away I wondered how I was going to sort this problem out. After more than two years' service I was beginning to look at the wider picture in relation to this type of situation. I could legitimately charge Ronnie with Breach of the Peace, but if I did so I would probably have to arrest the bus conductor for possession of an offensive weapon, namely the sword. By now if the Sikhs had any sense they would have hidden the weapon, giving me a problem, and then what? I could imagine the Evening News with headlines of police rampaging through a place of worship, resulting in telephone calls from the chief constable and others. We continued to march along the street ready to turn left and then on to the police station. My mind was now in overdrive and then I had a flash of inspiration. I had asked the conductor to contact Ronnie's father in an effort to distract their attention, but what if I could make use of his attendance to find a solution? Suppose we could resolve the matter at the station without allowing it to go any further? Why not ask Mr Singh to go surety for the good behaviour of his son for three months? I could draft an official piece of paper for him to sign and Ronnie could be warned and discharged, but would Tommy and the sergeant go along with this charade?

We went into the station and I pushed Ronnie into the back office and told him to sit down. He waved his handcuffs at me and I took them off, telling him to sit still. Tommy and Sergeant Fellows were in the front office and I explained the situation and my suggestion to deal with this problem. There was a silence after I had finished and then the sergeant asked for further information and I explained in greater detail how I had come to my solution. Tommy said that if Mr Singh and his family were prepared to accept the course of action then we should go ahead. We both looked at the sergeant; he stared at us and then smiled his acceptance. We drafted the document and Tommy typed it out, finishing off with the station stamp, officially dating it and we waited for Mr Singh to appear. I went to give Ronnie a cup of tea and told him his father was on his way.

Mr Singh and his wife bustled into the station with worried looks on their faces, but I had the feeling that they already knew what had happened. I brought Ronnie out to meet them and then gave them my version of events and what I had been told. They looked at Ronnie who nodded in agreement. I then said that we were prepared to help, but only if they were able to play their part in resolving this situation. They agreed and I took them into the Charge Office and the sergeant explained what was required of them and asked Ronnie's father if he would sign the form as surety for Ronnie's good behaviour for the next three months. If Ronnie played his part and no further trouble occurred the form would be destroyed at the end of this period, however, if he failed to mend his ways he would go straight to prison. This was agreed and I witnessed his signature and accompanied them out of the station, suggesting that Ronnie should apologise to the temple chairman for his behaviour. His father said that he had already arranged for that to happen. I watched them going down the road with Mrs Singh giving vent to her feelings down Ronnie's left ear, whilst Mr Singh was shouting at him from the other side. We didn't have the legal power to enforce such a requirement on the family, but it seemed to do the trick as far as Ronnie was concerned in that there was no more trouble, at least for the next three months. I found out later that Mrs Singh eventually found a suitable girl for Ronnie and I hoped that all went well, although I never found out because by then I had moved on.

I walked back into the station made my way to the back office and lit a cigarette. Sitting back, I went over in my mind what had taken place with Ronnie and the Sikhs and what steps I had taken to solve the problem. It seemed to me that I had learnt another lesson in the art of policing. At the Training Centre much effort was expended to drum into the minds of the new recruits the legal definition of the duties of a constable with its emphasis on upholding the law, preventing and detecting crime, together with protecting life and property, all of which I had experienced so far in my service. Only now was I beginning to recognise that was just a part of the role and that there were other issues which sometimes needed to be taken into consideration. At the Training Centre we had been told that a constable has the power to use his discretion when deciding how to use the law and perhaps the way we had dealt with Ronnie was a good example. For the first time I had thought about the need to protect the reputation of the Force, both in terms of the Sikhs and also the wider community. I finished the cigarette and walked back on my beat. Later that day I spoke to the chairman of the temple who told me that the sword was a part of the temple's regalia; I explained that if it was taken outside again I would seize it as an offensive weapon, confiscate it and arrest the individual concerned. We looked at each other and I thought for one moment he was going to object to what I had said, but he thought for a moment and nodded his head, saying that he would ensure that it would be kept secure in the temple in future.

CHAPTER SEVEN

Looking back, Inspector Murdoch's retirement was the start of the end of both a particular type of policing and the physically large breed of police officer who personified it. It was just before his sixtieth birthday and he and his wife were retiring to the West Country, which was not an unusual decision for police retirees to make. For me he was the typical old-time policeman; he was a smart military type, polite, kind and with a good sense of humour. He would not put up with any nonsense from his officers or the public, which included the black community. His views about that section of the community were common throughout society at the time; he felt that they had many good qualities in that they supported royalty, enjoyed cricket and were Christians. He felt that there would be no problems with them whilst they accepted their place in society, in that being recent arrivals they had to adjust, keep their heads down and make the best of things. In general these views were a reflection of those held by most of the white community, which included members of the police; they were not considered racist, although a minute's thought would have suggested that they created a climate of discrimination. There were white people who did not like the black community and that included some members of the police. Officers like Inspector Murdoch, were aware of this problem and tried to minimise it within the City Police by insisting on a sense of professionalism from his officers, which mitigated but did not eliminate racism by certain individuals. During my time as a uniform constable day-to-day policing using the foot beat system created a good atmosphere with the community, even if, according to Clarence Senior, we were too soft.

By now I had spent enough time in Hathersage to realise that these views about the black community played a part in the way that the area was policed. General policing matters such as road accidents and reports of crime were dealt with in accordance with normal procedure. Criminality by members of the black community had to be dealt with firmly. If a black criminal brought a brand new or fairly new vehicle, this became known and the local police would take action by consistently stopping and checking the driving details such as driving licence and certificate of insurance; although this behaviour was sometimes extended to any member of the white community who had the temerity to purchase a similar vehicle. In extreme cases I remember such vehicles being damaged, but whether that was by police officers or white members of the public was a matter for conjecture, either way I never remember anybody being arrested for such an offence.

Drug dealing and illegal drinking had a special place in enforcement. The drug of choice was mainly cannabis and its use was mainly confined within the black community; policing action in relation to drug use was light touch and left to the divisional Plain Clothes Department and the Force Drug Squad. Illegal drinking in the area did not require too much activity either, provided there were no complaints, by residents or members of the public, when raids would then be undertaken. Was there police corruption in relation to drugs or drink? Maybe, although during my time in uniform I did not come across any activity and I don't remember any officer being arrested for such offence.

How did the black community view the situation? From discussions with older members they were certainly aware of discrimination, not just in relation to policing but in other areas, such as housing and accommodation, but accepted that they were newcomers and this was part of the settling in process. The situation could not last and by the time the next generation had grown up they made it clear through the riots of 1981 that change could only be made by violent action, since there was little indication that the rest of society were making much effort to accept them as ordinary members of the community. By then the first black recruits were also joining the Police Service.

The inspector's retirement party was held in the Police Club and although the chief constable sent his apologies, everyone of note in the City Police, including the Chairman of the Watch Committee, were present. I stood back and listened to the speeches, drinking beer with friends and eating pies, sausage rolls and sandwiches. The chief superintendent, who was a similar vintage to the inspector, made a funny speech and Mr Murdoch accepted a clock as a retirement gift and said a few words in reply. Looking back Albert Murdoch was of a generation that had not been introduced to management principles, but his time in the Royal Navy, rising to be a chief petty officer, had given him leadership experience which he put to good practice. The first time I saw his dry wit in action was when I arrested a young lad for disorderly behaviour. The inspector was in the Charge Office when I brought the prisoner before him. The lad was a brash extrovert character, who thought he would make fun of the inspector by claiming he knew his 'rights' and should not have been arrested. The only problem was that the City Police did not recognise 'rights' in any form and if the lad had thought about it for one moment he might have tried a different approach. We were standing in front of the counter, behind which stood the inspector who had before him the large Charge Office book in which all the basic details of the prisoner were entered. The inspector asked the prisoner for his name; in reply the lad turned to me and said, 'What's my name?' I coughed in response. The inspector ploughed on, asking for his date of birth and his address. In each case the cocky young idiot turned and repeated the question to me.

After a short while Murdoch sighed and with a slight smile quickly closed the book, picked it up and hit the lad over the head with it. Turning to me he said, 'Did that hurt?' There was no more trouble afterwards.

I knew I was coming up in the world when the following Friday Sergeant Fellows asked me to look after the special constable patrol which took place once a month on a Saturday in the evening, normally from 8pm to midnight. Their usual watchdog had reported sick and the sergeant warned me to keep an eye on them and make sure they didn't get into trouble, which proved easier said than done. The role of the special constable within the City Police was much debated and caused endless arguments. On one side the Police Federation, which is the staff association for the junior ranks, wanted the 'specials' disbanded, saying there was no place for the 'hobby bobbies' in the era of professional policing. In this respect it was convenient for the Federation to ignore the fact that the Special Constabulary had a far longer role in the history of policing than the professionals. On the other side was the Watch Committee, who were firm supporters of the role of the Specials, praising them as public spirited members of the community, who performed a valuable service, whilst being unpaid. This latter element always struck a positive chord with the Committee, although to be fair the Specials were paid allowances for certain duties. In the middle of this maelstrom was the chief constable who took the easy way out by issuing an order to divisional commanders requiring them to make good use of special constables in an appropriate manner. The definition of 'appropriate manner' was never laid down, leaving divisions to make their own arrangements and our division let them loose once a month using their own car under the guidance of a regular officer. Their car was given a battery-operated Force radio and a temporary police sign which was fixed to the rear window of the vehicle. The Traffic Department, who were very obstructive when non-police vehicles were used for policing purposes, insisted on inspecting the vehicle, which was then given temporary police insurance and this allowed the Department to cast a baleful eye on the ability of the driver, who was always instructed never to exceed the speed limit. The Traffic Department further instructed that the 'Specials' were never to be allowed out on the road unless they were accompanied by a uniformed constable who could be relied on to keep them in check.

On this Saturday they came round to the station to pick me up in a smart Ford Cortina. There were three of them, who I had not met before. They introduced themselves; firstly there was Mr Bates their section leader and a building society manager, whose car we would be using, then a young fellow called George Prentice, who was hoping to join the police as a regular officer but currently worked in a local estate agency, and finally Arthur Jackson, a middle-aged man, who worked in the printing industry and told me he had seen service in the military police, which for me rang a few alarm bells. My experience of the military police in action, both in relation to members of our Armed Services as well as our Allies, had shown them to be heavy handed when dealing with outbreaks of violence and later that evening Mr Jackson did not let me down in this respect. It was the first time they had been accompanied by a younger officer and I gave them a brief resume of my career, which didn't take too long, and off we went. The first hour went without a problem; we went to the scene of a house fire and then a major traffic accident and by now I was beginning to relax since everything seemed to be in order.

It was just after 11pm when we spotted a car driving without lights. As keen as ever the Specials suggested that the car could have been stolen and I agreed we could stop it and give it look over. We used our Force radio but were told that it had not been reported as a vehicle theft. Mr Bates took the hint that he had received approval to exceed the speed limit and charged after the car, eventually overtaking it. We beckoned it to stop and before I could say anything all the Specials leaped out of the car to question the driver. As we walked towards to the vehicle it crossed my mind that I thought that the drivers face looked familiar and by the time we reached his door I knew we were looking at Detective Constable Arthur Mole, with another passenger slumped next to him. I told Prentice and Jackson to check the tyres while Mole wound the window down. I looked him in the eye and asked him if he knew that he was driving without lights. Without a pause Mole told me that his friend was ill and he was driving him home in his car to help him out, he went on to explain that he was unfamiliar with the light switch. There was a smell of drink coming from the vehicle and I was trying to crowd out Mr Bates, who was right behind me, from getting too close to hear the conversation or the smell of the alcohol. Mole switched the lights on and I told him to drive more carefully. The others returned from their inspection with nothing to report and I waved Mole off. I then explained to the others that the driver had been doing a good turn for the passenger who wasn't feeling well and was taking him home. Listening to myself my explanation seemed a bit thin even to me, but it was accepted without a murmur and we returned to our car.

IN THE 'NICK' OF TIME

As we got back into the car our attention was caught by a radio message to say there was a fight taking place at The George pub on Gladstone Street and once again Mr Bates put his foot down on the accelerator. When we got to the scene I watched the Specials go into action. Mr Bates and George tended to hang back and watch, whilst Arthur Jackson waded into the fight delivering blows left and right as he passed through the melee. We helped put the prisoners in the back of the van and then it was time for my Specials; you will note that by this time I had taken ownership of them, to drop me off at the station. I thanked them all for their efforts and returned to proper police work.

It was about this time that the first Indian restaurant opened up on the Lane. I had experienced eating curries in the Navy; they were usually minced beef cooked with tomato, curry powder, currents and coconut. I never really cared for them, but this new restaurant promised to be something different, although its name, 'The Duke of Richmond', seemed a bit strange. A week later I went with Charlie to the restaurant and within a few moments we met the owner, Mr Ali, who was more than happy to explain the intricacies of the menu. During the conversation I asked him how he had come to select the name of his restaurant. It turned out to be a convoluted story; Mr Ali's family came from Sylhet in East Pakistan and when they arrived in England they found that the locals believed that all their food came from India. Restaurants had names like Star of India and being a Pakistani Mr Ali could not bring himself to give his restaurant an Indian name and looked for an alternative. He thought an English name would attract customers to his new venture and his mother suggested the name of an English governor on a statute standing in her home town, and this was the name he selected.

I had chicken madras, pilau rice and chips; Charlie chose chicken biryani and rice, but I don't think he was too keen. In any event I enjoyed the meal and kept to that particular order, until I got married. I never had much trouble with 'The Duke of Richmond'; Mr Ali ran a tight ship, his brother did the cooking and his nephew served as waiter. There was the occasional incident where individuals couldn't or wouldn't pay, usually at weekends, but the restaurant remained in business until it was pulled down in the eighties as part of the council's clearance scheme and Mr Ali and his family moved on to a more superior establishment with a new name in the east side of the city.

It was after the visit to Mr Ali's place that I paraded for 'nights' and met Mr Murdoch's replacement, Inspector Stanley Baldwin. Baldwin was a thin, small officer, by the standards of the City Police, who had recently returned from the Police College. He seemed a solemn, pensive individual, who after introducing himself then spent the next twenty minutes explaining the importance of management theory which he said was going to transform policing efficiency. We were introduced to aims and objectives in our work, the importance of maintaining work performance against Force parameters and the way that a new appraisal system would assist in this process. I cast a surreptitious glance at my colleagues and found that some were looking dazed, whilst others seemed to have lost the plot. I have to confess that at that stage of my service I was not totally sure what he was on about, although later as I got to grips with the latest management theories which became popular in the police service, the mist started to clear. When he finished we left, not really knowing what to expect, although in hindsight I now realise that Baldwin was giving us an early introduction to extensive changes in police management and processes which we would be required to adopt in the future.

Before we left the station we were all caught by Tommy Hardy who told us that a 'found dog' had escaped and it needed to be located and returned. In the station yard were a couple of dog kennels, which were used to hold 'found dogs'. These were dogs brought in by the police and sometimes by members of the public, they usually did not have collars, and were found wandering in the area, apparently lost. If their owners turned up they recovered their pet, however if the dog was not claimed the local Dogs' Home sent a van and the animal was taken in and lodged there, hopefully to be handed over to new owners. We were told that the dog which had gone missing was a small black and white mongrel. Looking at my colleagues, who were still recovering from Inspector Baldwin's pep talk, I sensed that there would not be too much interest in recovering the animal, so I thought I would help Tommy by finding the dog.

For the first hour I saw no dogs, which was unusual since at night it was quite common to see these animals wandering about. About two o'clock, just before I was due for refreshments I spotted a small black and white mongrel coming towards me, it was quite a friendly animal and I fastened my dog lead round its neck and off we went to the station. In those days we were supplied with a leather dog lead to use if a member of the public handed in a lost dog to us if we were on beat duty. I felt happy that I had found the dog concerned and that Tommy would have no more problems. As I entered the station there seemed to be a lot of barking from the station yard, but I fastened my dog in the public office and went out to look for Tommy to tell him the good news. He was in the yard looking at the kennels, which seemed to be full of black and white dogs, some of whom were barking like mad. I told him I had brought a dog which might be the right animal he was looking for and suggested he might like to inspect it. He glowered up at me with a look of pure evil and said that if anybody brought any more 'effing' dogs into the station he would explode. Obviously I had misread the mood of my colleagues, all of whom must have been anxious to help, some of whom must have placed the dogs they had found in the kennels as a surprise without telling Tommy. I persuaded Tommy to look at my dog, but it was the wrong animal and I was forced to rush back to where I had found it and shoo it away.

Charlie and I had drifted effortlessly back into our exam study routine, but this time we were studying new subjects. Now we were concentrating on the Rules of Evidence, criminal offences found in the Larceny Act and the Offences against the Person Act, together with mentally wrestling with the definition of heavy locomotives, light locomotives and motor tractors, which formed part of the road traffic syllabus. We found the study interesting because it seemed more relevant to our work on the streets, although some of the subjects in the syllabus we thought were of little value to us, such as the Movement of Animal orders and other legislation which related to the rural, rather than urban environment in which we were used to working.

Charlie's wedding plans were moving along steadily and having had loads of advice about my role as Best Man I had now prepared a draft speech which I refused to show to Charlie. The time was coming up for the rehearsal and I now got to meet all the bridesmaids. Some of them I knew, but one called Diane Massey I had not met before; Barbara had asked Diane, who had become a friend from her teacher training college days, to be her chief bridesmaid. She was a tall blonde, slim girl, who I instantly took a liking to and who I thought might have the same feeling for me. After the rehearsal we all went to a nearby pub for a drink and during the course of the evening I managed to take her on one side and plucking up courage, asked her out on a date and much to my surprise she agreed.

The sun was shining on the day of the wedding and I turned up in my new suit; the wedding ring was in my jacket pocket and with my speech I was fully prepared. The ceremony went without a hitch; the bride looked lovely and so did the chief bridesmaid and afterwards we all made our way to the reception. I'm glad I had a few drinks as the Best Man's speech was beginning to weigh heavily in my mind as well as in my pocket. Fortunately the guests were full of good cheer and when my time came round for my speech, I found it caused much laughter and I was able now to relax and finish on a high note. Afterwards when it was Charlie's turn he ruefully informed the guests that having a Best Man who has known him since schooldays can bring back events you would prefer to forget, but he finished by thanking me and hoped he would get his own back one day.

A month after the wedding we sat the promotion exams and sometime after found we had both passed. I was later told that the pass rate for the City Police was pretty low, somewhere between twenty and twenty-five percent. This did not stop the older constables who sat the exam every year, since it gave them an extra day off shift work. Once you became a candidate for promotion the City Police had a well-laid path for career development purposes. You started with a twelve-month posting in the Plain Clothes Department and then if all went well you could apply to spend six months with divisional CID as an aide. So now I would have to watch my step and see how events played out. The actual system of promotion was a bit of a mystery which the Police Federation had tried to unravel, without much success. They had asked the chief constable for information, but he had refused saying that the Watch Committee played an important part in the process and they had declined to assist. What became apparent to me over the next couple of years was that as the pre-war and immediate post-war officers retired from the Force the process of promotion started to accelerate and this helped my chances of success.

On the first period of 'nights' after the wedding I was standing on the north corner of Fox Lane, near our local fire station, when the doors opened and one of their engines rushed out. It stopped alongside me and the front door of the vehicle opened and I was beckoned inside. I knew most of the crew since I was an associate member of their social club and the Leading Fireman at the front was a particular friend of mine. He told me they were off in answer to an alarm at the local hospital, which was at the southern end of my beat, and I sat back and enjoyed the ride. In those days fire engines operated a bell with blue light and when the vehicle swayed you could feel the water move in the tank, especially when the engine took a corner at speed. A few moments later we pulled into the hospital entrance and were directed to a block of wards at the rear of the premises.

The hospital had been built in Victorian times as a workhouse and the wards were in blocks of three storeys high and the fire had started in the middle floor of one of the blocks. The ward where the fire was located was unoccupied, but it was necessary to evacuate the patients from the bottom and top stories of the block. We all got out and I went over to see how the evacuation was progressing. The ground floor ward was being emptied but there seemed to be a problem with the top floor so one of the firemen and I went up the side of the building, using the outside fire escape, to see what was happening. When we reached the top we found that someone had piled a large number of canvas bags full of dirty laundry on the outside landing which was preventing the patients and staff from opening the fire doors in order to leave the building. Between the pair of us we started to throw the bags off the landing and the staff opened the doors and everybody was able to leave the ward. I later saw the Night Sister and told her forcefully that these circumstances must not occur again as they were putting life in danger. She agreed to make sure that the day staff would address the problem as an urgent matter.

Late evening a couple of days later I was walking along the entry at the back of the shops on the Lane when further ahead I heard a loud moan. I thought it was probably a local drunk suffering from a sore head and when I shone my torch around I noticed a man curled up against the wall looking as though he had been drinking. As I approached, however, I saw the floor was covered in blood; initially I thought that this man had been attacked and perhaps robbed. On looking more closely I saw that he had a knife in his right hand and seemed to be trying to cut off one of his fingers of his left hand. I took the knife off him and found some string which I used as a tourniquet to stop the flow of blood. By now he had fainted and I rushed round to the local phone box to summon an ambulance. I went with him in the ambulance to the city hospital casualty department, still none the wiser as to what had taken place. After the doctor had examined him he told me that the man had probably taken LSD which had led to the scene I had observed. Later I was told to return to the station and the Drugs Squad were informed and took over the matter. Eventually I found out that he had indeed taken LSD at a party on the north side of the city. After he recovered he explained that after he had taken the drug he had not experienced any effect and decided that he had been sold a bogus tablet made of sugar. However, when the party finished and he was travelling home on a bus he started to experience hallucinations. He left the bus before reaching home and started to believe that a snake was eating his fingers. This emotion was so powerful that he felt the only way stop this feeling was to cut off his finger, which he was attempting to do when I found him. Up to now my only experience of drug taking was related to cannabis, and this was my first experience in Hathersage of the new party drugs which were coming into fashion.

Up until now I had dealt with a number of missing persons reports; all those that concerned children had been found quickly and returned to their parents which gave me particular satisfaction. Investigating missing adults was more complex as these reports usually fell into two categories; those who had gone missing by accident or mistake, usually involving an excess of drink, and those who wanted to disappear without trace. If a person was not located within a reasonable period of time the report was passed to the Plain Clothes Department who would examine the circumstances in more detail, which sometimes led to locating the missing individual. I will discuss the work of the Plain Clothes Department in dealing with these types of incidents later.

My success rate in locating missing children took a turn for the worse about this time. I was working afternoons when Tommy asked me to go an address in Radford Street where the caller, a Mrs Johnson, wanted to report a missing child. It was about eight o'clock in the evening when I arrived to be met by an anxious set of parents. They reported that their youngest daughter, six-year-old Amy, had left school at the usual time and headed off with her friend Sylvia to spend time at her house. Sylvia lived near Princess Park and the two girls crossed the park and played in her bedroom until tea time after which Amy was due to return home. Her father had gone to Sylvia's home to collect his daughter, but was told that she left the house at the usual time and was last seen running back to her home through the park about seven o'clock. The family home was well kept and both parents were at a loss to explain their daughter's absence, assuring me that the girls took it in turn to visit each other's home, usually once a week. Amy was the youngest of three children, with two elder brothers. She was obviously a much-loved child and her parents went to great lengths to assure me that she had never been late before and when this remark was made I noticed tears started to form in her mother's eyes as the implications of what had been said became apparent. Her father said that after he been to Sylvia's home he had retraced Amy's path through the park without finding any signs of his daughter. As he said this Mrs Johnson started to cry asking me if Amy would be alright; I tried to reassure her but I could tell she was beginning to fear the worst.

Princess Park was a large public park covering an area of about a quarter mile square with small patches of woodland, together with large clumps of overgrown areas. I returned to the station and reported back to Tommy and the sergeant. Tommy knew the Park Keeper, Mr Newton, and was able to get in touch with him by phone. He agreed to turn out and open up the park, whereupon our new inspector assembled about ten officers with Mr Johnson and some neighbours and after arranging some extra lighting we assembled at the main gates. Sergeant Fellowes had obtained some of Amy's clothes from her mother and which he gave to our police dog handler for his dog Sabre to smell. After smelling the clothing Sabre lifted up his head and with that we entered the park, lined up with the dog in front and began to walk slowly across the park. Mr Johnson and some of the neighbours were calling out to Amy by name as we made our way into the centre, but there was no reply. Suddenly Sabre started to bark and made his way towards some bushes. Mr Johnson broke away and started to run after the dog and his handler, whilst the rest of us stopped, hoping that it was a false alarm.

The dog and the handler dived into the bushes whilst Sergeant Fellowes, who was nearest to hand, following Mr Johnson, accelerated into a run and managed the stop him going into the undergrowth after the police dog. There was a struggle between the two of them with Mr Johnson trying to break free of the sergeant's grasp and I dashed up and helped to restrain him. By now the dog was barking furiously and Andy the handler reappeared and motioned the sergeant to follow him, I stayed keeping a firm grip on Mr Johnson. I could see that tears were beginning to fall down his face and I noticed that Inspector Baldwin had gone to join the sergeant. Everybody else had formed around Mr Johnson in complete silence and I released my grip on him, joining the others, recognising a general feeling of grief; being men it was the best we could do in the circumstances.

The inspector reappeared and told me to get the Night Crime Patrol and the ambulance, although he was sure that the little girl was dead. I rushed off to Mr Newton's office and contacted the Information Room to give them the message after which I walked slowly back to the scene. Mr Johnson, who had recovered to some extent, was again asking to see his daughter, but Inspector Baldwin was adamant that this would not be possible at the present time, as the area was now a scene of crime and needed to be protected for forensic science purposes, promising that as soon all necessary measures had been taken arrangements would be made for him and his wife to see their daughter. I was later told by Sergeant Fellowes that although they wanted to protect the scene, the main reason why the inspector had taken this decision was that the girl's face and body had been badly assaulted and that it would be better for the parents to see their daughter at the mortuary after she had been made more presentable.

I left the park, never having seen the little girl or the crime scene and went home, leaving the Night Relief to take charge. The CID took over and the girl's body was taken to Casualty, pronounced dead and then conveyed to the mortuary. When I returned the following afternoon the district was crawling with detectives conducting door-to-door enquiries. Eventually the killer was identified as a local man who had been spotted keeping an eye on young girls. He had been seen hanging about the primary school watching the children playing in the yard and was seen in the park when Amy started her last journey from Sylvia's home. A search of his home address located bloodstained clothing which he had failed to dispose of, which matched Amy's blood group. He was found guilty of murder and given life imprisonment.

Charlie was posted to the Plain Clothes Department, whilst I and the rest of the section read the latest Divisional Order which announced that that at the beginning of next month the Hathersage Village section had been selected by the Force to run a new 'pilot' Unit Beat scheme for twelve months. The scheme was to transform the present policing system by introducing the use of motor cars and personal radios with cycle and foot beats taken out of policing to become relics of old-fashioned methods, a product of the past, no longer sufficient for the modern age. A new radio base station was to be installed at DHQ and the new section would be entirely self-sufficient during the period of the scheme with CID officers also drafted in to supply cover for the area. A list of officers was attached to the Order and I scanned the names and numbers to find that I had been posted to Unit Beat Car duties. Our section sergeant was George Armstrong, who I had met before and was a younger version of Sergeant Nelson.

A couple of weeks later and the officers selected to take part in the new scheme were summoned to a briefing session at DHQ. As we sat down in the main hall we found ourselves confronted by a bevy of top brass from Headquarters who all seemed anxious to tell us how important it was that we should get the scheme up and running properly from day one. They explained that the main objectives were to use the new radio system to provide a fast mobile response to public calls and that the panda cars should be seen by the public driving about the area on a constant basis, giving the impression of a Service which was providing a new modern policing responsive to public needs. Local intelligence was now to be collected and stored at DHQ on a card index with responsibility given to the new role of Collator, who would create the system and keep it up to date. It was explained that local knowledge which had been the preserve of beat officers should now be available to everybody working in the Force, and this presumably included the local CID, who were also expected to contribute to it, although it was noticeable that the detective chief inspector with the Headquarters team did not seem very supportive of that particular idea. Once again we were told that policing was leaving the old methods behind and replacing it with a more active system using new technology, such as radios and vehicles to provide a better service to the public.

Looking back I think our initial response to these new ideas was mixed; on one hand cutting down the staff by more than half did not seem much of an improvement. On the other hand the increased use of cars was accepted with alacrity, since here was the prospect of no more walking in the rain, no longer having to brave the cold in winter or having to walk along dark alleys at night. None of us at the time, and that seemed to include most of the senior officers, considered the negative impact that this loss of regular contact with the public would bring. However, one very important feature was the tremendous improvement radio communication gave in summoning help and assistance. The days of using telephone boxes or private telephones in order to contact the station were now gone; advice could be offered at the touch of a button as well as help from colleagues when dealing with a violent or disorderly prisoner. Certainly this new way of working gave a boost to working a beat from the uniform copper's perspective.

IN THE 'NICK' OF TIME

After a month certain amendments were made to the scheme when it was decided to include a couple of foot beat officers, one covering the north side, whilst the other covered the south side of the village. These officers were given twenty-four-hour cover for their beats and were responsible for dealing with outside enquiries and also encouraged to investigate complaints made by the public concerning minor crime or disorder issues. The other adjustment was to require Unit Beat car drivers to park up and patrol on foot when not dealing with public calls. This particular instruction was usually ignored by the officers concerned who found many ways to avoid this requirement.

Within a short time the public started to call the Unit Beat cars 'panda' cars due to their colour scheme of pale blue with a single white stripe painted around the middle of the car, and with it the policing system became known as the 'panda' system. More unintended changes followed this scheme as it was eventually rolled across the City Police area and of course became adopted nationally. The main change was the public's use of the 999 emergency call systems. In areas such as Belltown, where most of the residents did not possess their own telephone in the house, contact with the police was either by using public call boxes, going to the local police station or contacting the foot beat officer. The emphasis at the time was that the 999 system should only to be used by the public for genuine emergency calls. With the introduction of the panda scheme things gradually started to change because contact with local officers broke down which resulted in more use being made by the public of the emergency call system to convey information about incidents which were not genuine emergencies, such as cats stuck up trees or burst water mains. The response by the City Police was to accept the degrading of the 999 system because there was no alternative if contact with the public was to be maintained. This change in policy was not simply based on pragmatism but also the recognition that these changes to policing had never really been discussed in any detail with the general public. As a result it was accepted that if their support was to be gained for the new 'panda' system such changes were necessary.

On the first day at the start of the scheme we were each issued with a personal radio. In those days there were two pieces of equipment; one was a hand-held transmitter, which was carried in a uniform pocket, together with a separate receiver, which was pinned to the front of the tunic. There was no privacy when using the receiver which was broadcasting information which could be heard by any member of the public who was near at hand. At the end of each shift the radios were taken out of the equipment and put on charge and until we became used to operating them a number of problems could arise. For example, it was not unusual for one of us to forget to hand in one of the radio items, usually the transmitter, and sometimes you could find that the batteries were not fully charged and contact was lost before the end of a shift. I was occasionally asked to perform divisional van duties and found that you had to tune your ears to two separate radio channels, which sometimes were broadcasting different messages at the same time; one the local channel from DHQ, the other from Force Headquarters. Another major problem which emerged with the use of personal radios was the location of 'black spots'. These were geographical areas where messages could not be received or sent; this feature was quickly picked up by operational staff and large areas of Hathersage Village became blighted as 'black spots', much to the annoyance of supervisory staff. We all took advantage of this problem at one time or other, either to avoid work or to prevent sergeants from finding our location. In order to solve this problem the aerial at DHQ was increased in height and subsidiary aerials were provided, but this defect was never entirely eliminated until the introduction of more modern equipment which came along in due course.

Looking back now it seems that this new system led to the introduction of another major change. In the past men recruited into the uniformed branch had to adopt a particular attitude to police work. Working in the public domain, incidents had to be dealt with by individual officers, who normally could not rely on other members of the Force for assistance. The new system changed this approach, it was no longer necessary to recruit big men to enforce the law – with instant radio communication, assistance was only a few moments away and teamwork became more important. Policing was no longer the preserve of the individual officer to the same extent and working with others became a necessary aptitude for the modern-day uniformed officer on patrol.

Diane and I continued to see one another; I introduced her to my parents, who both liked her, and I in turn met her father and mother. As time went by our relationship grew and I realised that we both wanted to get married and so I arranged for us to spend a weekend away in the Lake District. On the Saturday night in a pub near Lake Coniston I proposed to her and she accepted. We decided to save up both for the wedding and also for a mortgage deposit on a house. We reckoned that would take twelve months, which was not unusual at that time. We returned home and told both sets of parents and our friends; Charlie suggested that we meet for a pint to celebrate. When I met him he seemed rather quiet and introspective, not his usual cheerful self. I looked at him and asked what the problem was. He thought for a moment and said that it wasn't working out. At that point in the conversation I thought he was talking about his marriage to Barbara, but he soon put me right. He told me that his wife had never been happy with his job in the police, especially shift work, and as he was talking my mind went back to the conversation he had recounted with Barbara with the remark he had made about the importance of Rent Allowance before their marriage. Apparently they had agreed to give it a try to see if she could adjust, but he said she had tried her best but this difficulty had not been resolved. Initially I was surprised at the turn of events and yet thinking back I realised that Barbara had never been happy with the situation. I remember her saying that Charlie could do a lot better for himself and when we had been out together at some point she would mention her reservation about his occupation, usually in a joking manner. I had never taken it seriously, saying to her that she could do a lot worse.

I asked him what he intended to do now that he had decided to leave the police and he replied that he wanted to go into teaching. Although he and I had a drink to celebrate my intended marriage the evening ended on a damp note. I later asked Diane if she knew what had been brewing between the two of them; she said that Barbara had not discussed it directly, but she knew something was up between them and was not surprised at what had happened. I told her that I had decided, unlike Charlie, to make the police my career and she grinned at me, saying that she had worked that out herself within a short time of us getting together. She went on to say that she had spotted it when she first met me and saw my enthusiasm for the job. Thinking about what she said I realised that she had put into words a decision I had come to accept and how perceptive she was in understanding my feelings.

Charlie and I remained friends, although our careers took different paths; he took to teaching like a duck to water and eventually became head of a large secondary school. We still occasionally reminisce over his decision to leave the police, but he always maintains that he made the right choice. A month later he had left the job and I must confess that after he had gone a guilty thought entered my mind that a vacancy would now occur in the Plain Clothes Department, and perhaps I might be selected. In any event I was still driving round in a panda car and settling down to this new form of policing. I enjoyed the radio communication and with it the feeling of keeping in touch with what was happening around the section, but on the other hand I knew that time spent with the public was beginning to diminish and that my colleagues and I were losing touch with them.

Harry Cornish had been given the foot beat on the north side of the village and we used to meet up with him, telling me how things had changed in this new role. How he could draw up his own work schedule, with the sergeant's approval, and take his personal radio home with him each day leading to a situation where he would very often contact DHQ from his kitchen to tell them he was starting duty in the morning or retiring in the evening. He was able to work split shifts if required and seemed to feel he had the best job in the Bobbies. I didn't think I could match that since I was beginning to learn that the job of a car beat officer was pretty straightforward without the advantages given to Harry and his foot beat responsibilities.

The first new situation whilst I was on panda car duties happened as a result of a conversation I had with Diane, who had taken up a new post as a primary school teacher at Hathersage Village School. I was having a meal with her at her parents' house when she suddenly asked me if I would visit the school with my car and radio and spend some time with the children explaining the role of the police officer. I told her that I wasn't a teacher and the children would be bored to tears, but she pressed on, saying that they would enjoy the experience and tellingly admitted that she had already discussed the matter with her head teacher who had told her it was a good idea. Eventually I agreed to raise the matter with my sergeant and if he approved I would arrange to come and see them. I saw Sergeant Armstrong the following day and put Diane's proposal to him; surprisingly he was full of enthusiasm for the idea and asked what I was going to do to entertain the children. I had been giving some thought to this problem and suggested that I would liaise with Albert

IN THE 'NICK' OF TIME

Duckworth, our radio operator, and we would arrange for some of the children to use the radio to speak to Albert. I asked if we would persuade the Dog Handler Bob Grove to show up with his dog, Prince, and by the time we had finished we had put together a programme of events which should last about an hour.

I spoke to Diane and arranged for us to attend the school the following week, which gave me time to practice my lines. The day soon came round and when I drove into the school yard I must admit that I was a bit nervous, but I was made very welcome and I got the programme underway without too many hiccups. All went well in that the radio communication fascinated the children; in fact I had too many volunteers who wanted to talk to Albert. Bob and his dog gave a wonderful display, with me as a volunteer who was caught by Prince, who fortunately only bit me and not the children in the process. Everybody seemed to enjoy themselves and our visit became an annual event to the school. A week later I received a large envelope from the school containing pictures in coloured pencil from the children about our visit. They varied from pictures of the car, many of Prince, and a good one of me being bittern in half by the dog; some I took home, the rest were pinned up in our canteen. It was just after our school visit that I was transferred to divisional van duty joining up with Joe Walsh. Up until that time we had been using Austin J-type vans, but as part of the new Unit Scheme we were given the first model of the Ford Transit van, which was a larger and a more powerful vehicle. I had known Joe from the past when I had worked at Harrison Street Station; he was slightly older in service and I knew he was hoping to join the Traffic Branch, having already passed the advanced driving course. He was married with a young family and I got used to the daily updates about his children, especially his daughter, who was three years old and who he called his 'young princess'. Although I didn't realise at the time our discussions about his family's trials and tribulations was to give me an inkling of what I has to experience in the future.

Our first job was nothing to do with police work but turned out to be an errand to help out Joe and his family. He lived in a police house at the edge of the village and he had bought some second-hand furniture from a local shop. He asked me to help him transport the furniture to his house as it would take only a couple of minutes from the shop in the village. We picked up the stuff and as we headed past the police station I noticed a Traffic car parked near the front entrance. We carried on and then I noticed that the Traffic car was following us and I asked Joe if he was expecting company; he couldn't see the driver, but thought it might be one of his friends from the Traffic Branch. We pulled up outside his home and before we could open the rear doors of the van the Traffic car stopped behind us and a traffic inspector got out. He had seen the van and since it was new wanted to know about the characteristics of the vehicle in comparison to the Austin van, which were of much interest to motoring enthusiasts in the Traffic Department. I left Joe and the inspector to discuss the respective merits of the two vans, whilst I wondered at what point he would ask to see the interior and how we were going to explain the presence of the furniture. To the relief of both of us he drove off without us having to open the van doors and we breathed a sigh of relief and carried the furniture into Joe's house in double quick time. I met Mrs Walsh over a cup of tea and was introduced to the rest of the family including his 'young princess'. I stayed on van duties with Joe for a further two months and then received the call I had been hoping for in that I was being posted to the Plain Clothes Department at the end of the month.

CHAPTER EIGHT

The Plain Clothes Department office was located on the first floor of DHQ; it consisted of a large room where the dozen constables were based, nearby was a small office in which resided the Plain Clothes sergeant, Norman Robinson, who was nearing the end of his time in charge. His replacement, Sergeant Reginald Cousins, was already sharing his office, getting to know the role of the Plain Clothes sergeant and the methods used by the Department and I met both of them on joining. I also met the deputy divisional commander, Superintendent David Allison, who was in overall charge of the Department as well as the Divisional administration. Allison was believed to be one of the future chief officers of the City Police. He was in his early forties, had been to the Police College on a number of courses and had served in the Chief Constable's Office. He had never stayed in any particular job for more than two years and was expected to be the officer most likely for promotion to chief superintendent, when the next vacancy occurred. I spent about five minutes with him when he gave me an introduction to my new duties and what he expected from me in a practiced manner which suggested he had made the same speech a number of times before.

I returned to the office and began the working introduction to my new duties. It was the practice of the Department to work in pairs and to share a desk and I was allocated to work with Eric Fuller. Eric had about ten years' service and had already been working in the office about six months; I found him to be a good partner to team up with and immediately settled down to learn the workings of the Department from him. He was a quiet reliable man, who had a good head on his shoulders and was hoping to move into the CID after his time in the office.

The first morning was spent with Eric giving me advice, issuing me with a diary in which I was expected to fill in each day with a description of the duties I had performed. He also introduced me to the rest of the staff, some of whom I already knew, and explained the hours of work. Normally the office worked split shifts; this allowed for attendance at the magistrate's court in the morning with a return to work in the evening. There was some flexibility, but most of the activity was centred in the evening and early morning when many of team operations were carried out. Officers were encouraged to develop their own contacts or 'snouts' in the community and there were limited funds to pay for information. According to Eric the work was split into three categories of investigation; firstly into the whole range of criminal vice offences, and then drugs offences and finally licensing matters. All these categories of work required the preparation of files, containing witness statements and other additional information which would assist the presentation at court by the prosecution solicitor. After the admin matters had been settled Eric suggested that we would work a split shift and he would take me out in the evening and introduce me to my new place of work.

I turned up later that evening and Eric took one of the plain clothes vehicles, which was a small dirty green van, and we set off for a tour of the area. The 'red light' district was a large square consisting of two main roads, Fox Lane in the north and Clarence Street in the south, separated by a number of small parallel roads together with a public park, Princess Park, almost in the centre. The women prostitutes used most of the roads, whilst the male sexual activity was centred in the park with particular use being made of the male public toilets situated by the park's main gates. According to Eric the women prostitutes could be divided into three groups. The high-class girls, who rarely walked the streets, preferring to run their activities from their own premises through the use of a telephone, they often had regular clients and charged at the top end of the market. They could make a lot of money and a few of them of them eventually went into business running their own brothels. The second group worked mainly on the street, sometimes bringing clients to a room in a house that they shared with other girls. Other members of this group, who were perhaps starting out in the trade, worked the streets looking out for clients in cars and then directed them to sites which were quiet enough to perform sex without disruption. The final group were at the bottom of the pecking order, charging the lowest rates and usually making use of back alleys. Some of these women operated on their own, whilst others had male pimps allegedly looking after them and taking a cut of their earnings. Finally there was a small sub group, who were women who made the occasional visit to the area, mainly to boost their finances; these included housewives and students.

After our tour Eric suggested that I should get to know the women working the area, he said that they were an invaluable source of information if treated properly. He went on to explain that they all accepted that they were going to be arrested for prostitution whilst operating as prostitutes, this was one of the facts of the trade, but there was an informal arrangement agreed by both Plain Clothes officers and the girls that these arrests would not happen too frequently. If a girl was a good source of information she might get arrested once every six months, in other cases once a month was the usual time limit. I had bought my car a few months previously and it was decided that because I was not yet known I would use the vehicle the following night, with Eric concealed in the back, to pick up and arrest some of the women, both as a way of introducing myself and also to become familiar with the charging procedure at DHQ.

The following evening I drove to the office in my car, a light blue Sunbeam Alpine, and Eric smiled when he saw the vehicle, saying that I would have no trouble picking up the girls, who initially would not recognise the vehicle. Plain Clothes work required changing vehicles frequently in order to keep one step ahead so that the women would not become too familiar with the vehicles that we were using, making it easier for us to approach them. As a result Plain Clothes Departments swapped cars and vans and we even occasionally raided the main transport office and borrowed ex-CID vehicles which had been taken out of service to be sold at the local car auction. That evening we prepared my car with Eric as comfortable as possible in the back, and after I disconnected the rear interior light we set off shortly about ten o'clock. He guided me round the area at a fairly slow speed when we spied a tall slim woman standing alone on a corner. Eric recognised her as Patti La Mar, an old regular, whose real name was Avril Soames. Eric said that she used her 'work name' because she thought it gave her a bit of class and consequently enabled her to charge a higher price when negotiating business. I pulled up beside her and wound the window down; she came over and asked me if I was looking for business. I nodded and smiled at her; I noticed that she was well made up with a watchful expression. She looked up and down the street and then told me what she was charging. Before I could reply she opened the car door and quickly jumped in. Eric sat up and I told her she was under arrest, she swore quickly and as she turned to open the door I drove off and was on the way to the station before she could leap out.

On arrival at the station Sergeant Anderson, in charge of the night charge office, heard my evidence and charged her with the offence of prostitution; a check with our Records Office revealed unsurprisingly that she had previous convictions, but no outstanding warrants and as a result she was bailed to attend court the following morning. Eric told me that as her previous conviction for this offence was over six months ago she would probably be fined. He said there was an unofficial policy at the magistrate's court, which was used when dealing with prostitution. Firstly the women were expected to plead guilty and provided they did not appear too often before the court they were fined. If on the other hand they made frequent appearances before the bench they could face imprisonment up to six months. Looking at the approach taken by the court it seemed to me that it appeared to be based on the recognition that these women provided a service, which although it was considered a crime should also be tolerated. As a result, this approach by the Court gave Plain Clothes staff considerable leverage with the girls which they used if they were going to mount an operation and information from the girls would help in insuring a successful result.

We resumed our patrol and this time, turning into Harrop Street picked up a woman who Eric said he had not seen before and must be new to our area. She was rough and unkempt, giving her name as Sheila Dawson, having recently arrived from the Liverpool area. Eric was suspicious of her account, telling me that he did not think she was telling the truth. Dawson was charged and bailed, since she appeared to have no previous convictions. Eric was still not convinced, but let the matter drop and we resumed our patrol.

We went out for a third attempt to see if I could again spring the trap, but initially we had no such luck. As we were deciding to return to DHQ and retire for the night we spotted a woman at the top of Fox Lane. As I drew up to her Eric said he knew her as one of his informants. I stopped the car and she got in and Eric introduced her to me as Sylvia Campbell, a cheerful Scottish woman who had arrived in the area about twelve months previously. She had left her husband in Glasgow, because she said he was a wife beater and since she had been unable to find work in her home city had moved south, saying that she had taken to prostitution until something better turned up. Talking to her I got the impression that she actually enjoyed her present job, which I found surprising since most of the women who I met during my time in Plain Clothes claimed to have taken it up as a last resort. It made me wonder if all the women engaged in prostitution were telling the truth about how they viewed their work. Maybe some of them enjoyed it, but felt the pressure to say otherwise in order to conform to the attitude prevalent within our society. During my time in the office I was never able to resolve this conundrum. Eric asked her if she had any news for him, but she said no as the area was pretty quiet at the moment. We dropped her off and returned to the office to retire from duty. Before Eric left Plain Clothes he handed over most of his informants to me, although by then I had also began to build up my own collection of 'snouts'. I had now begun to appreciate how important it was to have first-rate informants if you wanted to keep on top of your game as a Plain Clothes officer.

The following morning we both turned up at the magistrate's court to deal with the two arrests. Patti La Mar turned up on time, looking quite smart and anxious to get the hearing over, but there was no sign of our other prisoner, Sheila Dawson. I went up with Patti, whilst Eric hung on at Reception to collect Dawson as a late arrival. Patti pleaded guilty and was fined five pounds, but Sheila Dawson never turned up and I applied to the court and was granted a warrant for her arrest. On our way back we called at the address she had given, but she was not there and Eric said that if she had got any sense she would have left the area. Three days later I received a message from the Records Office saying that Sheila Dawson alias Joan Stapleton was wanted on warrant by the police in Liverpool for prostitution and larceny. In those days communication between police forces was far more leisurely than the instant response of today and many criminals were aware of this fact and took advantage of it whenever they could.

Having now finished my period of induction into the work of the department Eric told me it was now time to look at a couple of jobs that he and his previous partner had not been able to finish and were still outstanding as far as he was concerned. One in particular needed addressing and it involved the activities of one Leroy Franks. This young man had come to Eric's notice as a result of information he had been given which suggested he had been causing injuries to a young woman prostitute he was supposedly looking after as her pimp. The offence of living on immoral earnings or 'pimping' appears in principle to be straightforward in that the principle evidence is gained through the activities of the woman prostitute who is associated with the man. In practice, however, this can be more difficult than it seems. Many prostitutes will say that they live in fear of their lives from their handlers, which in many cases I knew to be true, and as a result will not come forward to offer evidence voluntarily. Others will say they are in love with their men, which again can appear to be true, and consequently maintain that they would never want to 'shop' them. Faced with these difficulties it was necessary to find different ways as well as observations to secure evidence leading to conviction.

The young woman in this case was called Mabel Brown who had been recently admitted to the local Casualty department with a broken nose and other facial injuries. Eric and his previous partner had managed to see her alone after the assault and found out that Franks had beaten her up during an argument over her perceived failure to service sufficient clients. Mabel would not give evidence against Franks because she said that he had been drinking and had apologised to her after he had recovered. They had made up when he agreed that he would never hit her again, however, she must have had second thoughts because she decided to give the officers details of where she worked and the role Franks played when she was picking up clients. Eric now wanted to get this enquiry back on track and I was more than happy to help him.

Mabel and Franks shared a first-floor flat in one of the large houses overlooking Princess Park. The area around the park spoke of shabby gentility; originally these houses had been built in Edwardian times for wealthy merchants working in the city. They were three-storey, large semi-detached properties with the occasional detached villa, as they were described locally, all of whom had now been converted into flats. Although the area was run down Mabel and Franks must have been finding a fair amount of money to cover the rent, since the rents on these flats were substantial, as the landlords knew or guessed the occupations many of their residents were engaged in and charged accordingly.

Her normal routine was to pick up men from the top of the Lane and then arrange for them to drive her to the flat. She said that Franks was sometimes hidden in the flat, ostensibly to keep an eye on her, but also to keep a lookout to see if the client had anything worth stealing. Sometimes she worked in the afternoons with regular clients, but more usually at night making sure to finish around midnight, which allowed Franks and herself to visit a night club before going to bed in the early hours of the morning. Eric and I checked the house and found that their routine had not changed from the details she had given previously. We decided to take observations over the next couple of nights, using the Division's mail van as our observation point. We parked it about one hundred yards from the address and found that Mabel was a busy worker with us recording eight men during the two-day period visiting the flat. We recorded the car details of each client, although we were hoping not to use them, but if Franks was going to plead 'not guilty' then we might require them as witnesses. Later at the office we discussed how we were going to present the case and we agreed that, if necessary, we would summon Mabel as a hostile witness, which would offer her some protection, since she could then claim to her 'boyfriend' that she had not assisted the police in their investigation should his solicitor challenge her appearance at court during the trial.

The following morning Eric and I went to see Reggie Cousins, who had now settled into the job of running the department as Plain Clothes sergeant. After discussing what we had found it was agreed that we had enough evidence to arrest Franks for the offence of immoral earnings, but Reggie wanted us to plan the arrest as we had to get into the flat and up to the first floor without causing too much disturbance and possible damage. He asked whether it would be possible to enlist the help of one of the other residents, ideally on the ground floor to gain entry; we agreed to make inquiries to see if we could set this up. We knew that the best time to get into the house to make inquiries would be early in the morning when Mabel and Franks would be sleeping off the effects of the previous night.

Before leaving the office the following morning we decided to initially use a fictitious missing person inquiry when interviewing the residents we came across which would help us assess whether the individual would be supportive and give us assistance. Once we had identified the right person we could reveal our true intentions and ask for their help. We got to the house just after nine and I scanned the doorbells; there were four flats in total, two on the ground floor and one each on the next two floors. Franks' flat and the one above had no name with the bell, but the two on the ground floor offered some hope. One gave the name of Miss Annabel Potts and the other a Mr Herbert Jones.

Mr Jones was not at home so I tried for Miss Potts, eventually the door opened and a delightful old lady stared up at us through some very thick glasses. We introduced ourselves and she invited us into her flat, which was well kept, complete with old-fashioned chairs and dark furniture. Miss Potts was a well-spoken lady whose eyesight might have deteriorated, but whose brain was still as sharp as a razor. We mentioned a missing person from the neighbourhood for a while and as we talked she offered us a cup of tea. Eric then asked if there were any problems with the rest of the residents in the house and with that her eyes lit up and she began to describe the activities of Franks and Mabel. As she spoke it became obvious that she had no time for Franks, who she described as a bully, but she obviously liked Mabel, who she said had been led astray. After hearing this I looked at Eric and he nodded and we then told Miss Potts the real reason for our visit and asked her if she would help us. She became quite excited at the prospect of a police raid and said she would give us all the assistance she could. Rather than ask her to open the door to allow us access we suggested that we obtain a copy of her front door key which we would use for the raid. She gave me her key without any hesitation and I headed off to obtain a copy whilst Eric continued his conversation with her. About a quarter of an hour later I returned with a copy and returned her original key to her. Before leaving we crept upstairs to the first floor to examine the entrance to the flat occupied by Franks and Mabel. The front door did not look too secure and I reckoned a well-placed blow from our trusty lump hammer would gain entry without much trouble. We crept back down stairs and left the house to plan the operation for the next night.

We discussed the options with Reggie and decided that a small team from our office, including Reggie, together with a uniformed constable would suffice. Eric and I would leave about ten o'clock and see if Mabel was at work and if we could locate Franks, after which we would use the Force radio to inform Reggie who would then come and join us with the rest of the team. When Mabel brought in her next client we would enter the house after them and hope to catch them all in the flat. At nine thirty we briefed everybody and Eric and I left the station in a borrowed CID car and parked up not far from the house. Eric left the car and went into the park, creeping along the boundary wall until he was level with the house, whilst I stayed in the vehicle and waited. Time went by with no sign of activity and then a car pulled up outside and Mabel and the driver got out and went into the house. Eric emerged from the bushes and beckoned that the raid was on. I made the radio call and moved the car up to the house. Eric crossed over the road and told me he had seen Franks at the window after which he had watched him draw the curtains together when he saw the client's car pulling up outside. I took the hammer out of the car and we walked quietly up the path to the front door as the Plain Clothes van drew up and I carefully opened the front door, noticing Miss Potts had opened her window curtains to peer out at us; I waved to her and entered the house followed by the rest of the team.

We made our way up the stairs as silently as we could and gathered on the landing at Frank's flat door. I looked at the door, took aim and hit the woodwork as hard as I could; the door shuddered and then opened. All thought of silence had been replaced by speed and we dashed in through the living room into the bedroom. We burst in to see Mabel in bed with her client, who looked as though he was having heart failure. I peered under the bed, but Franks was not there whereupon Eric and I, as of one mind, headed for the wardrobe, opened it and found him inside staring at us in surprise. We hauled him out, cautioned him and told him he was under arrest for immoral earnings. By this time Mabel had recovered, although her client still looked as though he had not properly recovered from the shock of our entry and we took him to one side to obtain his name and address, after which we told him he could leave the premises. Two members of the team took Franks down to the van and as they did so I heard a shout coming from the landing. I turned and saw the client returning with the uniformed constable who had caught him trying to rush out of the house still dressed only in his underpants. Trying not to smile, I told him to get dressed after which he left the building. We had a brief discussion with Mabel and told her that her boyfriend would be staying the night at DHQ and given his previous record we would be objecting to bail when he appeared at court. She asked if she would be needed as a witness at court and Eric said it depended on whether Franks was prepared to plead guilty.

The following morning Franks appeared before the Stipendiary Magistrate who after looking at his previous record, which included convictions for robbery and larceny, decided to remand him in custody to appear at the Crown Court when the case would go ahead. We left the court knowing that our next job was to prepare a file for the prosecution barrister proving the facts of the case, and on the way back I dropped off the extra key with Miss Potts. We had another cup of tea and I told her what had happened, after which she told me that Franks had got what he deserved. Two months later Franks was convicted and received three years' imprisonment, whilst Mabel stayed on at the flat for a while and then moved down to London to start life afresh, or so she told me. Did I believe her? No, not really, Mabel was a good-looking girl and during the short time I had got to know her I gained the impression that she was used to the good things in life, which included spending money and going to night clubs. Once she settled down in London I reckoned it wouldn't be long before she was back on 'the game', there would be too many temptations for her to ignore in her new environment.

As I have already mentioned one of our responsibilities within the Plain Clothes Department was to investigate adult missing person reports, where the uniform members of the division had made preliminary enquiries but had not been able to find the person concerned. Our objective was to establish whether they had suffered harm, leading perhaps to their death or an accident leading to memory loss. Once we were satisfied that there was no cause to suspect foul play we tried to locate them, but some of them had obviously decided to go missing with the objective of starting a new life and had made plans to help them achieve their objective. In such circumstances many of them were able to disappear without trace, making them impossible to find. Our office did have the occasional success in tracing them, but if they did not want their whereabouts to become known to their family there was little we could do, other than inform their relatives that they were safe and well.

One of my successes in tracing an adult missing from home involved a long-distance lorry driver whose wife reported him missing. The reporting officer had made some enquiries without any success and I was given his report with a request to assess if the matter could be progressed any further. His wife had already been interviewed but I decided to see her again to find out if she had remembered any other facts which might prove useful. Mrs Rushton was in her late thirties with two teenage children, she seemed a woman who had the weight of the world on her shoulders, conscientious, but without much humour. We went over the information she had provided, but she couldn't bring any new facts to light. Her husband, Harold, had left for work at the usual time, he wasn't staying overnight, as sometime happened if he was on a long-haul journey, and she expected him back about six o'clock that evening for his meal. When he didn't return at the usual time she did not initially have any concern until a couple of hours elapsed and then she rang the haulage firm he worked for to see if they could give her some information. She contacted the night watchman at Belltown Haulage, who hadn't seen her husband, but gave her the manager's home telephone number. The manager must have been out, because he did not get back to her until after ten o'clock, telling her not to worry as the lorry must have broken down and they would sort things out in the morning.

When she rang the firm the following morning she found that the lorry had been returned that evening at the normal time and her husband had left the premises as usual. Everybody who she spoke to at the premises told her that they assumed he was returning home, having seen him get into his car and drive off. The constable who took the initial report from Mrs Rushton had requested observations locally for the car, but had not received any response. He had also contacted the local hospitals, but again there was no information about Mr Rushton. His wife told me that there were no problems within the marriage and she had no idea why he had gone missing. I asked her to give me the names of her husband's friends and relatives, but other than his brother, who lived in the London area, all the others that she knew of were people from the haulage firm. I thanked her and got back in the car, but before turning on the engine I stopped and went over in my mind what I had been told.

I sensed that Mrs Rushton had told me the truth from her perspective, but that was only half the story. There was no evidence, so far, to indicate that Harold Rushton had come to some harm and therefore the circumstances seemed to indicate that he had done 'a runner', as we unofficially classified these types of reports. The circumstances seemed to suggest that he had left home and moved elsewhere. Given the picture which I was beginning to build up it seemed to me that enquiries at the haulage firm might provide some answers to completing the puzzle as to why Harold Rushton had felt to need to disappear and where he might be.

I drove to the firm's address, which was located near the railway viaduct in Belltown close to the docks. Most of the yard was empty of vehicles and I parked my car next to a Bentley, near an office building at the rear. Inside I was introduced to Mr Rawson, the owner, and Mr Fields, the office manager. I told them the nature of my visit and asked them if they could shed any light on Harold Rushton's disappearance. Mr

IN THE 'NICK' OF TIME

Rawson, who was obviously used to taking centre stage, started by saying that Harold had worked for him for about six years, was a good driver and employee, who had never been in any trouble. I noticed that while this was going on Mr Fields was fiddling with a pen and looking out of the window. When Mr Rawson finished I turned to Mr Fields and asked him if he had any ideas as to why Rushton had gone missing. He replied by saying that he wasn't sure, coughed and then said nothing came to mind. I changed the subject by supplying both men with the three names given to me by Mrs Rushton, who said that they were friends of her husband, and asked them if these drivers were available for interview. Mr Rawson didn't know and referred the answer to Mr Fields, who thought for one moment and said that two of them would be back about 6pm, whilst the third was on an overnight stop, returning in the following afternoon. I arranged with the two men for me to return later in the day to speak to the other two drivers. Before I left Mr Rawson asked if this matter would get in the press, saying that this might have an adverse effect on his firm. In reply I said that they would not be interested in this story at this stage, but we might have to resort to them if circumstances changed for the worst.

I left the firm thinking that Mr Fields gave the impression that he might have some more information that could be useful, but that it would be probably better to speak to him without Mr Rawson or anybody else being present. I returned to the office and wrote up the report giving an account of what had taken place. I then spent the next couple of hours writing up a prosecution file for licensing offences at one of our more notorious pubs and returned to Belltown Haulage at about 5pm. By now the yard had filled up with lorries and I noticed that the Bentley had left, which I took to mean that Mr Rawson had probably gone home. I went into the office and found Mr Fields at his desk. I recounted what Mrs Rushton had told me when she had contacted him the evening her husband had failed to return home and asked him if that was correct. Mr Fields looked embarrassed and admitted that he had no idea what Rushton was up to and had made the story about the lorry breakdown, not wishing to upset her at the time. I asked him what had taken place when Harold Rushton had returned with his vehicle to the depot on the final day after completing his delivery. Fields told me that Rushton had parked up, walked over to the office and said to him that he was leaving and asked to be paid up. Fields said he was surprised since this was the first he had heard of Rushton's wish to leave and asked him what the problem was, to which Rushton had replied that it was nothing to do with the job, but he had felt it was time to move on since he was having problems at home. According to Fields Rushton gave him no indication he was leaving his family and he had no idea where he might have gone in answer to my last question that I put to him.

Before leaving the yard I spoke to Rushton's two colleagues at work whose names had been supplied by Mrs Rushton, but they claimed to have no knowledge as to why Rushton had left his wife and family. From their responses to my questions I didn't believe them, but in the circumstances there was little I could do. As I was walking back to the car I had a sudden brainwave and went back to the office asking Fields if

I could have Rushton's work sheets going over the previous six months. He gave me Rushton's records for the previous twelve months and I returned to our office to see if I could trace any common pattern which might indicate whether Rushton was doing anything out of the ordinary. I enlisted Eric's support and we went through the paperwork together to see if anything of significance came to light. After about half an hour it struck us that every fortnight and sometimes on a weekly basis he was visiting northeast England, especially Hartlepool, and significantly it was always accompanied with an overnight stay. I decided to enlist the help of the local police in Hartlepool to see if Rushton's location could be found by asking them if they could find his car.

After two weeks they came back and told me Rushton's vehicle had been found on a second-hand car lot in the town and after making enquiries with the staff obtained the name and address of the owner. I supplied them with Rushton's description and armed with this information they went to the address which had been given during the sale and located my missing person. They found that Rushton had started another home in the area, with a woman and a young child. He had decided to leave his family in Belltown and had now moved in with his second family. He asked for his present location to remain secret, saying that he intended to divorce his wife and remarry when his finances improved. It only remained for me to see his first wife, tell her that her husband was safe and well and that he that he had promised to get in touch with her in the future. It was not a pleasant interview in that on hearing the news she not surprisingly got most upset, giving me her views on Rushton and men in general. I was glad to leave the house in one piece.

During that summer Diane and I spent a holiday together in Germany. She had a German pen friend called Elizabeth, who was married to Hans whose parents had a holiday cottage situated in the Black Forrest area of south-west Germany. The plan was to meet up with Hans and Elizabeth and spend a week with them in the cottage. However, just before we were ready to start our holiday they told us that there had been a fire at the cottage and the arrangements had been changed; we were now meeting them at a gasthaus in the village near the cottage. We drove into France and then Germany and eventually found the village near the headwater of the Danube. The gasthaus was on one side of the road whilst directly opposite was an inn with a large veranda, full of tables and chairs, all occupied by the locals drinking and eating in the sunshine. We booked in as husband and wife, although there was a problem over our passports, which told a different story. The innkeeper accepted our excuse that we had not yet had chance to change Diane's passport; in response he looked as though he had heard that story before, but he gave us the benefit of the doubt and showed us to our room. We settled in with Diane using the communal bathroom first, since she wanted to go over to the inn to see if Elizabeth and Hans had arrived, leaving me to follow on after.

When she finished I went in and locked the door and spruced up for the introduction to her friends, and when I finished I turned the key back to unlock the door. I was flummoxed when it wouldn't open, I turned the key again in both directions for a few times, but still the door refused to budge; I was now in a quandary, what to do next? I banged on the door to attract attention and shouted for assistance, but there was no reply and nobody came to investigate; I knew Diane had left and it seemed that the building was empty. I made a couple more attempts to open the door and again without success and now I started to think of other avenues of escape. There was a window and I thought perhaps that offered a way out; I opened it and stared out directly across the road towards the inn and the veranda opposite which was still full of the locals having a good time. I closed the window and made one more attempt to open the door, again no effect. I decided that the time had come for action and opened the window and looked down onto the pavement, which was a drop of about five feet below. There was nothing for it and I started to climb out on to the window ledge; at that point the locals started to take an interest and I could see them pointing and nudging each other at my activities. My imagination started to work overtime and I thought they would be saying, 'Is that how the English normally leave the bathroom?' but by now I couldn't care less since I had decided that I was not going to spend my holiday locked in that room. I jumped down on to the pavement and strolled across the road trying to look nonchalant, but without much success.

I could see Diane and her friends looking at me with amazement and after I joined them I had to give an explanation for my behaviour. When I told them of my difficulties with the lock my new German friends laughed and said I had fallen victim to a double lock which was commonly fitted to most houses in Germany. I must have turned the key twice, without knowing when I originally locked the door, and because of this became trapped in the room. By now the locals were also anxious to hear my explanation and as a result, everyone in the inn was amused, however it did not last long and we settled down to a very enjoyable holiday. One incident which did cause a slight problem was that Diane told her friends that I was a Plain Clothes detective and over time this information passed round the inn and before I knew it I had become a Scotland Yard detective or perhaps a rival to Sherlock Holmes. We decided afterwards that in future when we were on holiday or anywhere else for that matter and somebody asked after my occupation, we would tell them I was a lorry driver.

Returning to the office after the holiday I found that the department had become embroiled with an expected visit by HM Inspector of Constabulary who was making his annual inspection of the Force and this year our division had been selected as part of his inspection. Everything in the office was examined by Reggie; the place was tidied up, the paperwork filed in order and a sample of recent case files laid out ready for his inspection. I was working 'days' during his visit and because of my holidays had escaped most of tidying up and with little to do I was gazing out of the window waiting to spot the HMI's car. Nothing was happening and I looked around and saw a large green bushy plant in a pot near to me on the windowsill. This was in its normal spot and I remember Eric telling me that it was a cannabis plant which had been seized during one of the drug raids which the Department had organised before I joined. Staff members used to water it regularly and as a result it now seemed to thrive in our office environment. I turned back to the window and noticed that the HMI had arrived and having exchanged a salute was now shaking hands with our chief super. I came out of my reverie and wondered if Reggie knew about the plant and whether I should move it, but he had disappeared. Suddenly I saw him coming along the corridor towards me and I mentioned the plant to him, but he obviously had no idea of its identity and a worried look crossed his face. I suggested removing it before the HMI turned up and Reggie agreed, telling me to hide it somewhere in the station; he suggested that it would not look out of place on the canteen windowsill. So I went back into the office and collected the plant and went back along the corridor with the intention of going down the stairs to the canteen, but before I could get there I ran into the HMI and the chief super coming up the stairs. I came to a halt at the top of the stairs, smiled politely at everybody and waited for the inevitable question about my possession of a cannabis plant. My mind was working overtime to find a suitable explanation, but nothing came to mind, my brain had frozen and then I realised that the HMI was speaking to me. He was saying what a good idea it was to have plants around the station and relief came over me when I realised that he had no idea what sort of plant I had in my arms. The chief super on the other hand looked at me and the plant with a slightly puzzled look, nodded, and they both walked on to his office and I quickly went downstairs and placed the plant in the corner of the canteen.

The inspection went off without a hitch; our office was complimented on its work and tidiness, whilst the

CID got a 'black mark' for not having its paperwork up to date. When the HMI had left the chief super turned up in our office and inquired about the plant, which had now been restored to its rightful place in our office. Reggie identified the plant to Dougie Fairbanks and said it was useful for teaching purposes, but our chief super was not impressed and told him to get rid of it. Disposing of the plant made me realise that Eric and I had not concentrated our efforts to any great extent on the drugs scene in Hathersage and maybe it was time to take a look.

The opportunity for us to get involved arrived in a somewhat unusual manner a short time later. I was in the office late one evening with Eric finishing some paperwork when the phone rang and it was Fox Lane station telling us there was a problem at the Congo Club. It seemed that a number of members from the club had been taken ill and suspicion pointed to the cannabis they had been using. The initial reaction from most of our colleagues present in the office was to say that it served the members right for smoking rubbish. I thought differently, in that it seemed to me that it might open up an opportunity to identify some of the major local dealers and producers of the drug. Eric agreed with me and so did Reggie. We got in the car and I drove to the scene.

There were about thirty people inside together with a couple of uniformed officers present when we arrived. Three members had been taken to hospital and half a dozen said they felt woozy, but did not want to go to the Casualty Department. We started to take names and addresses and I searched the floor, finding some discarded cigarettes which I inspected, although nothing seemed amiss. However, I put them in an evidence bag for them to be examined by our forensic laboratory. None of the members were very forthcoming and the enquiry looked as though it was going to be hard work, until I spotted Clarence Dawson Junior in the crowd. I looked at him and nodded towards the entrance; he nodded back and left immediately and I counted twenty and slowly followed him out of the premises. I don't think anyone was paying any attention since Reggie had gathered the club members around him at the time and was trying to gain their co-operation in order to deal with the situation, telling them that he didn't want anybody else to fall ill.

I met Clarence outside and we drifted round to the back of the club, and when the coast was clear I asked him what had happened. He told me that two men had come to the club selling cannabis, which they claimed was top quality at a very good price and as a result many members had taken up their offer. He knew they were major suppliers who had been there before and they were using a house in Harefield Street situated near Somerford City's ground. He then gave me their names and addresses and I thanked him and told I would do everything possible to keep him out of the picture, and he left for home and I returned to the club. Sergeant Cousins was thanking the members for their co-operation, stressing that any information supplied would be treated as confidential; the members still seemed to require some more persuasion. I thought one or two would contact us as anonymous callers with some information the following day and before we left I took Reggie to one side and put him in the picture.

We all went back to our office to discuss the situation and Reggie said that we should act quickly before the problem with the drug caused more illness. He left to get a search warrant from a magistrate who lived nearby and we began to collect as many of our colleagues as we could as well as three uniform constables. Half an hour later we all assembled and held a short briefing session, after which we made our way to the house. I parked our van down the street and two of the uniformed lads went round the back, leaving the rest of us to quietly move to the front of the house. There were lights on downstairs and we waited for everybody to get into position and then Reggie said, 'Go.' I had the inevitable hammer, but we didn't require it since we found that the door was ajar and we were all in the house in seconds. We did not want to give them time to flush the drugs down the toilet, which was one of the usual ways of disposing of such property. The plan worked well in that we arrested three men and seized a large quantity of cannabis.

When the club members were told of the arrests they confirmed the information given to me by Clarence, in fact two of those in hospital, all of whom recovered, were more than happy to act as witnesses. Reggie requested that nobody from the club should be prosecuted, which was accepted. However, the operation was criticised by the Drug Squad who were quick to complain that they had not been consulted and we could have jeopardised one of their operations. In response Reggie told them that given the circumstances time was at a premium and that as he had also secured the backing of Deputy Div Commander Supt. Allison, who agreed that we should respond with speed, he consequently had no option but to mount a quick operation. His actions paid off because not only did we arrest the drug dealers, Reggie's name was put forward by the chief superintendent for a commendation for good police work. After the science lab had examined the drugs we had seized they told us that it had been mixed with a quantity of sawdust to bulk it up; the sawdust, however, had contained a toxic substance which introduced a mild poison to the mixture. The three drug dealers were dealt with at Crown Court and given extended prison sentences to take into account the harm they had caused.

CHAPTER NINE

It was time for Eric to return to uniform duties and the office gave him a good send-off, after which he and I had a quiet pint at our local pub, the White Hart. He had been an excellent partner to team up with and I had learnt a lot from working with him. I knew he was anxious to join the CID and two months later his application was granted and he began a CID aide course which later led to him eventually being transferred full-time into the CID. Eric was one of those officers who were never able to pass the promotion educational exams, although he passed the law exams without a problem. He had to wait for about ten years when a change took place and it was decided that the educational requirement within the promotion examination was no longer necessary. As a result that part of exam was removed from the system and shortly after Eric was promoted detective sergeant and before retiring was moved up to detective chief inspector. We remained friends and he and I kept in regular touch over the years.

My new partner Jimmy Dolan did not arrive straight away after Eric had left which meant I was given a month's special duty. But first I was asked to look after a detective constable who was arriving by train from Metropolitan Police to collect one of our prisoners, who was wanted on warrant by the Met, and escort him back to London. I drove to the main station, parked the car and walked to the barrier to await the London evening train expected to arrive about six o'clock. The only description I had been given about this officer, who was coming from West End Central Police Station, was that he would be wearing a blue suit; I had mentioned in response that I would be in my grey suit wearing a red tie. I stood and watched the London train pull into the platform and watched as a large number of people get off and slowly made their way through the barrier and into main the station concourse. I assumed that that this police officer would be a similar height to myself and subconsciously looked out for a man about six foot or over in a dark blue suit. Initially I couldn't spot anybody who fitted this description until I realised that a small figure in a light blue suit with a pink shirt was making his way towards me. He smiled and introduced himself as DC Malcolm Westgate and I suddenly realised why the Met Police had been given the nickname of the 'metronomes' by others in the Police Service. We went back to the car and I drove to the small hotel on the Division which we had booked for him to spend the night before his return to London the following morning.

Initially I had some suspicions of a man who wore a light blue suit and especially a pink shirt, which in those days was associated with being a queer. But I was assured by this member of the Vice Squad that this dress sense was acceptable in the scene in which he operated, such as Soho, where formal suits were not the order of the day. Within a short period of time I found Malcolm Westgate to be a confident, well-spoken, affable character who had never been 'up north' before and was interested in the City and our policing methods. As we swapped stories I realised how insular policing could be with us all working in our respective police forces with very little contact between us. Malcolm wanted to see the City's night life and it was my job to introduce him to our clubs and bars. We started in the Grosvenor Club, where we had a meal and some drinks. He said he had been given expenses and pulled out a thick wad of banknotes which reminded me of a second-hand car salesman. It was then that it was brought home to me that the Met Police were in a different league when it came to expenses. I had been told that if I spent more than five pounds during the evening I would have to fund the difference, but given Malcolm's desire to prove how generous the Met could be I had now become more relaxed thinking that money would not be a problem.

We finished the night about three o'clock and I dropped him off at his hotel, promising to return about nine o'clock that morning. I managed to fulfil my promise, but my head was still feeling the effects of the night before. Malcolm on the other hand appeared bright and breezy having eaten a full English breakfast. I took him to the DHQ where he signed for the prisoner and I took them both back to the main station, secured an empty compartment for them and wished Malcolm a safe journey back to London.

After ten years at Sommerford, Chief Constable

Captain Goldworthy retired and was replaced by an officer from a southern force. The new man took his time visiting the divisions and it was a year after his appointment before I saw him in the flesh. However, as soon as he took over he started to make waves by making it very clear in the local press that he felt that the city centre had far too many night clubs which were attracting a rowdy element into the city. In the circumstances he promised that the police would take a far tougher policy in bringing this problem under control. From his description to the press it seemed to the locals that the city centre had been suddenly turned into Sodom and Gomorrah and that the writing was on the wall for many of the clubs. It was in light of this change in policy and the fact that my new partner had not arrived which resulted in my selection to help implement this new approach to the City's nightlife by inspecting the clubs, a task which caused envy amongst my colleagues. I was told that I was being seconded to the Licensing Department for a month and to go the following Monday to Force HQ and report to Chief Inspector George Appleton.

When I arrived I found Mr Appleton to be a jovial character who obviously enjoyed his work and who turned out to be a friend of Reggie Cousins. He told me that my job for the next month was to visit, as an undercover officer, every club in the city centre and take observations as to how the club was being operated; this included the performance of the live acts, together with the conduct of the staff and the public. Apparently all the officers in the Licensing Department were well known to the management of the various clubs and it had been decided that an officer from out of town would be a more reliable guide in reporting the conduct of these premises.

I was given a list of clubs to be visited and a special entertainment allowance to buy food and drink whilst visiting these premises. On the face of it the job seemed to be a dream appointment and I decided to spend the weekend before starting on the Monday, dividing the city centre into areas and then working out how I was going draw up observations for each of the clubs. I knew I could not sit in the premises laboriously writing up a report and had to devise a short-hand code which I could use as an aide memoir. The other crucial point was to how to remain sober throughout, whilst not showing myself up by continually asking for fruit drinks instead of drinking alcohol, which the club members would be consuming.

On the Monday I started my new duties on the north side of the city centre, in an area which I was relatively unfamiliar with, as I tended to visit the south side, but I was full of enthusiasm for the task in hand. The first club I went in seemed a pretty average sort of establishment; the decor needed smartening up, the beer was watery, the food tasteless and the entertainment would have probably suited an insomniac. The premises was nearly empty, which was not unusual on a Monday night, but overall I thought this club was one of those the chief constable had in mind and my report was written up to that effect. All these factors meant that I was in a remarkably sober condition when I visited the next club feeling hungry and looking forward to being entertained. This place was larger with a brighter, smarter interior. The beer whilst still fizzy was more to my taste, the food was better prepared and the floor show seemed more energetic with strippers who were good looking and giving the appearance of enjoying themselves. There were plenty of people inside and the premises seemed well run and overall it gave a good impression. The third and fourth clubs were about average and by now I was feeling a bit bloated and was getting fed up with the staple diet of chips with pie or burgers. I was beginning to realise as time went by that the club scene was 'much of a muchness' as my grandmother used to say, and I was finding it difficult to keep up the required level of interest. I took some time out and had a walk round the Town Hall Square to freshen up before visiting the fifth and last club of the evening.

After the third week was over I began to realise that I was going to find the final week difficult to manage. The quality of the beer left a lot to be desired and I was beginning to accept that there was not much chance of me becoming drunk; my weight was beginning to increase under the strain of eating the monotonous diet of chips with something else, usually beef burgers or a pie, and I was also beginning to meet the same performers on more than one occasion as they rotated round the clubs. As time went on I was classifying the clubs into good and bad and at this point had found that about two thirds of them fell into this latter category; it would appear the new chief constable had a point. I finished the final week and completed the assignment, promising to see Mr Appleton the following Monday with my last report. I had updated the chief inspector on a regular basis during my stay and as the picture built up of my observations he did not appear to be surprised at the findings. We had our last meeting and he thanked me for my efforts, leaving me to return to my office with much relief. Sometime later the Licensing Department started to crack down on the clubs and many of them started to close. I assumed that my observations must have played a part, although the number of clubs which did close were nowhere near the total amount I had identified; maybe I was too keen, however I think it was more likely that some club owners kept on the right side of the Licensing Department and in particular the chief inspector.

When I returned to the office Jimmy Dolan was already in post; he was an Irishman who was small for a City Policeman, about my age, married with two children. Although he had slightly more service on the Division than me, our paths had never crossed, so he would have to prove himself as far as I was concerned. He seemed willing to learn and so I gave him a similar introduction to the work of the Department as I had received from Eric. During this induction period we used his car, a Ford Anglia, to arrest a couple of prostitutes and I liked his confident approach to the job. I told him that I had a couple of enquiries which needed his assistance to complete and we decided to investigate some information I had been given, by a prostitute, who had been a reliable source in the past, about a brothel which had been set up in Newgate Street. My informant had told me that a woman had set up the premises at number 27 and that she was using two local girls and a third woman, who had recently arrived in the area from out of town. The woman running the brothel was known as Marion and from her accent it was believed that she came from the south and as far as I could tell she also had arrived in our area fairly recently. Marion was operating mainly from the premises during the afternoons, although there was some activity in the evening.

Before I became a member of the Department I had imagined that every other street in our 'red light' district would have a brothel run by a middle-aged 'madam', but in practice I found that such premises were few and far between. When I received the information about the brothel in Newgate Street I checked the office records and found that the last time our department had dealt with similar circumstances involving a woman running a brothel was a conviction recorded over three years ago. Perhaps our area was not genteel enough or maybe there was a shortage of 'madams' in Somerford. In retrospect I should have dug deeper in trying to establish the identity of Marion before commencing our observations, as events were later to show.

My first job was to see whether the department had any contacts in Newgate Street, but nobody could help so I extended my enquiries to the CID and then to Uniform. Initially I did not have any success with either department, until a uniformed constable called Jones told me he had sorted out a dispute between neighbours at number 14 and 16 over children from number 16 playing in the entry at the rear of both houses, causing enough noise to wake up the man at number 14, who worked the night shift at the local rubber factory. Apparently these two families had never got on and trouble flared up between them from time to time, which sometimes led to violence. I was looking for somewhere to use as an observation point and these two addresses did not fit the bill, but

I found that on two occasions we had been told about outbreaks of trouble between the two families from an old couple who lived at number 18, perhaps they might help, I thought. We went to see them and they were more than happy to let us use their front downstairs room for our observations.

At the end of the first day we had the names of the two local girls and I assumed that the older of the two other women was Marion, but the other girl's identity was still unknown. By the end of the second day it was obvious that the women were picking up clients in cars, but they were not using pickup points in our area. I decided that these men were probably being brought from the city centre, since they were all smart, clean-shaven types wearing business suits. We contacted our colleagues on the A Division and Jimmy and I went to see if we could locate the pickup points these girls were using, and eventually we found them at work in the city centre near one of the main hotels. I had also discovered that the house was rented and after some time spent on the phone making enquiries with local estate agents was given Marion's surname as Jennings. The next step was to obtain a warrant from the court to enter the house and when everything was completed we assembled a small team with the intention of raiding the house the following afternoon.

After lunch I briefed my team of colleagues and two uniformed constables and split them into two groups. Jimmy and myself with one uniformed officer went in our car, whilst the rest followed in a Plain Clothes van. We dropped the van off round the corner and Jimmy and I carried on to the rear of the premises. The uniformed constable who was with us was left in the entry at the back of the house and we made our way along a passage turning right along the side of the house. Once we had a good observation point we stood back and waited. Time passed and then a car drew up at the front of the house and the driver and one of the girls got out; there was a brief conversation between the two of them after which they both made their way into the house. We kept back because I was hoping that another of the girls would appear with a client before the previous pair had finished. As luck would have it another car did pull up and I alerted the van and told them to slowly move towards the house. The driver of the second car and the girl walked slowly up to the front door and I waited for them to open the door. By this time Jimmy and I were on their heels and as she opened the front door we rushed up and bundled them into the hallway, by which time I could hear the van pulling up outside with the rest of the team joining us.

The client, who was a big middle-aged man with a red face, was pushed up against the wall as the team moved past into the house. He turned to me and demanded to know what was going on; in reply I smiled and told him we were the City Police raiding a brothel. He looked at me and gave me the impression of a balloon slowly deflating. I asked one of the team to take his details and walked up the hallway to meet a woman who I took to be Marion Jennings. I introduced myself and explained the situation; she was of average height, slightly dumpy and looked in her thirties. I was struck by the fact that she seemed quite calm and composed and not at all put out with what was happening. She was well spoken, with a southern accent, did not raise her voice and gave me the impression she had seen it all before. I asked her to confirm her name and then told she was being arrested for running a brothel. By this time the couple from upstairs had been brought down and we arranged to take the two girls and Jennings to the station. The prisoners were taken out of the house and Jimmy brought the red-faced client to me and introduced him as Councillor Phillips. The councillor now had a worried look on his face and asked if he could have a quiet word with me, I nodded and we both went into the front living room. He began by telling me that he was a friend of the chief constable and before he could get any further I replied by saying that this raid was a matter for the court and because this was seen as a serious offence it was usually dealt by the Stipendiary Magistrate. He paused and we now came to the point that was troubling the councillor when he asked me if he could be kept out of the court proceedings. I told him it depended on whether Miss Jennings was prepared to plead guilty and if so the proceedings would only require police witnesses. He brightened up at this possibility and then wandered round the house looking for Jennings, not realising that she had already left for the station. We ushered him out, secured the house and Jimmy locked up and we too left for the station.

I charged Marion Jennings with brothel keeping and after fingerprinting her spoke to our Criminal Records Office, commonly known to members of the Force as SOMCRO (Somerford Criminal Office). I gave them her details and asked if there was anything known about a Marion Jennings, but they had nothing on her in their system. Although she appeared to be a first offender I still wasn't convinced that this was the case but that was all I could do at the time and there the matter rested. I took one of the girls to one side and asked what she knew about Marion. She wasn't able to supply much more information about her, except that Marion had appeared in the area about a couple of months previously, told her she was going to start a brothel and asked her if she would like to use the facilities. They agreed the financial arrangements and once the operation started she said the premises were well run and everybody taking part had made a lot of money. The only personal information about Marion that she had gleaned was that she had come up from the south coast and been told that Marion needed the money to help with her son's private school fees. I still felt that there was more to this woman than met the eye but I was stymied for the moment.

The following morning we all turned up at the Stipendiary's court where Marion went in the dock and pleaded guilty. The Stipendiary, after hearing that she had no previous convictions, gave her a good telling off and let her off with a hefty fine. I met her as she stepped out of the dock and took her to the Fines Office where she took out her chequebook and wrote a cheque for the amount required. As we left the court she turned to me and said she had learnt a lesson and she would not be troubling us again because she was leaving the district to start a new life. She was true to her word since we never saw her again. About a week later the SOMCRO got in touch to say that the Metropolitan Police Central Record Office had examined the forms we had sent of her fingerprints and confirmed that her real name was

Joyce Carter and she had a record for prostitution and brothel keeping as long as your arm. Once again she was an example of a professional who knew the system and had no doubt moved on to new pastures with a new name to carry on doing what she did best. Although she had put one over us on this occasion I felt that my suspicions had been vindicated.

Male prostitution was not a big part of the work of our Department, unlike the City Centre Plain Clothes. On their patch they seemed to specialise in arresting 'queers' as they were then known, operating in the public toilets found across their division. Thinking back it was probably that we were fortunate in having the most active area for vice in the city and there was more than enough to keep us occupied, without dealing with Gross Indecency as male prostitution was called, to any great extent. When our Department were required to deal with it, the circumstances usually arose by way of a complaint. Eric and I had never cause to investigate an incident of Gross Indecency and it wasn't until Jimmy arrived that I got involved with a complaint alleging such behaviour in the male toilets at the main entrance to Princess Park.

We took it in turns to answer the office phone during the day, whilst the others were at court or on daytime enquiries, and on this day it was my turn. When the phone went I picked it up and found I was talking to the uniformed clerk at the public desk. He told me that a Mr Butters had come to the station to make a complaint about lewd behaviour at the men's public toilet at the entrance to Princess Park. I went downstairs and introduced myself to the complainant who I found to be a man in his fifties, small and thin, dressed in what reminded me of my father's old demob suit. I took him up to the office and listened to his complaint. He said he was a stranger to the area, having come for a job interview in the city centre. He said he had finished the interview, got in his car and drove out along Fox Lane back south towards the Midlands when he decided to find a men's toilet, before settling down for the journey home. He asked directions from a passer-by who suggested he use the toilets by the park. He located the toilets and went in; finding them apparently empty, he started to urinate when one of the toilet cubicles opened and out stepped a young man who was wearing women's lipstick. This man smiled at him and asked if he required his services, saying that there was enough room in the cubicle for them both to enjoy themselves. Mr Butters said he was horror struck to be propositioned in this manner and told the man that he should be ashamed of himself, whereupon the man starting shouting at Mr Butters saying that he was only trying to make a living and there was no need for Mr Butters to get on his high horse. Mr Butters said he thought this man was becoming aggressive and so rushed out of the toilet, jumping into his car and eventually finding the station to report what had taken place.

I asked Mr Butters if he was prepared to make a statement, since if this man was arrested he would be required as a witness. There was a few moments' silence whilst my request was digested by the complainant. He eventually declined saying he could not afford the time off work. I took some details off him, including a description of the young man who had accosted him, and with that he left the station heading back to his home. I looked through the prisoners book and found that the last time the department had locked up males for Gross Indecency had been about six months previously. The queers had obviously thought we had forgotten about their activities in the toilet. The usual way the department set up an operation to catch them was to use a good looking, slightly effeminate member of the office as bait. This officer would enter the toilet, smile sweetly and wait to be approached. If he was propositioned he would arrange to take the man to his car, where his colleague would appear and the individual would be arrested and taken to the station to be charged. There were other variations, such as if the toilet was empty, a colleague would hide in a cubicle and wait for the officer to be approached, after which the arrest took place.

Looking at all the current members of our office there was no one who fitted the bill as bait and so I asked Reggie if we could approach the A Division Plain Clothes Department for assistance. Reggie agreed and a few days later a young fresh-faced Plain Clothes officer, called Vincent Shaw, turned up and offered to help. We took him to the gents' toilets by the park and spent some time examining the premises. Fortunately nobody was using the facility at the time and we were able to have a good look round. Vin, as he was known, soon spotted a number of holes in the cubicle walls, saying that the toilets were obviously well used for this type of activity. From previous experience we knew that the 'queers' operated from late afternoon onwards and we decided to start the operation the following day from 4pm onwards.

IN THE 'NICK' OF TIME

That afternoon the three of us left the station by car and parked up near the park gates and spent some time observing the toilet to see whether there was any activity, but everything seemed quiet. Vin and I got out of the car and went over; he decided to go in and I counted thirty before I followed him into the toilets. When I went inside I found him talking with a young man who answered the description given by Mr Butters. I found out his name was Wilfred Soames and that he had previous convictions for Gross Indecency. We arrested him and took him back to the station; he pleaded guilty and was given two months' imprisonment. There is an interesting follow-up to this tale. A couple of years later I heard that Vin had left the Force and I caught up with him again after a fair amount of time had elapsed when I had progressed to be an inspector with the Discipline and Complaints Department, or Internal Affairs as it would now be known. This time Vincent, as he preferred to be addressed, was now a solicitor, and represented an officer I was investigating for corruption. We exchanged pleasantries and I found he was living with his partner, a man, on the north side of the city. As we continued our conversation he explained that it was during his time in Plain Clothes that he realised he was a queer, and decided that trying to keep his secret was not an option so he left the Force. As we agreed whilst he was in Plain Clothes he had been a good example of the saying 'setting a thief to catch a thief'. Policing in those days had no time for homosexuality within its ranks and if Vincent had decided to remain in the City Police he would have had to keep his feelings very private and resist the possibility of blackmail, if he had formed a relationship with someone who wanted exploit the possibilities that his job might have offered.

My last job as a member of the department was the most difficult I had encountered so far in my career in Plain Clothes. I had made a previous attempt without success and it involved trying to gain enough evidence to bring a charge of Immoral Earnings on a man called Thomas Calderwood. Calderwood was using two sisters for prostitution and I had been told that he liked to inflict a great deal of violence on both of them when the mood took him. He was a big man, about as tall as myself, but a lot heavier, and was subject to fits of rage when crossed. It seemed that both women lived in terror of him and there was a story in the neighbourhood about the eldest sister, Mavis, having her arm broken when she had tried to run away on one occasion. Various efforts had been made by me and other officers to persuade she and her sister to give evidence against him, but they were both terrified of him and refused to help.

The problem I needed to overcome related to the location of Calderwood's address. He lived in a terraced house in a small cul-de-sac off Fox Lane called Emden Street. There were some ten houses in the street and it was a known centre of criminal activity in the area. All the occupants were involved in one sort of crime or another and nobody wanted to co-operate with the police, and as a result direct observations on the premises had been difficult to set up. From the information I had been given both women operated at the same times during the day and the evening and Calderwood had taught them to be careful and to look out for police activity whilst they were working.

We went along Fox Lane and as Jimmy and I passed Emden Street we took the time to discuss how we could tackle this problem. As we looked around I noticed that council workmen were digging up the road near the junction with George Street. Watching them suddenly gave me an idea; I knew that the manager of the local council highways depot, Len Thompson, played bowls with my father and I wondered if he could be persuaded to help. Later that afternoon I went round to the depot and spoke to Mr Thompson; I gave him a brief description of the problem I was up against and asked him if we could borrow one of the canvas tents they sometimes used when working on road repairs. He did not need much persuasion and agreed straight away to provide some assistance. We arranged for Jimmy and myself to meet him at the depot the next morning from where he would take us in a van and help us assemble the tent over a sewer cover, which could then be used as our disguise for the duration, whilst we were at the junction of Fox Lane and Emden Street. He also offered to lend each of us a pair of the department's overalls, which would be a further help whilst we were taking observations on the house.

The following morning we met up early at the depot and Mr Thompson loaded up the gear, whilst we put on the overalls and then climbed into the back of the van. After stopping at the junction we helped erect the tent and climbed in together, with some tools, which we used to remove the grid. We settled down to take observations, but nothing happened during the morning. At lunchtime we saw

Calderwood leave the house, presumably for his daily visit to his local pub for a drink. About 2pm we saw the first signs of activity with Mavis leaving the house, followed by her sister, Susan. About half an hour later Susan returned in a car with a client. Mavis returned on foot also with a client about twenty minutes later. Calderwood returned to the house about three thirty. During the afternoon up to five o'clock when Mr Thompson came to collect us, both women brought a total of five clients to the house and we returned to the Highways depot feeling that we had made a good start. We arranged with Mr Thompson to make a final visit to Emden Street the following day.

We were up bright and early the next morning and once again Mr Thompson dropped us off and we set up our tent. After the previous day's experience we had decided to start later in the morning and we no sooner sat down to commence our observations when Mavis left the house. This time she turned out to be shopping and by the time she had returned Calderwood had left the house. Both women commenced work at 2pm, with Mavis the first one back in a car with a client. During the course of the afternoon the women collected a total of six clients, after which Mr Thompson picked us up and we finished our observations. By this time we felt we had enough evidence to arrest Calderwood and the next problem was to decide how we were going accomplish this objective. I went back to his house in Emden Street and walked along the entry past his back gate, which did not look very substantial. I knew the internal layout of the premises, which was similar to those I had been in on other occasions, and decided to mount an operation to gain entry to the house through the back door. I returned to the office and discussed my plan with Reggie and Jimmy and they agreed with my proposals, suggesting that the best time would be early in the morning when Calderwood and the sisters and most of the inhabitants of the street would be asleep, offering little in the way of resistance. Later that day I obtained a warrant to enter the premises and arrest Calderwood from the court.

At six o'clock the following morning I briefed the team and we set off for Emden Street. Jimmy shinned over the rear gate and once more I used the lump hammer to force open the back door. We found the kitchen empty with some used cups and plates on the table and went through and up the stairs as quickly as we could. By now both women were screaming and Calderwood was bellowing. He came out of his room just as I got up to the top of the stairs; I didn't stop and dived straight at him, catching him in a rugby tackle around the knees. He fell backwards with me on top of him, Jimmy had followed immediately behind me and between the pair of us we had the handcuffs on him before he could move. I got my breath back and told him he was under arrest; by now everyone, including Calderwood, had calmed down and we took them all to the station, after they had dressed.

As we led them into the Charge Office I noticed that Susan had a recent bruise under her right eye. I took her to one side and asked her if Calderwood had struck her; she looked away and I noticed that she had started crying. She turned back towards me and I again asked if Calderwood was responsible, she took a deep breath and nodded. I took her into the Interview

Room and asked one of the uniformed policewomen, who had been with us on the raid, if she would get Susan a cup of tea and take a statement from her, because I sensed she was now ready to tell us her side of the story. I then took Mavis into another Interview Room and told her that Susan had decided to make a statement giving us the whole story. Mavis looked at me with a thoughtful expression and asked what was likely to happen to Calderwood. I told her that the last man I had dealt with for this offence had gone down for four years and with Calderwood's record he could look forward to a much longer stretch in prison. She looked down at her hands, nodded to herself and then said that she would follow her sister's decision and also make a statement. I got her a cup of tea and left her with another policewoman whilst she made her statement. Considering the circumstances the case was going better than I had hoped because with the girls on our side I reckoned we could now secure a straight forward conviction against Calderwood.

At the Crown Court both women gave evidence against Calderwood, who was given six years' imprisonment. About six months later I saw Mavis in the city centre, she looked very smart in a dark business suit. She recognised me and we stopped for a talk for a few minutes. I found out that she was now working in an insurance office, whilst Susan had moved down south to the Birmingham area working in a women's dress shop. She told me that both of them were happy with their lives, hoping now that the past was behind them; I wished her well and we both went our separate ways.

CHAPTER TEN

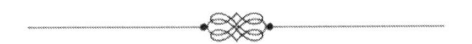

It was now time for me to transfer out of Plain Clothes; I had enjoyed my time in the Department, which had given me another perspective on police work and for the first time provided a greater degree in the use of my own initiative. One of the changes I noticed whilst being in Plain Clothes was the attitude which the rest of the Division showed towards members of the Department. It was as if we had suddenly become endowed with greater authority, power and knowledge. Nobody challenged any request or instruction that I issued and initially I found this change in status difficult to adjust to, but over time I quite enjoyed it and it helped me in gaining experience for the next rank. Although I had moved on I had not finished with the work of the Department, since for another six months I was required to attend court to settle various cases which were still outstanding.

I had hoped to become a CID aide after leaving Plain Clothes, but I had to wait a further six months before a vacancy occurred. I spent this intervening time back in uniform mainly on divisional van duties and for a period of a month as acting sergeant based at Harrison Street station. The area had changed during the years I had been away. The Corporation had been applying Compulsory Purchase Orders to the area in an effort to implement their new policy of replacing the old terraced housing with new council building. As a result large areas of the district had been replaced with vacant land waiting for the Council Direct Works Department to start the building programme. I found it odd to move around an area I had once known when it was full of houses and people, now empty with the occasional isolated building, usually a pub, highlighting all that was left of the area. Most of the people had been moved to Corporation council estates miles away, some outside the city boundary. I used to see some of the old residents making a return visit, wandering round trying to find where their particular home had been located. One or two new tall council flats had been built in one corner of the district near to some new shops, one of which sold newspapers. As I moved past this shop I stopped to examine the window. Around the edge of the window were a neat row of postcards and on examination I found that they were all from previous tenants of Belltown who were anxious to return to the area and hoping to do a swap with families who had already moved into these new flats.

The role of sergeant had also changed in that there was no more striking the pavement kerb with a stick at night to summon a constable, no more meeting officers at specific points to give a 'visit', the only element of work which had remained the same was the amount of paperwork which seemed to have increased. When I moved to Harrison Street as acting sergeant I thought that I might have a problem managing officers who I had previously worked with, but in practice that proved not to be the case. During my time away most of my contemporaries had moved on and there were only two officers I knew from the past and they were younger in service. The new policing system with its panda cars and personal radios had settled down, with everybody now familiar with the new arrangements.

I arrived at my old station having been given an armband with three stripes to wear, and spent some time walking round reliving past memories. The place hadn't changed much; the smell of bleach still hung in the air, the tiles had not changed and were still the same colour, and once again in my opinion the station could do with a new lick of paint. The station officer was now George Greenwood, who I remembered as a beat PC when I had worked at the station. He was the first station officer I had seen who did not wear medal ribbons from the Second World War. It was a sign of the times, I thought, the passing of the old guard, there couldn't be many of the old veterans left. After a word with him I picked up the correspondence and information bulletins and went into the Parade room, and found my flock sitting round a table. Gone were the days of standing in a line, producing staffs and notebooks, instead everybody sat round chatting amiably with each other. There were six constables present, down from the ten officers I remembered when I first started as a probationary constable. They looked up and watched me walk towards them. I knew that they would be aware of my background and I had already decided what to say in laying down the ground rules, explaining what I expected from them. I told them that if they kept what I said in mind we would get on well during the next four weeks.

Looking at the officers, I identified two who would need watching. The first was an experienced constable called Edwin Butcher. Butcher had a reputation of being a bully; he was physically a tall, heavily built man who tried to use his physical size to intimidate people and that included members of the public as well as colleagues. Looking at him I thought he wasn't big enough as far as I was concerned, and smiled to myself at the thought. He caught my eye and then looked away; I wondered if he had read my thoughts? The second officer was a probationer constable, PC Williams; he was a thin, lanky individual who I had been told had previously been employed in the Planning Office of the Town Hall. He had six months' service and seemed to be a bundle of nerves. I decided I would spend some time with him and find out if there was a problem which needed my help. The remaining four officers all had about five years' service and had a reputation of being smart, reliable types. I went through the briefing, gave out the refreshment times and got them all out and on their way. I then took the opportunity to take Williams to one side and told him we would patrol together whilst he told me how he was getting on with his new career.

We left the station and walked towards his beat and I opened the conversation by explaining to Williams that this was the first area I had been posted to as a beat constable. He asked me questions about policing in the past and I began to feel like a police pensioner as I explained the differences between the old methods and current system of policing. After the first five minutes Williams began to relax and slowly he began to describe the problems which he was experiencing. He said that his previous sergeant, Ben Wilkinson, had told him that he wasn't satisfied with his performance and that he needed to show more effort if he was to successfully complete his probationary period. According to Williams the sergeant had not given him any indication as to what the problem was and as his six-monthly appraisal report was due to be submitted in the near future he was at a loss to know how he was supposed to improve. All this was news to me but I told him that I would be completing his next performance report and in the meantime I would help him get organised.

Over the next four weeks I watched him deal with members of the public, looked at the quality of his report writing and assessed whether he had a nose for investigating crime. Gradually he started to regain confidence and when it was my turn to complete his report I could say in all honesty that he had the makings of a constable. Looking at the circumstances I came to the conclusion that the problem might have stemmed from a personality issue in that I formed the impression from speaking to the other officers that Sergeant Wilkinson didn't like the officer, and that had probably played a part in creating the situation. It was a lesson which I would remember for the future, to try not to let personal feelings overcome objective reporting.

The other officer I had identified as a possible cause for trouble, Constable Butcher, did not cause any problem until the final week of my appointment.

We were on 'afternoons', it was close to 10pm and I was returning from DHQ when I heard the divisional radio operator ask for an officer to attend to some trouble at the Crown Inn on Alma Street, and I heard that Butcher had volunteered to attend. The pub had a reputation for being the source of trouble and I wondered whether he would need some backup and decided to make my own way to the premises. I stopped the car and went inside to find Butcher was in the midst of a fight in which two men were giving him a good pasting. I went over and pulled one of the assailants off, whilst Butcher gained control of the other one. By this time the divisional van crew had also turned up and we placed both men in the back of the van which headed off to DHQ to have them charged with disorderly behaviour. We left the pub and I asked Butcher what had happened; initially he seemed a bit reticent, saying that one of the prisoners was drunk and had been causing trouble and that when he had tried to arrest him his friend had intervened to prevent the arrest. He then left me to follow the prisoners in his own panda car to complete the charging procedure whilst I returned to Harrison Street Station to check the inevitable paperwork before completing the shift and retiring my officers off duty.

The following day I returned to the station for the last time and heard the full story of Butcher and the two drunks. It seems that Butcher went to the pub following a call from the landlord who had thrown out one of his regulars who had been causing trouble. This man had not caused any further problems by making his way home. When the officer arrived at the pub he saw the landlord and after finding out that the incident had been resolved was about to resume patrol when another pub regular had accosted him in the bar and accused him of sleeping with his wife. Butcher had initially tried to calm the situation down, without admitting the allegation, but his accuser refused to quieten down and the officer decided that the only option available was to arrest him and remove him from the scene. When he tried to arrest the aggrieved husband his friend stood up and got involved and the pair of them then set to with fists flying, and assaulted the officer which was about the time that I entered the scene.

Both men appeared before the magistrates, and although the complaint about the officer's conduct was made, it didn't stop them being found guilty of being drunk and disorderly and fined. But the husband was still feeling aggrieved and as a result went on to make a formal complaint to the inspector about Butcher's behaviour. In those days the police complaints system in dealing with non-criminal issues was fairly relaxed, and when the man's wife refused to support her husband's allegation it was decided that the best way of handling the matter was to transfer Butcher to the C Division with a cautionary word as to his future conduct.

Events also moved on for me because as I finished my period as acting sergeant I was told that I was transferring to the divisional CID office to work for six months as an aide. On hearing the news I went home and selected a dark grey suit from my much-improved wardrobe. The next job was to ask my father if I could borrow his grey trilby hat for the next six months. My mother, who was a big fan of the television programme 'Fabian of the Yard', watched me put it on approvingly and said I had now become the picture of the great detective. This caused us both to laugh at the idea.

The divisional CID office was located on the first floor of the DHQ with all the detective sergeants and constables being based in a large office on the corner of the building; next door were two separate offices for the detective chief inspector or DCI, and his deputy the detective inspector or DI. The previous DCI, Reg Carter, had moved on, becoming detective superintendent in charge of the Headquarters Serious Crime Squad; his replacement was Jack Morrison who was in his forties, but looked twenty years older. He presented an untidy appearance in a seedy green tweed suit with each pocket packed with pipe tobacco, matches, pens and pencils. He was a calm, unflappable officer, continually smoking a pipe and universally liked across the Division. His number two, DI Gordon Blake, was a small ginger-haired man, who had a fussy manner, continually rearranging objects around his desk. His predecessor, DI Corbell Watson, had returned to CID Headquarters Administration, to the relief I was told, of all the members of the office. Their overall assessment of Watson was that he was excellent with paperwork, but did not know how to deal with people and that included staff as well as prisoners and witnesses. As for his successor, a lot of officers on the Division had no time for Blake, who was considered officious and abrupt, but as I got to know the officer I found him to be a good boss to work for. I found that under the veneer of a man who had no time for idiots, there lurked an intelligent individual who, once he had the measure of the person he was dealing with, was quite happy to give advice and assistance.

I had been told to report to the CID office at 9am, for the morning briefing, when either the DCI or DI discusses with the staff the Night Crime Patrol Report and any other matters which have come to notice. I waited for Jack Morrison to finish and then followed him into his office, which reeked of tobacco. My new boss lit his pipe and ushered me to a chair, welcomed me as an aide, told me that I had come with a good reputation and then explained what he looked for in a potential detective. Firstly I should remove any notion in my mind about trying to emulate Sherlock Holmes or Fabian of the Yard; being a detective, he said, was a combination factors – attention to detail, do the facts of the case add up, and assessing the evidence and also the calibre of the witnesses. However, he assured me that I was unlikely to be involved in any crime too complicated until I had mastered the basics. One fact that the potential CID officer had to come to terms with was the amount of paperwork involved; he made it clear that if an aide cannot deal with it there was no future in the CID for that officer. However, he said that having had experience in Plain Clothes and putting prosecution files together, I should not find the paperwork to be too difficult. Finally he told me that he expected I would make mistakes as I settled into the job and that was accepted as a fact of life, but he said I should learn by my mistakes and aim to not the same mistake again, and certainly if I made it a third time I would be back in uniform. With that, he said that DI Blake kept a watching brief over aides and conducted me into the office next door and introduced me to his deputy.

DI Blake carried on with the introduction to the department, giving me a more detailed description of the paperwork involved, explaining that each crime report was given a number and then allocated to a detective. The more serious crimes, such as wounding and robberies, were given to the sergeants and more experienced officers; lesser crimes were allocated down the hierarchy with aides given the bottom of the pile, such as stolen motor vehicles or reports of minor larceny or theft as it would now be called. When the crime reports were given out the DCI or DI would insert a follow-up date which required the officer to interview the complainant and describe in the crime report what steps he had taken to progress the investigation. What this meant in practice was that the detective saw the complainant at least once and if it was a more serious crime on a number of occasions, until the crime was solved either directly by the arrest of the criminal or indirectly when this previous crime is admitted after the arrest of the criminal for another matter. He told me that the main office was divided into four sections, corresponding to the Divisional layout, with each section comprising a detective sergeant or DS and three or four detective constables, DC's, with one aide assigned to each section.

He then took me into the main office where I joined the First Section, covering Belltown, and introduced me to DS Charlie Hanson with DCs Jeff Reed, Ronny Hurst, and Steve Bellamy. He needn't have bothered since I had worked with them all in the past, especially Steve who was also an ex-Marine. After the introductions Charlie showed me to my part of the

IN THE 'NICK' OF TIME

desk that I shared with Jeff who then pointed out the huge pile of crime files which had now become my responsibility. All this paperwork had been left for me by my predecessor who had now returned to uniform. Jeff suggested that I read through them quickly and decide what priority to give them, he also mentioned that nobody expected me to solve them overnight, but that if I could begin to write them off that would be a good start. I could see that I was going to have to devise a plan to file this paperwork before I became overwhelmed. Turning first to stolen cars, many of the reports looked as though they were the actions of a joy rider, who had dumped them close to home. I would come back to these later to see if there were any leads which might identify any of our local criminals. This category, I could sort out easily, the small number remaining related to the theft of expensive models, such as Rovers and Jaguars, they could be part of an operation to recycle them for resale or even export. Reading the reports these vehicles had been stolen from either suburban homes in Hathersage or parked at the north end of Belltown near the city centre. I reckoned that this latter category were drivers who had left them parked up before going to the night clubs in the city centre, since it was a common practice which most people, including myself, made use of when visiting the area. I noticed that these expensive cars were generally not recovered and wondered if they were being stolen to order and then repainted and renumbered before leaving the area. I discussed my theories with Jeff who smiled and said that it was certainly possible and advised me to give it a go.

I knew a young mechanic in Belltown who had been recommended to me in the past and who I now used to service my car, and I wondered if he knew what was going on in the trade regarding stolen cars and whether he could throw any light on this matter which would be of help. Arthur Bailey loved cars and whenever I visited him he was always under a car sorting out some problem. His garage was occupied a railway arch near the docks. I went to see him and asked if he had heard of anybody in the area dealing with stolen cars, such as giving them a change of colour and a new registration number; he said he couldn't bring anybody to mind, but he would let me know if anything came to light. I returned to the office and began the task of writing off stolen cars which had been recovered. I then looked at the other reports of minor crime and divided them into those where there were no leads and others which might be solved by a few enquiries. I was beginning to realise how important it was to keep abreast of paperwork if I was going to make my mark in the office.

A couple of days later Arthur rang me back and said that he might have some information which could help. That evening we met at his local pub and I bought him a pint and we settled down to discuss what he had discovered. Briefly he had heard a whisper on the street that the people running the scrap metal yard in Navigation Street were taking in cars and changing the colour and number plates. He assumed that they were probably using the number plates from scrapped vehicles and transferring them onto stolen cars of the same make, which wasn't unknown in the car business. I knew something of the scrap yard he mentioned, which was owned by two brothers called Briggs. In those days before the change to unit car beat methods uniform foot beat officers used to circulate information about stolen property to likely places like pawnbrokers or scrap yards, where such property might be offered for sale by the thief or thieves. In the past I had occasionally visited Briggs' yard on such errands and had met the brothers, who had been convicted of handling stolen property in the past. Whilst I had been on that beat I had never heard of them being involved with stolen cars, but perhaps times had changed. I talked the matter over with Charlie and Jeff but, the information was news to them and I asked Charlie if I could take some observations to see if there was any truth in the story I had been told. He took me to see the DI who agreed with my suggestion but told me to keep in radio contact with DHQ and restrict myself simply to observations and not to get involved whatever happened. Diane was away on a course so I had plenty of free time to take up observations on the scrap yard.

I reckoned that if that sort of activity was going on, the cars would be taken into the yard at night, so I decided to spend a couple of nights observing the yard to see what was happening. It was fortunate that I knew the area since there were only a couple of places I could use as observation points without being seen, and so before settling down I went past the yard, but there were no lights or any other signs of activity and I watched until well after midnight without any success. I decided to call it a day and went home still feeling that something would happen to confirm my suspicions. The next night I returned to the scene and thought there was someone in the yard, but I couldn't be sure. There was a dim light in the office but I could see no signs of activity and thought that the light might have been left on by mistake. I decided to carry on but nothing happened until after midnight when a black Rover 90 was driven into the yard; I couldn't make out the driver, but I took down its number and waited to see if there was going to be any further activity. Time went by and I waited and by two o'clock I was thinking of going home when a green Triumph sports car appeared and this vehicle also went into the yard. Again I took its number while the car was driven to the back of the yard. This time I saw the elder brother Walter Briggs close the yard gates, which I thought might imply that work was over for the night. I left the scene and drove out of the area and checked the two car numbers on my personal radio to see if anything was known about them, but there were no reports of them being stolen, so I went home.

The following morning on returning to the office I again checked the car numbers and this time I found that they had both been reported stolen; the Rover from our Division and the Triumph from the city centre. I spoke to Charlie and put him in the picture and we both went to the DI and I repeated what I had found out. Blake asked a few questions and then said that in these situations time was at a premium and we needed to raid the yard before the cars were removed. We were not sure whether the brothers were paint spraying in the yard or whether the work was undertaken elsewhere in which case they would simply change the plates and move the cars to the new location fairly confident of not being stopped. In these types of operations there was no shortage of volunteers in the office and Blake assembled six of us and we went straight to the yard and found the gates locked. This did not present much of a problem since with the right amount of physical pressure we forced open the gates and began to search the yard.

As we started our search the yard the office door opened and Walter Briggs rushed out demanding to know what was going on. Whilst the DI was explaining our visit to him I made my way round to the rear of the premises where I knew was a large brick building used by the brothers to store scrap metal. The doors were ajar and inside I spotted the two cars I had seen the previous night. I went over to the DI telling him what I had found and he brought Briggs over to the cars and confronted him with the evidence, telling him that he and his brother were being arrested.

We arranged for the Traffic department to remove the cars and both brothers were charged with larceny and handling stolen property. As is usual in these matters Charlie rang the headquarters-based Stolen Vehicle Squad and informed them what had taken place. After he had made the call he looked thoughtful and said that the detective sergeant he had spoken to had not been happy and was coming round to conduct his own interview with both the brothers and then have a word with Charlie. I didn't think anything further about the matter and got on with preparing the paperwork, since I was hoping that I would now be able to clear up a number of car thefts as the Briggs brothers had obviously been working at this operation for some time. Initially the brothers were not very co-operative when questioned, but this changed when we were able to identify the car mechanic they were using to respray the vehicles and who when approached turned out to be very forthcoming with evidence which clearly implicated the brothers with the stolen vehicles. Once they found out what had happened the brothers realised the game was up, changed their minds and agreed to talk. I went back to the yard and went through their files to see what information I could find. Unusually for criminals they kept precise records of which cars they had stolen and from their paperwork I was able to clear up a number of car thefts which were added to the list of charges.

Returning to the office I found that DS Frank Browne of the Stolen Vehicle Squad had made an appearance. He and Charlie were having an animated conversation in the far corner of the office away from other members of staff. Looking at them I could see that both men were angry, but at this point I had no idea what was causing the disagreement. Eventually Browne left and I asked Charlie what had happened, he hesitated for a moment and told me that Browne had said that we should not have done anything without telling the Stolen Vehicle Squad first, since they had the yard under observation and we might have jeopardised an important operation. In response Charlie had replied that he didn't believe him, since I had been there two evenings and had not spotted any other indication of police activity and nobody from the Squad had seen me, and if they had spotted me they should have contacted our office and we would have stood down if requested. He then went on to say to me that the Squad had a dubious reputation within the CID, since there was a general belief that most of its officers were corrupt and he included Browne in that category. He suspected that the Briggs brothers may have been paying members of the Squad to leave them alone and unfortunately for them I had come along and ruined their scheme. I smiled at the thought and carried on finishing the paperwork.

Diane and I were now busy looking for a suitable house to buy and this objective was proving harder to achieve than I had anticipated. The problem was that the prices of houses in the district where we wanted to live in were higher than we could afford. I had lined up Mr Bates, my contact from the Specials, who was prepared to let us have a mortgage, but we hadn't yet found the house of our dreams at a price we could afford. In those days only the husband's income qualified for a mortgage and as a constable with about eight years' service this did not leave us with much room to spare, together with the fact that we had a wedding coming up over the horizon.

Two weeks before I was due to finish my time as an aide I was called into the DCI's office. I knocked and entered and found that as well as myself and the DCI, also present were DS Roy Grant, DC Albert Small and another CID aide, Bob Fraser. Roy Grant was a fat, amiable officer who was in charge of the Hathersage Village CID section. Albert Small had been a detective for about ten years, having served a period in the Serious Crime Squad. His stature belied his surname since he was as tall as myself. Bob Fraser was like me, coming to the end of his aide's attachment period and was someone I knew well, since he and his family lived in a police house not far from my parents' address. Jack Morrison nodded at me and lit his pipe, after which he told us all that we were being drafted to the B Division for a week to assist in a murder enquiry. We were initially going to help them with house-to-house enquiries, he said, and then proceeded to let us know how low he rated B Division CID. 'Every time they get a serious crime the first thing they do is ask for help. Whilst I've been on this division I have never asked anyone for any assistance,' he assured us. He made it clear that he was only going to release us to them for a week, not a day longer! After supplying us with some more information, such as to report next Monday at 2pm at B Div DHQ Station at Newport Street, he ushered us out of his office.

As we trooped out of his office I wondered how we had been selected. The selection of Bob and myself was easy enough to work out; we were both coming to the end of our attachment, so our absence wouldn't be missed. Al Small was highly rated as a good detective and initially I had no idea why he had been selected, however, I later found out that he had previously served on the B Division and had volunteered for the job. He would probably spend his time renewing old friendships. Sergeant Grant had the reputation of being the laziest man in the office and since the Hathersage Village section had the lowest crime rate it was not too difficult to work out why he had been picked. Bob and I stopped in the Main Office to discuss travel arrangements to Newport Street which was on the north side of the City. We decided to take in turn to use our cars and I volunteered to start off by picking him up on Monday.

Monday dawned and I collected Bob and we made our way to Newport Street Police Station. The station was situated in the district of Newport which was identical to Belltown, having been built about the same time. Once more there were row upon row of terraced houses all built in Victorian times. This was another area which was due to be cleared, but unlike Belltown, the City had not yet got round to demolishing the properties. We turned a corner and saw the station for the first time; the building was about the same age as Harrison Street, but was a lot bigger. We drove through the main gate into the courtyard which was surrounded on two sides with three floors of living accommodation. There was washing draped across the balconies of most of the married apartments and some was secured to washing lines at ground level. I parked the car and we walked across to the Main Office, where we were directed up to the second floor where the Divisional Murder Squad had their offices.

We went into the main office and found that Roy Grant and Al Small were already there. We were introduced to DI Ian Morris who spent the next few minutes explaining the details of the murder. The body of a forty-year-old man had been found in an entry at the rear of King Street, which is one of the main roads leading north out of the City. He had been stabbed a couple of times in the back and chest and had been visually identified as a local villain, 'Mad' Mitch Warren. From local knowledge within the office it was believed that this murder was part of a violent struggle between two local gangs which had erupted recently over a dispute over territory and the circulation of drugs. There were no witnesses to the murder and the DCI had decided to implement a large house-to-house enquiry covering the immediate area of the murder scene and two other locations in which both gangs operated. Bob and I were given a number of streets near where the murder had taken place, together with some forms which we were to fill in giving details of addresses and people interviewed and any information which might help the enquiry.

We were each given three streets to cover and armed with a B Division radio, a clipboard and the forms we were taken by car to our locations. It had just finished raining and looking at my list I saw that each of my streets had been given the name of a flower. Looking at the dismal scene outside I wondered what had led the City Fathers to give the area such names; was it to inspire hope or did someone have a twisted sense of humour? I could not supply the answer to the question and in any case the car was pulling up and I was the first one to get out. I had been dropped off opposite Iris Street and I set off across the street to look at what would be required to cover the addresses. I found there were thirty-four houses and starting at number one I slowly made my way along the street. By about four o'clock I had finished; there were three addresses where I had not seen the occupiers, but from local information I was confident I could complete my enquiries after tea time. I then walked on to Lavender Street, which was the next street along, and again started at number one. I moved along the street without any problems until I reached the end terrace at number seventeen. All the curtains were closed which indicated in those days that the occupiers were way from home. I went back to number fifteen and spoke to the old lady I had just finished interviewing. I asked her about her next-door neighbours; she told me that they were a brother and sister, called Barry and Ann Wainwright. She had been told that the sister had recently moved to live with a relative in London, whilst her brother was in the process of changing jobs. She hadn't seen the brother for a couple of days, but she had heard movement in the house and assumed he must be at home.

I thanked her and knocked again on the door of number seventeen, but there was no reply. Initially I was going to move on and return later, but I wondered why he had drawn the curtains. Something seemed a bit odd. I stood on the corner and wondered what my next move should be and then I saw a red GPO van at the other end of the street with a postman delivering a parcel. On the spur of the moment I went back to the house lifted up the lid to the letter box and shouted that I had a parcel for number seventeen. When nothing happened I opened the lid again and said I was leaving it on the step and walked round the corner, creeping back to see whether there was going to be a response. A few minutes passed and I was beginning to feel that Wainwright may have left the house, when the door slowly moved, without waiting for it to be fully opened I walked back on to the step and pushed my way in.

I apologised to the surprised Barry Wainwright and introduced myself and the reason for my call. He was a slim fellow about average height with a white tired face, who I thought was slightly younger than myself. I pulled out one of my forms and suggested we go in the kitchen, whilst I wrote down the details. As I was filling in the form I noticed that he had started to cry – tears were running down his cheeks at an ever-increasing rate. I stopped my form filling and asked him what was the matter, and in reply he asked me to follow him upstairs. We went up the stairs and into the back bedroom and two things hit me. Firstly there was a young woman lying on the bed who looked to me as though she was dead, and secondly she seemed to be lying in a pool of blood. I went up to the bed and examined her as best I could, satisfying myself that she was indeed dead, but I couldn't see any marks of violence. There was blood on the floor and as I turned back towards Wainwright I saw a blue bowl in the corner of the room, which also seemed to be full of blood. Walking over to it I saw the form of a very small baby, also dead. On the face of it looked as though I had walked into the scene of a miscarriage or perhaps an unsuccessful abortion.

I looked at Wainwright, who was still convulsed with tears, and took him down stairs. I asked him what had happened and he told me that his sister had been pregnant, but had not wanted to advertise the fact. She went to see a local backstreet abortionist and came back telling him that she had been given some pills to take and everything was going to be alright. That night she had started to give birth, but things had gone wrong and the next thing he knew she had died soon after the baby was born, who also turned out to have died. 'I didn't know what to do,' he kept saying. The anguish on his face was clear to see and I felt a wave of sympathy. Given the circumstances a picture of what might have led to the pregnancy started to emerge in my mind, but there was one crucial question that needed to be asked before the jigsaw would be complete.

I asked him who the father was; in response to my question he looked away from me and stared through the kitchen window. A minute passed and then I asked him again, 'Who was the father?' He turned slowly towards me and admitted that he was the father. The picture was complete. He claimed they had never meant for this to happen, but they had been overcome by events. Their father had died ten years ago and their mother followed him some two years later. Their mother's elder sister had made the occasional visit from Leeds, but made it clear that she was not going to take them in and that in practice they were now on their own.

'We were lonely and afraid,' he said. 'We only had each other.' In response I now understood what had happened.

I went into the hallway and radioed the B Division giving brief details of the circumstances. I was told that DI Morris would be around shortly and a few moments later there was a knock on the door. I opened it to find the DI with a DC and a uniformed constable. I took Morris upstairs and after looking round the room he agreed with my conclusion, but said the body would be examined to confirm our suspicions. I told him what Wainwright had said to me by way of explanation and he replied, 'The dirty bugger.' By now I had worked out that Morris saw things in 'right or wrong', there were no shades of grey in his mind. We went back downstairs and he told me to return with him and Wainwright to the station, leaving the others to await the arrival of the Mortuary van which had already been summoned. At the station I took Wainwright into the Interview Room. I knew that my job would be to take a detailed record of the interview which would be conducted under caution by the inspector. By now Wainwright had calmed down, in fact he gave the impression that he was glad he had been released from the pressures he had been under. Under questioning he gave the same story I had heard and when Morris had finished he looked over to me to see whether there were any gaps in the facts Wainwright had given him, but I reassured him that everything was in order. I finished off the paperwork and then went back to Morris and told him I was ready to resume my house-to-house enquiries. He smiled when I appeared and told me that they had arrested a man for the murder and I could return to my Division.

When I got back I went up to the CID office and coincidently bumped into my DCI, who was just coming out. Jack Morrison asked me how I had got on and I gave him a brief account of my case of incest. He listened with interest and when I had finished remarked, 'Poor bugger,' and walked off into his office. As he left I thought unlike Morris he was the type of detective I would want to be, someone who was empathetic and could see that life was not simple, but that didn't stop him enforcing the law and doing 'the job' effectively and competently.

About six months later I met up again with DI Morris to give evidence at Crown Court at Wainwright's trial for incest. He pleaded guilty and his barrister had persuaded his aunt from Leeds to give evidence on his behalf and also his next-door neighbour in an effort to show extenuating circumstances. It worked in as much as the judge sentenced him to three years' imprisonment. Wainwright seemed more relaxed in court and I got the feeling from looking at him that he would have accepted life imprisonment for failing to prevent the death of his sister.

I came to the end of my attachment with the CID and went to see my DCI before I left. He started off by saying I had made a good impression in the office and he would endorse Mr Blake's recommendation that I be transferred into the CID when a suitable vacancy occurred. He said I had fitted in well with the rest of the office, had improved my interrogation techniques and that my paperwork was better than average. Overall he would be glad to welcome me back. I thanked him for all the advice and support I had received and said I hoped to return. I went next door and had a few words with the DI before returning to clear my desk. Charlie Hanson told me that at least I had made some effort to reduce the files, although there were still some left for my replacement. After I had finished clearing up my desk we all went out to the Red Lion, that was the preferred pub the CID liked to use, and I bought them all a round of drinks. In those days it was not uncommon for one or more of the local crime reporters to make an appearance at CID pubs when there was a celebration taking place. There were two members of the press there that I had got to know quite well during my time in the office; Roy Meadows from the local evening paper and Paul Mathers from one of the nationals, who worked from their northern offices in Somerford. Usually the DCI or DI dealt with them, although I knew that certain older detective sergeants and constables would also provide information on occasion. As an aide I didn't have much dealings with them, although they did buy me the odd pint and as this was my leaving 'do' Roy, who was there, wished me well and bought me a drink.

In the event the opportunity to transfer into the CID did not happen, since two weeks later I received a message to see my chief superintendent. The previous office holder, Douggie Fairbanks, had retired and had been replaced by Chief Superintendent Tony Wilshaw, a fat pleasant character who had moved from Headquarters as a replacement whilst I was undergoing my CID Aide's Course. He seemed to be another senior officer who was fan of man management theories, telling me that these new theories were the way to the future and that he was going to use them as the basis for changes that were going to be made to the division. After finishing with this information he eventually got round to telling me the main reason for my interview. He told me that he had received a memo from HQ notifying him that I was to attend a promotion parade at Force Headquarters in three days' time when I was to be promoted to uniformed sergeant and transferred to the city centre A Division with immediate effect. He congratulated me and wished me well in the future; I was surprised since although I hoped that promotion was in the offing I did not expect it to come so quickly.

What I didn't know was that this parade would be the last one in which the Watch Committee would take part. The following April the Watch Committees would be disbanded and replaced by a Police Authority with a different set of responsibilities. Up until this time all promotions had to be sanctioned by the Watch Committee, in the future any promotions would solely the preserve of the chief constable.

There were other changes to the police service such as the reduction in the number of police forces in England and Wales, but those issues were of little importance to me at that time, I had more pressing matters to resolve.

I careered through the station looking for a vacant phone to contact Diane, my mother, and also make an appointment to visit the Uniform Stores. On a personal level I hoped the house buying problem would now be resolved since I had been given a pay rise. I later gave Diane the important task of sewing on my new stripes, which I thought would be straight forward but she found more difficult than I anticipated; apparently the thickness of the uniform didn't help. The promotion parade took place in the Chief Constable's Office; there were twelve officers present – six constables to sergeants, three sergeants to inspector, two inspectors to chief inspector and one chief inspector to superintendent. The chief constable and the Watch Committee chairman each shook our hands in turn and congratulated us; there was a short speech from both of them and then we were given tea and sandwiches after which it was all over. Thinking back to that moment I realised that a particular journey had ended and a new door was opening; overall it had been an eventful time as a constable punctuated by periods of boredom, some sadness, but in the main highlighted by humour, surprise and satisfaction.

ABOUT THE AUTHOR

After a short period of service in the Royal Navy the author joined a northern city police force in 1961. After serving for over 30 years he retired as chief superintendent and then went into academia, becoming a member of staff at his local university.

Printed in Great Britain
by Amazon